"Nice try, sweetheart." His low chuckle seemed to vibrate straight through her.

"I didn't say I would agree to anything. I said we'd talk."

She took a deep breath. "All right, cowboy. I'll stay with you at the Big Blue. But I want you to promise that you'll keep an open mind and give me a fair chance to change it."

"Only if you'll drop the matter if I decide against doing it," he said, extending his hand to shake on their deal.

The moment her palm touched his an exciting little shiver slid up her spine, and Felicity couldn't help but wonder what she had gotten herself into. Chance Lassiter was not only the best choice for redeeming his family in the eyes of the public, he was the only man in a very long time to remind her of the amazing differences between a man and a woman.

* * *

Lured by the Rich Rancher
is a Dynasties: The Lassiters novel—
A Wyoming _____ of _____ _____ ption!

LURED BY THE RICH RANCHER

BY
KATHIE DeNOSKY

Published in Great Britain 2014
by Mills & Boon, an imprint of Harlequin (UK) Limited,
Eton House, 18-24 Paradise Road, Richmond, Surrey, TW9 1SR

© 2014 Harlequin Books S.A.

Special thanks and acknowledgement are given to Kathie DeNosky for her contribution to the Dynasties: The Lassiters miniseries.

ISBN: 978-0-263-91472-6

51-0714

Kathie DeNosky lives in her native southern Illinois on the land her family settled in 1839. She writes highly sensual stories with a generous amount of humor. Her books have appeared on the *USA TODAY* bestseller list and received numerous awards, including two National Readers' Choice Awards. Kathie enjoys going to rodeos, traveling to research settings for her books and listening to country music. Readers may contact her by e-mailing kathie@kathiedenosky.com. They can also visit her website, www.kathiedenosky.com, or find her on Facebook.

This book is dedicated to the authors of Dynasties: The Lassiters. It's been a pleasure working with you and I hope to do so again in the near future.

And a special dedication to my good friend and partner in crime, Kristi Gold, whose sense of humor is as wicked as my own. Love you bunches, girlfriend!

One

At the designated time on the Fourth of July, Chance Lassiter and his half sister, Hannah Armstrong, approached the doorway to the massive great room in the Big Blue ranch house. "This seems wrong. I just learned two months ago that I have a sister and now I'm giving you away," he complained.

"That's true," she said, smiling. "But since you and Logan are good friends, I think we'll probably be seeing each other quite often."

"You can count on it." He gazed fondly at his five-year-old niece waiting to throw flower petals as she preceded them down the aisle. "I told Cassie I would come over and take her into Cheyenne for ice cream at least once a week. And I'm not letting her down."

"You're going to spoil her," Hannah teased good-naturedly.

Grinning, he shrugged. "I'm her favorite uncle. It's expected."

"You're her only uncle," Hannah shot back, laughing. "You have to be her favorite."

When he first discovered that he had a half sister from the extramarital affair his late father had some thirty years ago, Chance had experienced a variety of emotions. At first, he'd resented the fact that the man he had grown up believing to be a pillar of morality had cheated on Chance's mother. Then learning that Marlene Lassiter had known her husband had a daughter and hadn't told him had compounded Chance's disillusionment. His mother had been aware of how much he missed having a sibling and he felt deprived of the relationship they might have had growing up. But in the two months since meeting Hannah and his adorable niece, he had done his best to make up for lost time.

Chance tucked Hannah's hand in the crook of his arm. "Besides the standing ice-cream date, you know that all you or Cassie have to do is pick up the phone and I'll be there for you."

"You and your mother have been so good to us." Tears welled in Hannah's emerald eyes—eyes the same brilliant green as his own. "I don't know how to begin to thank you both for your love and acceptance. It means the world to me."

He shook his head. "There's no need to thank us. That's the beauty of family. We accept and love you and Cassie unconditionally—no matter how long it took us to find you."

As they started down the aisle between the chairs that had been set up for the wedding, Chance focused on the red-haired little girl ahead of them. Cassie's curls bounced as she skipped along and her exuberance for throwing flower petals from the small white basket she carried was cute as hell. Of course, like any proud uncle, he thought everything the kid did was nothing short of amazing. But with an arm like that there wasn't a doubt in his mind that she could play for a major league baseball team if she set her mind to it.

Approaching the groom standing beside the minister in front of the fireplace, Chance waited for his cue before he placed his sister's hand in Logan Whittaker's. He kissed Hannah's cheek, then gave his friend a meaningful smile as he took his place beside him to serve as the best man. "Take care of her and Cassie," he said, careful to keep his tone low. "If you don't, you know what will happen."

Grinning, Logan nodded. "You'll kick my ass."

"In a heartbeat," Chance promised.

"You don't have anything to worry about," Logan said, lifting Hannah's hand to kiss the back of it as they turned to face the minister.

When the bespectacled man of the cloth started to speak, Chance looked out at the wedding guests. Except for Dylan and Jenna, the entire Lassiter clan had turned out in force. But his cousin and his new bride's absence was understandable. Their own wedding had only taken place a little over a week ago and they were still on their honeymoon in Paris.

As Chance continued to survey the guests, he noticed that his cousin Angelica had chosen to sit at the back of the room, well away from the rest of the family. She was still upset about the terms of her father's will and refused to accept that J. D. Lassiter had left control of Lassiter Media to her former fiancé, Evan McCain. Chance didn't have a clue what his uncle had been thinking, but he trusted the man's judgment and knew there had to have been a good reason for what he'd done. Chance just wished Angelica could see things that way.

He shifted his attention back to the ceremony when the minister got to the actual vows and Logan turned to him with his hand out. Chance took from his jacket pocket the wedding ring his friend had given to him earlier and handed it to his soon-to-be brother-in-law. As he watched Logan slide the diamond-encrusted band onto Hannah's ring finger, Chance couldn't help but smile. He had no intention of going down that road himself, but he didn't mind watching others get married when he knew they were meant for each other. And he had yet to meet two people better suited to share their lives as husband and wife than Hannah and Logan.

"By the power vested in me by the great state of Wyoming, I pronounce you husband and wife," the minister said happily. "You may kiss the bride."

Chance waited until Logan kissed Hannah and they turned to start back down the aisle with his niece skipping along behind them before he offered his arm to the matron of honor. As they followed the happy couple toward the door, a blonde woman seated next to his cousin Sage and his fiancée, Colleen, caught his eye.

With hair the color of pale gold silk and a complexion that appeared to have been kissed by the sun, she was without question the most gorgeous female he'd ever had the privilege to lay eyes on. But when her vibrant blue gaze met his and her coral lips curved upward into a soft smile, he damn near stopped dead in his tracks. It felt as if someone had punched him square in the gut.

Chance had no idea who she was, but he had every intention of remedying that little detail as soon as possible.

Felicity Sinclair felt as if something shifted in the universe when she looked up to find the best man staring at her as he and the matron of honor followed the newly married couple back down the aisle. He was—in a word—perfect!

Dressed like the groom in a white Oxford cloth shirt, black sport coat, dark blue jeans and a wide-brimmed cowboy hat, the man was everything she had been looking for and more. He was tall, broad-shouldered and ruggedly handsome. But more than that, he carried himself with an air of confidence that instilled trust. She could only hope that he was related to the Lassiters so that she could use him in her PR campaign.

When he and the matron of honor continued on, Fee turned to the couple seated next to her. "Sage, would you happen to know the name of the best man?"

"That's my cousin Chance," Sage Lassiter said, smiling as they rose to their feet with the rest of the wedding guests. "He owns the majority of the Big Blue now."

Excited by the fact that the best man was indeed a member of the Lassiter family, Fee followed Sage and his fiancée, Colleen, out onto the flagstone terrace where the reception was to be held. She briefly wondered why she hadn't met him at the opening for the newest Lassiter Grill, but with her mind racing a mile a minute, she dismissed it. She was too focused on her ideas for the PR campaign. The Big Blue ranch would be the perfect backdrop for what she had in mind and there wasn't anything more down-to-earth and wholesome than a cowboy.

When her boss, Evan McCain, the new CEO of Lassiter Media, sent her to Cheyenne to take care of the publicity for the grand opening of the Lassiter Grill, she'd thought she would be back in Los Angeles within a couple of weeks. But she'd apparently done such a stellar job, her stay in Wyoming had been extended. Two days ago, she had received a phone call assigning her the task of putting together a public relations campaign to restore the Lassiter family image and Fee knew she had her work cut out for her. News of Angelica Lassiter's dissatisfaction with her late father's will and her recent association with notorious corporate raider Jack Reed had traveled like wildfire and tarnished the company's happy family image, and created no small amount of panic among some of the stockholders. But by the time she hung up the phone, Fee had already come up with several ideas that she was confident would turn things around and reinstate Lassiter Media as the solid enterprise it had always been. All she needed to pull it together was the right spokesperson in the right setting. And she'd just found both.

Of course, she would need to talk to Chance and get him to agree to appear in the television spots and print ads that she had planned. But she wasn't worried. She'd been told all of the Lassiters had a strong sense of family. Surely when she explained why she had been asked to extend her stay in Cheyenne and how important it was to restore the Lassiters' good name, Chance would be more than happy to help.

Finding a place at one of the round tables that had been set up on the beautifully terraced patio, Fee sat down and took her cell phone from her sequined clutch to enter some notes. There were so many good ideas coming to her that she didn't dare rely on her memory.

"Do you mind if I join you, dear?"

Fee looked up to find a pleasant-looking older woman with short brown hair standing next to her. "Please have a seat," she answered, smiling. "I'm Fee Sinclair."

"And I'm Marlene Lassiter," the woman introduced herself as she sat down in the chair beside Fee. "Are you a friend of the bride?"

Shaking her head, Fee smiled. "I'm a public relations executive from the Los Angeles office of Lassiter Media."

"I think I remember Dylan mentioning that someone from the L.A. office had been handling the publicity for the Lassiter Grill opening here in Cheyenne," Marlene said congenially. She paused for a moment, then lowering her voice added, "And when I talked to Sage yesterday, he said you were going to be working on something to smooth things over after Angelica's threats to contest J.D.'s will and her being seen with the likes of Jack Reed."

"Yes," Fee admitted, wondering how much the woman knew about the board of directors' concerns. Something told her Marlene Lassiter didn't miss much of what went on with the family. "I'll be putting together some television commercials and print ads to assure the public that Lassiter Media is still the solid, family-friendly company it's always been."

"Good," the woman said decisively. "We may have our little spats, but we love each other and we really are a pretty close family."

They both looked across the yard at the pretty dark-haired woman talking rather heatedly with Sage. It was apparent she wasn't the least bit happy.

"I know it's probably hard for a lot of people to believe right now, but Angelica really is a wonderful young woman and we all love her dearly," Marlene spoke up as they watched the woman walk away from her brother in an obvious huff. Turning to Fee, Marlene's hazel eyes were shadowed with sadness. "Angelica is still trying to come to terms with the death of her father, as well as being hurt and disillusioned by his will. That's a lot for anyone to have to deal with."

Compelled to comfort the older woman, Fee placed her hand on top of Marlene's where it rested on the table. "I'm sure it was a devastating blow to her. She worked so hard for the family business that many people just assumed she'd be running it someday."

"When J.D. started cutting back on his workload, Angelica knew he was grooming her to take over and we all believed she would be the one leading Lassiter Media into the future," Marlene agreed, nodding. "When he left her a paltry ten percent of the voting shares and named Evan McCain CEO, the girl was absolutely crushed."

Fee could tell that Marlene was deeply concerned for Angelica. "It's only been a few months since Mr. Lassiter's passing," she said gently. "Maybe in time Angelica will be able to deal with it all a little better."

"I hope so." Marlene shook her head. "There are times when even grown children have a hard time understanding the reasons their parents have for making the decisions they do. But we always try to do what's in our children's best interest."

It was apparent the woman's focus had shifted and she was referring to someone other than Angelica. Fee didn't have a clue who Marlene was talking about, but she got the distinct impression there might be more than one rift in the family.

"I don't have children, but I can imagine it's extremely difficult sometimes," she agreed. Deciding to lighten the mood, she pointed to the bride's table, where the wedding party would be seated. "I don't know who did the decorations for the reception, but everything is beautiful."

All of the tables were draped with pristine white linen tablecloths and had vases of red, white and blue roses for centerpieces. But the table where the newly married couple and their attendants would sit had been decorated with a garland made of baby's breath and clusters of red and blue rosebuds. It was in keeping with the holiday and utterly stunning.

"Thank you," Marlene said, smiling. "Hannah left the reception decorations up to me and I thought red, white and blue would be appropriate. After all, it is the Fourth of July." Marlene smiled. "We'll be having fireworks a bit later when it gets dark."

"Grandma Marlene, can I sit with you for dinner?" the adorable little red-haired flower girl asked, walking up between Fee and Marlene.

"Of course, Cassie," Marlene said, putting her arm around the child. "As long as your mother says it's okay."

"Momma said I could, but I had to ask you first," Cassie answered, nodding until her red curls bobbed up and down. She seemed to notice Fee for the first time. "I'm Cassie. I got a new daddy today."

"I saw that." Fee found the outgoing little girl completely charming. "That's very exciting, isn't it?"

Cassie smiled. "Yes, but Uncle Chance says that I'm still his best girl, even if Logan is my new daddy."

"I'm sure you are," Fee said, smiling back.

While the child walked around her grandmother's chair to sit on the other side of Marlene, Fee felt encouraged. She hadn't realized she had been talking to her new spokesman's mother and niece. Surely if Marlene knew about the public relations campaign and was all for it, her son would be, too. And with any luck, he would be more than willing to play a role in the publicity she had planned to help restore the Lassiters' reputation.

Seated next to his new brother-in-law at the head table, Chance was about as uncomfortable as an eligible bachelor at an old-maids convention. He didn't like being on display and that was exactly the way he felt. Every time he looked up from his plate, someone was either smiling at him, waving to him or just plain staring at him. It was enough to make the succulent prime rib on his plate taste about as appetizing as an old piece of boot leather.

Finally giving up, he sat back from the table and waited until he had to toast the bride and groom. Once he got that out of the way, as far as he was concerned, his duties as the best man would be over and he fully intended to relax and enjoy himself.

At least, Logan had decided they would wear sports coats and jeans instead of tuxedos or suits.

Hannah called Logan's choice of wedding clothes "casual chic." Chance just called it comfortable.

As he scanned the crowd, he looked for the little blonde that had caught his eye at the wedding. He hoped she hadn't skipped the reception. She was definitely someone he'd like to get to know.

He was almost positive she wasn't from the area. None of the women he knew looked or dressed like her. From her perfectly styled hair all the way down to her spike heels, she gave every indication of being a big-city girl, and he would bet every last penny he had that the red strapless dress she was wearing had a famous designer's name on the label. But it didn't matter that they came from two different worlds. He wasn't looking for anything permanent with anyone. All he wanted was for them to have a little summer fun while she was around.

When he finally spotted her, he barely suppressed a groan. She and his mother seemed to be deep in conversation and that couldn't be good. Since his mother had gotten a taste of what it was like to be a grandmother with Cassie, she had made several comments that she wouldn't mind him giving her another grandchild or two in the near future. Surely his mother wouldn't be talking him up as husband and father material.

He frowned. Of course, he couldn't be sure. She'd shocked the hell out of him a couple of months ago when she had admitted that she'd known all about the affair his late father had thirty years ago. Then his mother had surprised him further when she admitted that she was the one who paid child support to Hannah's mother all those years after his father's death. His mother's secrets had caused him no end of frustration and it had only been in the past few weeks they had started to repair the breach those issues had caused in their relationship. Surely she wouldn't run the risk of creating more problems between them.

Lost in thought, it took a moment for him to realize that Logan had said something to him. "What was that?"

"Time for your toast," Logan said, grinning. Lowering his voice, he added, "Unless you'd rather make us wait while you sit there and ogle the blonde seated next to Marlene."

"Did anyone ever tell you what a smartass you can be, Whittaker?" Chance grumbled as he took his champagne flute and rose to his feet.

He ignored his new brother-in-law's hearty laughter as he sincerely wished the couple a long and happy life together, then gifted them a thousand acres on the Big Blue ranch to build the new house he knew they had been planning. Now that the toast was out of the way and he had given them his gift, he was free to enjoy himself. And the first thing he intended to do was talk to the blonde.

Hell, he might even ask her to dance a slow one with him. Not that he was all that great at doing more than standing in one place and swaying in time to the music. He wasn't. But if the lady was willing to let him put his arms around her and sway with him, it would be worth the risk of looking like a fool.

Ten minutes later, after listening to several more toasts for the bride and groom, Chance breathed a sigh of relief as he headed over to the table where his mother, Cassie and the blonde sat. "I'm glad that's over," he said, smiling. "Now it's time for some fun."

"You did a fine job with the toast, son," his mother said, smiling back at him.

"Uncle Chance, would you dance with me?" Cassie asked as she jumped down from her chair and skipped over to him.

"You're my best girl. Who else would I dance with?" he teased, winking at the blonde as he picked Cassie up to sit on his forearm. "But we'll have to wait until the band starts. Will that be okay with you?"

Cassie nodded. "I hope they hurry. I'm going to pretend we're at the ball."

"Fee, this is my son, Chance," his mother introduced them. Her smile was just a little too smug as she rose to her feet. "While we wait for the dancing to begin, why don't you and I go inside the house to see if we can find your princess wand, Cassie?"

"Oh, yes, Grandma Marlene," Cassie agreed exuberantly. "I need my wand and my crown for the ball."

Chance set the little girl on her feet as the band started warming up. "I'll be waiting for you right here, princess." When his mother and niece started toward the house, he placed his hand on the back of one of the chairs at the table. "Mind if I join you, Fee?"

Her pretty smile caused an unexpected hitch in his breathing. "Not at all, Mr. Lassiter."

"Please, call me Chance." He smiled back as he lowered himself onto the chair his mother had vacated. "I don't think I've ever known anyone with the name Fee."

"It's actually short for Felicity." She brushed a wayward strand of her long blond hair from her smooth cheek as they watched Hannah and Logan dance for the first time as husband and wife. "My grandmother talked my mother into naming me that. It was her mother's name."

"Are you a friend of my sister?" he asked, wondering if she might be one of the teachers Hannah worked with in Denver.

"No, I'm a public relations executive with Lassiter Media," she answered as she picked up her cell phone from the table and tucked it into her purse. When she looked up, he didn't think he'd ever seen anyone with bluer eyes. "I work out of the Los Angeles office."

That explained why he'd never seen her before, as well as her polished career-girl look. But although she probably bought everything she wore from the shops on Rodeo Drive, Fee Sinclair had a softness about her that he found intriguing. Most of the career women he'd met were aloof and all business. But Fee looked approachable and as if she knew how to kick up her heels and have a good time when she decided to do so.

"I'll bet you worked on the publicity for the grand

opening of Lassiter Grill," he speculated, motion-
ing for one of the waiters carrying a tray of filled
champagne flutes. Asking the man to bring him a
beer, Chance took one of the glasses of bubbling
pink wine and handed it to Fee. "My cousin Dylan
said he couldn't have been happier with the way you
handled the opening."

"I didn't see you that evening," she commented.

He shook his head. "No, I had to be over in Lara-
mie on business that day and didn't get back in time."

She seemed to eye him over the rim of her glass as
she took a sip of the champagne. "I've also been put
in charge of getting your family's image back on track
what with all the controversy over J. D. Lassiter's will
and Angelica's association with Jack Reed."

"So you'll be here for a few weeks?" he queried,
hoping that was the case. "Will you be staying here
at the ranch?"

"Lassiter Media has rented a house in Cheyenne,
where they have employees from the L.A. office stay
while they're in town on business," she said, shaking her head. "I'll be here at least until the end of
the month."

Chance waited until the tuxedoed waiter brought
him the beer he had requested and moved on before
he commented. "I don't envy your job. Our reputation of being a solid family that got along well took
a pretty big hit when Angelica pitched her little hissy
fit right after my uncle's will was read. Do you know
how you're going to go about straightening that out?"

"I have a few things in mind," she answered evasively.

Before he could ask what those ideas were, Cassie skipped up to them. "I'm ready to dance now, Uncle Chance. I have my wand and my crown."

"You sure do," he said, laughing as she tried to hang on to her pink plastic wand while she adjusted the tiara his mother had bought for her a few weeks ago. As if on cue, the band started playing a slower tune. Turning to Fee, he smiled. "I'm sorry, but I can't keep the princess waiting. I'll be right back."

Fortunately, all he had to do was stand in one place and hold Cassie's little hand as she pirouetted around him. The kid had definite ideas on the way a princess was supposed to dance and who was he to argue with her? He just hoped she didn't make herself too dizzy and end up falling flat on the floor.

When the dance was over and he and Cassie returned to the table, Chance held out his hand to Fee. "Would you like to dance, Ms. Sinclair?"

She glanced at her uncomfortable-looking high heels. "I...hadn't thought I would be dancing."

Laughing, he bent down to whisper close to her ear. "You witnessed the extent of my dancing skills with Cassie. I'm from the school of stand in one place and sway."

Her delightful laughter caused a warm feeling to spread throughout his chest. "I think that's about all I'll be able to do in these shoes anyway."

When she placed her soft hand in his and stood up to walk out onto the dance floor with him, it felt as if an electric current shot straight up his arm. He took a deep breath, wrapped his arms loosely around her and smiled down at her upturned face. At a little over six feet tall, he wasn't a giant by any means, but everything about her was petite and delicate. In fact, if she hadn't been wearing high heels, he could probably rest his chin on the top of her head.

"Chance, there's something I'd like to discuss with you," she said as they swayed back and forth.

"I'm all ears," he said, grinning.

"I'd like your help with my public relations campaign to improve the Lassiters' image," she answered.

He didn't have any idea what she thought he could do that would make a difference on that score, but he figured it wouldn't hurt to hear her out. Besides, he wanted to spend some time getting to know her better and although she might not be staying in Wyoming for an extended period of time, that didn't mean they couldn't have fun while she was here.

Before he could suggest that they meet for lunch the following day to talk over her ideas, she gave him a smile that sent another wave of heat flowing through him. He would agree to just about anything as long as she kept smiling at him that way.

"Sure. I'll do whatever I can to help you out," he said, drawing her a little closer. "What did you have in mind?"

"Oh, thank you so much," she said, surprising him with a big hug. "You're perfect for the job and I can't wait to get started."

He was pleased with himself for making her happy, even if he didn't know what she was talking about. "I don't know about being perfect for much of anything but taking care of a bunch of cattle, but I'll give it my best shot." As an afterthought, he asked, "What is it you want me to do?"

"You're going to be the family spokesman for the PR campaign that I'm planning," she said, beaming.

Because he was marveling at how beautiful she was, it took a moment for her words to register. He stopped swaying and stared down at her in disbelief. "You want me to do what?"

"I'm going to have you appear in all future advertising for Lassiter Media," she said, sounding extremely excited. "You'll be in the national television commercials, as well as…"

Fee kept on telling him all the things she had planned and how he figured into the picture. But Chance heard none of it and when the music ended, he automatically placed his hand at the small of her back and, in a daze, led her off the dance floor.

His revved up hormones had just caused him to agree to be the family spokesman without knowing what he was getting himself into. Un-freaking-believable.

Chance silently ran through every cuss word he'd ever heard, then started making up new ones. He might be a Lassiter, but he wasn't as refined as the rest of the family. Instead of riding a desk in some corporate office, he was on the back of a horse every day herding cattle under the wide Wyoming sky.

That's the way he liked it and the way he intended for things to stay. There was no way in hell he was going to be the family spokesman. And the sooner he could find a way to get that across to her, the better.

Two

The following day, Fee programed the GPS in her rented sports car to guide her to the restaurant where she would be meeting Chance for lunch. After their dance last night, he had insisted that they needed to talk more about his being the family spokesman and she had eagerly agreed. She was looking forward to getting her campaign started and his sister's wedding reception hadn't been the right time or place to discuss what she needed Chance to do.

When the GPS instructed her to turn north, Fee nervously looked around and realized she was heading in the same direction they'd driven the afternoon before on the way out of Cheyenne to the wedding. Sage and Colleen had invited her to accompany them to the Big Blue ranch for the wedding because she was alone in town and unfamiliar with the area. She'd been more than happy to accept the offer because her biggest concern when she'd learned that she would be spending more time in Wyoming was the fact that she was going to be completely out of her element. She had been born and raised in the San Fernando Valley and the closest she had ever been to a rural setting was her grandmother's pitiful attempt at a vegetable garden on the far side of her swimming pool in Sherman Oaks.

When the GPS indicated that her destination was only a few yards ahead, she breathed a sigh of relief that she wouldn't have to venture out of the city on her own. Turning into the gravel parking lot of a small bar and grill, she smiled when she parked next to a white pickup truck with Big Blue Ranch painted on the driver's door. Chance was leaning against the front fender with his arms folded across his wide chest and his booted feet crossed casually at the ankles.

Lord have mercy, the man looked good! If she'd thought he looked like a cowboy the night before in his white shirt, black sport jacket and black hat, it couldn't compare to the way he looked today. Wearing a blue chambray shirt, jeans and a wide-brimmed black cowboy hat, he was the perfect example of a man who made his living working the land. The type of man men could relate to and women would drool over.

"I hope I didn't keep you waiting long," she said

when he pushed away from the truck to come around the car and open her door.

"I've only been here a couple of minutes," he said, smiling as he offered his hand to help her out of the car.

Her breath caught. Chance Lassiter was extremely handsome at any time, but when he smiled he was downright devastating. She had noticed that about him the night before, but attributed her assessment to the excitement she'd felt at finding the perfect spokesman to represent his family. But now?

She frowned as she chided herself for her foolishness. Her only interest in the man or his looks was for the purpose of improving his family's image. Nothing more.

But when she placed her hand in his, a delightful tingling sensation zinged up her arm and Fee knew her reaction to his smile had nothing whatsoever to do with being anxious to start her ad campaign and everything to do with Chance's raw sexuality. He wasn't as refined as the men she knew in Los Angeles, but something told her that he was more of a man than any of them ever dreamed of being. She took a deep breath and ignored the realization. Her interest in him was strictly business and that's the way it was going to stay. Maybe if she reminded herself of that fact enough, she would remember it.

"I have some of the mock-ups of the print ads I'd like to run," she said, reaching for her electronic tablet in the backseat.

"Let's have lunch and talk before we get into any

of that," he said, guiding her toward the entrance to the restaurant.

"I suppose you're right," she agreed as they walked inside. "I'm just excited about starting this project."

His deep chuckle sent a warmth coursing throughout her body. "Your enthusiasm shows."

When they reached a booth at the back of the establishment, he asked, "Will this be all right? It's a little more private and we should be able to talk without interruption."

"It's fine," she answered, sliding onto the red vinyl seat. Looking around, Fee noticed that although the bar and grill was older and a little outdated, it was clean and very neat. "What's the special here?" she asked when Chance took his hat off and slid into the booth on the opposite side of the table.

"They have a hamburger that's better than any you've ever tasted," he said, grinning as he placed his hat on the bench seat beside him. "But I'm betting you would prefer the chef's salad like most women."

His smile and the sound of his deep baritone sent a shiver coursing through her. The man's voice alone would charm the birds out of the trees, but when he smiled, there wasn't a doubt in her mind that he could send the pulse racing on every female from one to one hundred.

Deciding to concentrate on the fact that he had correctly guessed her lunch choice, she frowned. For reasons she couldn't explain, she didn't like him thinking that she was predictable or anything like other women.

"What makes you think I'll be ordering the salad?" she asked.

"I just thought—"

"I can think for myself," she said, smiling to take the sting out of her words. "And for the record, yes, I do like salads. Just not all the time."

"My mistake," he said, smiling.

"Since it's your recommendation, I'll have the hamburger," she said decisively.

He raised one dark eyebrow. "Are you sure?" he asked, his smile widening. "I don't want you thinking I'm trying to influence your decision."

"Yes, I'm positive." She shrugged. "Unless you're afraid it won't live up to expectations."

He threw back his head and laughed. "You're really something, Felicity Sinclair. You would rather eat something you don't want than admit that I was right. Do you even eat meat?"

"Occasionally," she admitted. For the most part she lived on salads in L.A. But that was more a matter of convenience than anything else.

When the waitress came over to their booth, Chance gave the woman their order. "I can guarantee this will be the best hamburger you've ever had," he said confidently when the woman left to get their drinks.

Curiosity got the better of her. "What makes you say that?"

"They serve Big Blue beef here," he answered.

"It's the best in Wyoming, and several restaurants in Cheyenne buy from our distributor. In fact, my cousin Dylan and I made a deal when he decided to open a Lassiter Grill here to serve nothing but our beef in all of his restaurants."

"Really? It's that special?"

Chance nodded. "We raise free-range Black Angus cattle. No growth hormones, no supplements. Nothing but grass-fed, lean beef."

Fee didn't know a lot about the beef industry, except that free-range meat was supposed to be healthier for the consumer. But she did know something about Dylan Lassiter and the Lassiter Grill Group.

A premier chef, Dylan had started the chain with J.D.'s encouragement and had inherited full control of that part of the family business when J.D. died. Dylan was well-known for serving nothing but the finest steaks and prime rib in his restaurants, and Fee was certain that was why every one of them bore the coveted five-star rating from food critics and cuisine magazines. If he was confident enough to serve Big Blue beef exclusively in his restaurants, it had to be the best. And that gave her an idea.

"This is perfect," she said, her mind racing with the possibilities. "I'll have to give it a little more thought, but I'm sure we can use that for future Lassiter Grill advertisements, as well as the spots about the Lassiter family."

"Yeah, about that," Chance said slowly as he ran a hand through his short, light brown hair. "I don't think I'm right for what you have in mind for your ad campaign."

Her heart stalled. "Why do you say that?"

He shook his head. "I'm not a polished corporate type. I'm a rancher and more times than not I'm covered in dust or scraping something off my boots that most people consider extremely disgusting."

"That's why you're the perfect choice," she insisted.

"Because I've stepped in a pile of...barnyard atmosphere?" he asked, looking skeptical.

Laughing at his delicate phrasing, she shook her head. "No, not that." Now that she'd found her spokesman, she couldn't let him back out. She had to make Chance understand how important it was for him to represent the family and that no one else would do. "Not everyone can identify with a man in a suit. But you have that cowboy mystique that appeals to both men and women alike. You're someone who will resonate with all demographics and that's why they'll listen to the message we're trying to send."

"I know that's what you think and for all I know about this kind of thing, you might be right about me getting your message across to your target audience." He shook his head. "But I'm not real big on being put on display like some kind of trained monkey in a circus sideshow."

"It wouldn't be like that," she said earnestly. "All you'll have to do is pose for some still pictures for the print ads and film a few videos that can be used for television and the internet." She wasn't going to mention the few personal appearances that he might have to do from time to time or the billboard advertising that she had already reserved. Those were sure to be deal breakers, so she would have to spring those on him after she got a firm commitment.

When he sat back and folded his arms across his wide chest, she could tell he was about to dig in his heels and give her an outright refusal. "What can I do to get you to reconsider?" she asked out of desperation. "Surely we can work out something. You're the only man I want to do this."

A mischievous twinkle lit his brilliant green eyes. "The only man you want, huh?"

Her cheeks felt as if they were on fire. She was normally very clear and rarely said anything that could be misconstrued. "Y-you know what I meant."

He stared at her across the table for several long moments before a slow smile tugged at the corners of his mouth. "Come home with me."

"E-excuse me?" she stammered.

"I want you to come and stay at the Big Blue for a couple of weeks," he said, his tone sounding as if he was issuing a challenge. "You need to see how a working ranch is run and the things I have to do on a daily basis. Then we'll talk about how glamorous you think the cowboy way of life is and how convincing I would be as a spokesman."

"I didn't say it was glamorous," she protested.

"I think you referred to it as 'the cowboy mystique,'" he said, grinning. "Same thing."

"Is that the only way you'll agree to do my PR

campaign?" she asked, deciding that staying in the huge ranch house where the wedding had been held the night before wouldn't be an undue hardship.

The Lassiter home was beautiful and although a little rustic in decor, it was quite modern. If all she had to do to get him to agree to be part of the advertising was stay at the ranch for a week or so, she'd do it. She had a job promotion riding on the outcome of this project and she wasn't about to lose the opportunity.

"Nice try, sweetheart." His low chuckle seemed to vibrate straight through her. "I didn't say I would agree to anything if you came to the ranch. I said we'd talk."

Staring at him across the worn Formica table, Fee knew that she didn't have a lot of choices. She could either agree to go home with him and try to convince him to represent the Lassiters or start looking for another spokesman.

She took a deep breath. "All right, cowboy. I'll stay with you at the Big Blue. But only on one condition. You have to promise that you'll keep an open mind and give me a fair chance to change it."

"Only if you'll respect my decision and drop the matter if I choose not to do it," he said, extending his hand to shake on their deal.

"Then I would say we have an agreement," she said, extending her hand, as well.

The moment her palm touched his an exciting little shiver slid up her spine and Fee couldn't help but wonder what she had gotten herself into. Chance

Lassiter was not only the best choice for redeeming his family in the eyes of the public, he was the only man in a very long time to remind her of the amazing differences between a man and a woman.

Why that thought sent a feeling of anticipation coursing through her at the speed of light, she had no idea. She wasn't interested in being distracted by him or any other man. She had a job to do and a career to build and protect. As long as she kept things in perspective and focused on her goal of putting together a campaign that would redeem the Lassiters for any and all transgressions, she would be just fine.

The following morning, Fee had just put the finishing touches on preparing brunch when the doorbell rang, signaling her guest had arrived. "You have perfect timing," she said, opening the door to welcome Colleen Faulkner. "I just took the scones out of the oven."

"I'm glad you called and asked me over." Colleen smiled. "Sage is out of town for the day and I can definitely use a break from all of the wedding plans."

"Have you set a date yet?" Fee asked as she led the way down the hall to the kitchen.

"No." Seating herself at the table in the breakfast nook, Colleen paused a moment before she continued, "Sage is hoping if we wait a bit, things will settle down with Angelica."

Pouring them each a cup of coffee, Fee set the mugs on the polished surface and sat down on the opposite side of the small table. "When I saw her at the wedding the other night, I could tell she's still extremely frustrated with the situation. Has she given up the idea of contesting her father's will?" Fee asked gently.

She didn't want to pry, but it was no secret that Angelica Lassiter and the rest of the family were still at odds, nor was there any mystery why. The young woman wanted to break the will and regain control of Lassiter Media, while the rest of the family were reluctant to go against J.D.'s last wishes or bring into question the other terms of the will and what they had inherited.

"I don't think she's going to give up anytime soon," Colleen admitted, shaking her head. "Angelica is still questioning her father's motives and how much influence Evan McCain had in J.D.'s decision to take control of Lassiter Media away from her." Colleen gave Fee a pointed look. "But J.D. had his reasons and believe me, he knew what he was doing."

Fee had no doubt that Colleen knew why J. D. Lassiter had divided his estate the way he had—leaving his only daughter with practically no interest in Lassiter Media. Colleen had been his private nurse for some time before his death and she and J.D. had become good friends. He had apparently trusted Colleen implicitly, and with good reason. To Fee's knowledge, Colleen hadn't revealed what she knew about the matter to anyone.

"I just hope that I'm able to turn public opinion around on the matter," Fee said, dishing up the breakfast casserole and crisp bacon she had made for their brunch. "The Lassiters have for the most part been known as a fairly close, happy family and that image has taken its share of hits lately." She didn't want to mention that Sage had distanced himself from J.D. sometime before the older Lassiter died or that they had never really resolved the estrangement. It was none of her business, nor did it have anything to do with her ad campaign.

"The tabloids are having a field day with all this," Colleen agreed. They were silent for several long moments before she spoke again. "I'm a very private person and I'm not overly thrilled by the idea, but if you can use our wedding plans in some way to shift the focus away from whatever legal action Angelica is planning, I suppose it would be all right."

Taken by surprise at such a generous offer, Fee gave the pretty nurse a grateful smile. "Thank you, Colleen. But I know how intrusive that would be for you and Sage during a very special time in your lives."

"If it will help the Lassiters, I'll adjust," Colleen answered, looking sincere. "I love this family. They're very good people and they've welcomed me with open arms. I want to help them in any way I can."

Smiling, Fee nodded. "I can understand. But I think—at least I hope—I've found the perfect angle for my campaign and won't have to use your wedding."

"Really?" Colleen looked relieved. "May I ask what you're planning?"

As she explained some of her ideas for the videos and print ads featuring Chance as the family spokesman, Fee sighed. "But he's not overly happy about being in front of the camera. In fact, he's invited me to stay at the Big Blue for the next two weeks to prove to me that he's completely unsuitable."

Colleen grinned. "And I'm assuming you're going to use that time to convince him the exact opposite is true."

"Absolutely," Fee said, laughing. "He has no idea how persistent I can be when I know I'm right."

"Well, I wish you the best of luck with that," Colleen said, reaching for a scone. "I've heard Sage mention how stubborn Chance could be when they were kids."

Fee grinned. "Then I'd say he's met his match because once I've made up my mind I don't give up."

"The next couple of weeks should be very interesting on the Big Blue ranch," Colleen said, laughing. "What I wouldn't give to be a fly on the wall when the two of you butt heads."

"I'm not only hoping to have his agreement within a week, I'd like to get a photographer to start taking still shots for the first print ads," Fee confided in her new friend. "Most of those will start running by the end of the month."

"It sounds like you have things under control." Colleen took a sip of her coffee. "I'll keep my fingers crossed that you get Chance to go along with all of it."

"Thanks," Fee said, nibbling on her scone.

She didn't tell Colleen, but she had to get him on board. Her entire campaign was based on him and his down-to-earth cowboy persona. The Lassiter family had been ranching in Wyoming for years before Lassiter Media became the communications giant it was today. Besides the down-to-earth appeal of a cowboy, it just made sense to capitalize on the family's Western roots. She wasn't going to let a little thing like Chance's reluctance to be in front of the camera deter her from what she knew would be an outstanding promotion.

On Monday afternoon when Chance parked his truck in front of the house Lassiter Media had rented for visiting executives, he felt a little guilty about the deal he had made with Fee. He had promised that he would consider her arguments for his being part of her PR campaign and he did intend to think about it.

It wasn't that he didn't want to help the family; he just couldn't see why one of his cousins wasn't more suitable for the job of spokesman or for that matter, even his mother. She was the family matriarch and had been since his aunt Ellie had died over twenty-eight years ago. They all knew more about Lassiter Media than he did. He was a rancher and had been all of his life. That's the way he liked it and wanted it to stay. Besides, he'd never been the type who felt the need to draw a lot of attention to himself. He had always been comfortable with who he was and hadn't seen any reason to seek out the approval of people whose opinions of him didn't matter.

All he wanted was to get to know Fee better and that was the main reason he'd suggested that she stay with him on the ranch. They could have some fun together and at the same time, he could prove to her that he wasn't the man she needed for her ad campaign. He knew she wasn't going to give up easily and would probably still insist that he was the best choice. But he seriously doubted she was going to make a lot of headway with her efforts.

Getting out of the truck, he walked up to the front door and raised his hand to ring the bell just as Fee opened it. "Are you ready to go?" he asked as his gaze wandered from her head to her toes.

Dressed in khaki slacks and a mint-green blouse, she'd styled her long blond hair in loose curls, making her look more as if she was ready for a day of shopping in some chic, high-end boutique than going to stay at a working cattle ranch. He hadn't thought it was possible for the woman to be any prettier than she had been two days ago when they'd had lunch, but she'd proved him wrong.

"I think I'm about as ready as I'll ever be," she said, pulling a bright pink suitcase behind her as she stepped out onto the porch.

His eyebrows rose when he glanced down at the luggage. It was big enough to fit a body and if the bulging sides were any indication, there just might be one in there already. It was completely stuffed and he couldn't imagine what all she had in it.

"Think you have enough clothes to last you for two weeks?" he asked, laughing.

"I wasn't sure what I would need," she answered, shrugging one slender shoulder. "Other than attending the wedding the other night, I've never been on a ranch before."

"My place does have the convenience of a washer and dryer," he quipped.

"I thought it would," she said, giving him one of those long-suffering looks women give men they think are a little simpleminded. "That's why I packed light."

When he picked up the suitcase, he frowned. The damn thing weighed at least as much as a tightly packed bale of hay. If this was her idea of "packing light," he couldn't imagine how many pieces of luggage she'd brought with her for her stay in Cheyenne.

Placing his other hand at the small of her back, he noticed she was wearing a pair of strappy sandals as he guided her out to his truck. "I'm betting you don't have a pair of boots packed in here," he said, opening the rear door on the passenger side of the club cab to stow the suitcase.

"No. I didn't expect to be needing them," she answered. She paused a moment before she asked, "What would I need them for?"

He laughed. "Oh, just a couple of things like walking and riding."

"I…I'm going to be riding?" she asked, sounding a little unsure. "A…horse?"

"Yup." He closed the rear door, then turned to help her into the front passenger seat. "Unless you want me to saddle up a steer so you can give that a try."

She vigorously shook her head. "No."

"You do know how to ride, don't you?"

There was doubt in her pretty blue eyes when she looked at him and he knew the answer before she opened her mouth. "The closest I've ever been to a horse is seeing them in parades."

"Don't worry. It's pretty easy. I'll teach you," he said, giving her what he hoped was an encouraging smile as he placed his hands around her waist.

"W-what are you doing?" she asked, placing her hands on his chest. The feel of her warm palms seemed to burn right through the fabric and had him wondering how they would feel on his bare chest.

"You're short and…the truck is pretty tall," he said, trying to ignore the hitch he'd suddenly developed in his breathing. "I thought I'd help you out."

"I assure you, I could climb into the truck," she said.

"I'm sure you could," he said, smiling. "But you want to shoot me a break here? I'm trying to be a gentleman."

Staring down at her, it was all he could do to keep from covering her lips with his and kissing her until the entire neighborhood was thoroughly scandalized. His heart stuttered when he realized she looked as if she wanted him to do just that.

He wasn't sure how long they continued to gaze at each other, but when he finally had the presence of mind to lift her onto the seat, he quickly closed the truck door and walked around to climb in behind the steering wheel. What the hell was wrong with him? he wondered as he started the engine and steered away from the curb. He'd never before been so completely mesmerized by a woman that he forgot what he was doing. Why was Fee different? What was it about her that made him act like an inexperienced teenager on his first date?

"I still don't understand…why you insisted on coming to get me," she said, sounding delightfully breathless. "I could have driven…to the ranch."

"You could have tried," he said, focusing on her statement instead of her perfect coral lips. "But that low-slung little sports car wouldn't have made it without drowning out when you forded the creek. That's why I suggested you leave it here. If you need to go somewhere, I'll be more than happy to take you."

"When we drove to the ranch for the wedding, I don't remember anywhere along the way that could happen," she said as if she didn't believe him. "The roads were all asphalt and so was the lane leading up to the ranch house." She frowned. "I don't even remember a bridge."

"There isn't one," he answered. "Most of the year it's just a little slow-moving stream about three or four inches deep and about two feet wide," he explained. "But July is the wettest month we have here in Wyoming. It rains almost every day and the stream doubles in size and depth. That little car sits so low it would stall out in a heartbeat."

"Why don't you build a bridge?" she demanded. "It seems to me it would be more convenient than running the risk of a vehicle stalling out."

He nodded. "Eventually I'll have the road to my place asphalted and a culvert or bridge put in. But I only inherited the ranch a few months ago and I've had other things on my mind like cutting and baling hay, mending fences and moving cattle from one pasture to another."

"Hold it just a minute. Your place?" She frowned. "You don't live on the Big Blue ranch?"

"I've never lived anywhere else," he admitted. "I just don't live in the main house."

"There's another house on the ranch?" she asked, her tone doubtful.

"Actually there are several," he said, nodding. "There's the main house, the Lassiter homestead where I live, as well as a foreman's cottage and a couple of smaller houses for married hired hands."

"The only buildings I saw close to the ranch house were a couple of barns, a guest cottage and a stable," she said, sounding skeptical.

"You can't see the other places from the main house," he answered. "Those are about five miles down the road where I live."

"So I won't be staying with Marlene?" she inquired, as if she might be rethinking her decision to stay with him.

"Nope. The actual ranch headquarters is where we'll be staying," he said, wondering if Fee was apprehensive about being alone with him. She needn't be. He might want to get to know her on a very personal level, but he wasn't a man who forced his attentions on a woman if she didn't want them.

Frowning, she nibbled on her lower lip as if deep in thought. "I was led to believe that the main house was the ranch headquarters."

Chance almost groaned aloud. Nothing would please him more than to cover her mouth with his and do a little nibbling of his own. Fortunately, he didn't have time to dwell on it. They had arrived at the stop he'd decided to make when he learned she didn't have a pair of boots.

Steering his truck into the parking lot at the Wild Horse Western Wear store on the northern outskirts of Cheyenne, he parked and turned to face her. "My uncle built the main house when he and my late aunt adopted Sage and Dylan. That's where we have our family gatherings, entertain guests, and Lassiter Media holds corporate receptions. The actual ranch headquarters has always been at the home my grandfather and grandmother built when they first came to Wyoming. I renovated it about seven years back when my uncle turned the running of the ranch over to me. I've lived there ever since."

She looked confused. "Why not have the headquarters at the main house? Doesn't that make more sense?"

Laughing, he shook his head. "Headquarters is

where we sort cattle for taking them to market and quarantine and treat sick livestock. A herd of cattle can be noisy and churn up a lot of dust when it's dry. That's not something you want guests to have to contend with when you're throwing a party or trying to make a deal with business associates."

"I suppose that makes sense," she finally said, as if she was giving it some serious thought.

"Now that we have that settled, let's go get you fitted for a pair of boots," he suggested, getting out of the truck and walking around to help her down from the passenger seat. "How many pairs of jeans did you bring?"

"Two," she said as they walked into the store. "Why?"

"I'm betting your jeans have some designer dude's name on the hip pocket and cost a small fortune," he explained as he walked her over to the women's section.

"As a matter of fact, I did get them from a boutique on Rodeo Drive," she said, frowning. "Does that make them unsuitable?"

"That depends," he answered truthfully. "If you don't mind running the risk of getting them torn or stained up, they'll be just fine. But if they're very expensive, I doubt you'll want to do that. Besides, they probably aren't boot cut, are they?"

"No. They're skinny jeans."

He swallowed hard as he imagined what she would look like in the form-fitting pants. "We'll pick up a few pairs of jeans and a hat."

"I don't wear hats," she said, her long blond hair swaying as she shook her head.

Without thinking, Chance reached up to run his index finger along her smooth cheek. "I'd hate to see your pretty skin damaged by the sun. You'll need a hat to protect against sun and windburn."

As she stared up at him, her pink tongue darted out to moisten her lips and it was all he could do to keep from taking her into his arms to find out if they tasted as sweet as they looked. Deciding there would be plenty of time in the next two weeks to find out, he forced himself to move. He suddenly couldn't wait to get to the ranch.

"Let's get you squared away with jeans and boots," he advised. "Then we'll worry about that hat."

Three

Fee glanced down at her new jeans, boots and hot-pink T-shirt with *I love Wyoming* screen-printed on the front as Chance drove away from the store. When had she lost control of the situation? When they walked into the store, she hadn't intended to get anything but a pair of boots and maybe a couple pairs of jeans.

She had to admit that Chance had been right about her needing the boots. Her sandals definitely weren't the right choice of footwear if she was going to be around large animals. Even his suggestion about getting new jeans had made sense. She'd paid far too much for the stylish denim she'd purchased in one of the boutiques on Rodeo Drive to ruin them.

But when he had suggested that she might want

to start wearing the boots right away to get them broken in, that's when her command of the situation went downhill in a hurry. She'd had to put on a pair of the new jeans because the legs of her khaki slacks hadn't fit over the tops of the boots. Then she'd taken one look at her raw silk blouse with the new jeans and boots and decided to get something more casual, motivating her to get the T-shirt. She glanced at the hat sitting beside her on the truck seat. She'd even given in to getting the hat because his argument about protecting her skin had made sense.

Looking over at Chance, she had to admit that a shopping trip had never been as exhilarating as it had been with him. When she stepped out of the dressing room to check in the full-length mirror how her new jeans and T-shirt fit, she'd seen an appreciation in his brilliant green eyes that thrilled her all the way to her toes. It certainly beat the practiced comments of a boutique employee just wanting to make a sale.

She sighed heavily. Now that they were actually on the road leading to the ranch, she couldn't help but wonder what she'd gotten herself into. On some level, she had been excited about the new experience of being on a working ranch. It was something she'd never done before and although she felt as if she would be going into the great unknown, she had thought she was ready for the challenge. But if the past hour and a half was any indication of how far out of her element she was, she couldn't imagine what the next two weeks held for her.

Preoccupied with her new clothes and how ill-prepared she had been for her stay at the ranch, it came as no small surprise when Chance drove past the lane leading up to the main house on the Big Blue ranch. They had traveled the thirty or so miles without her even realizing it.

Now as she watched the lane disappear behind them in the truck's side mirror, Fee felt the butterflies begin to gather in her stomach. It was as if they were leaving civilization behind and embarking on a journey into the untamed wilderness.

She was a born and bred city dweller and the closest she had ever been to any kind of predatory wildlife was in the confines of a zoo. There was a certain comfort in knowing that there were iron bars and thick plates of glass between her and the creatures that would like nothing more than to make a meal out of her. But out in the wilds of Wyoming those safety measures were nonexistent and she knew as surely as she knew her own name there were very large, very hairy animals with long claws and big teeth hiding behind every bush and tree, just waiting for the opportunity to pounce on her.

"Do you have a lot of trouble with predators?" she asked when the asphalt road turned into a narrow gravel lane.

Chance shrugged. "Once in a while we have a mountain lion or bobcat wander down from the higher elevations, but most of the time the only wildlife we see are antelope and deer."

"Doesn't Wyoming have bears and wolves?" she asked, remembering something she'd read about their being a problem when she'd gone online the night before to research ranching in Wyoming.

"Yeah, but they're like the big cats. They usually stay up in the mountains where their food sources are," he said slowly. "Why?"

"I just wondered," she said, looking out the passenger window.

She didn't like being afraid. It took control away from her and made her feel inadequate. Fee couldn't think of anything that she hated more than not being in charge of herself. But that was exactly the way she was feeling at the moment. But as long as the really big, extremely scary wildlife stayed in the mountains where they belonged, she'd be just fine.

As she stared at the vast landscape, hundreds of black dots came into view. As they got closer, she realized the dots were cattle. "Are all those yours?"

"Yup. That's some of them."

"How big is this ranch?" she asked, knowing they had been on the property for several miles.

"We have thirty thousand acres," Chance answered proudly. "My grandparents settled here when they first got married. Then when Uncle J.D. inherited it, he kept buying up land until it grew to the size it is now." He laughed. "And believe it or not, I'm going to be checking into leasing another ten or twenty thousand acres from the Bureau of Land Management next year."

"Isn't the ranch big enough for you?" she asked before she could stop herself. It seemed to her that much land should be more than enough for anyone.

"Not really." He smiled as he went on to explain. "The Big Blue has around six thousand head of cattle at any given time. Since our cattle are grass-fed year-round we have to be careful to manage the pastures to keep from overgrazing, as well as make sure we have enough graze to mow for hay in the summer to put up for the winter months. That's why we keep a constant check on grazing conditions and move the herds frequently. Having the extra land would give us some breathing room with that, as well as expanding the herd."

His knowledge about the needs of the cattle he raised impressed her and Fee made a mental note of the information. Since he supplied beef for the Lassiter Grill Group, it was definitely something she could envision using if she was assigned future promotions for the restaurant chain.

When Chance stopped the truck on top of a ridge, Fee's breath caught at the sight of the valley below. It looked like a scene out of a Western movie. "This is where you live?"

Smiling proudly, he nodded. "This is the Lassiter homestead. The house wasn't always this big, though. When I did the renovations before I moved in, I added several rooms and the wraparound porch on to the original log cabin."

"It's really beautiful," Fee said, meaning it. She pointed to two small houses on the far side of the valley. "Are those the cottages you mentioned for the married hired hands?"

"Slim and Lena Garrison live in one and Hal and

June Wilson live in the other," Chance answered. "Slim is the ranch foreman and Hal is the head wrangler." He pointed toward a good-size log structure not far from the three barns behind the house. "That's the bunkhouse, where the single guys stay."

"This would be the perfect place to film some of the videos I'm planning," Fee said, thinking aloud. She noticed that Chance didn't comment as he restarted the truck and drove down into the valley. "You do realize that I'm not going to give up until you agree to be the Lassiter spokesman, don't you?"

"It never crossed my mind that you would," he said, grinning as he parked the truck in front of the house. He got out to come around and open her door. "You're here to try to talk me into taking on the job and I'm going to try to convince you that you'd be better off finding someone else."

Anything she was about to say lodged in her throat when he lifted her from the truck and set her on her feet. She placed her hands on his biceps to steady herself and the latent strength she felt beneath his chambray shirt caused her pulse to race and an interesting little flutter in a part of her that had no business fluttering.

"Why do you keep…doing that?" she asked.

"What?"

"You keep lifting me in and out of the truck," she said, even though she enjoyed the feel of his solid strength beneath her palms. "I'm perfectly capable of doing that for myself."

"Two reasons, sweetheart." He leaned close to

whisper, "I'm trying to be helpful. But more than that, I like touching you."

Her breath caught and when her gaze locked with his, she wasn't sure if she would ever breathe again. He was going to kiss her. And heaven help her, she was going to let him.

But instead of lowering his head to capture her lips with his, Chance took a deep breath a moment before he stepped back and turned to get her luggage from the backseat. She did her best to cover her disappointment by looking beyond the house toward the fenced-in areas around the barn.

"What are all these pens used for?" she asked.

"We use the bigger ones for sorting the herds during roundup," he answered as he closed the truck door. "The smaller ones are for sick or injured animals that need to be treated or quarantined. The round one we use for training the working stock or breaking them to ride."

"You have all that going on at one time?" she asked, starting toward the porch steps.

"Sometimes it can be pretty busy around here," he said, laughing as he opened the front door for her.

When Fee entered and looked around the foyer, she immediately fell in love with Chance's home. The log walls had aged over the years to a beautiful warm honey color and were adorned with pieces of colorful Native American artwork along with cowboy-related items like a pair of well-worn spurs hanging next to a branding iron. Although the Big Blue's main ranch house, where she had attended the wedding, was quite beautiful, it had a more modern feel about it. Chance's home, on the other hand, had that warm, rustic appeal that could only be achieved with the passage of time.

"This is really beautiful," she said, gazing up at the chandelier made of deer antlers. "Did you decorate it?"

"Yeah, I just look like the type of guy who knows all about that stuff, don't I?" Laughing, he shook his head. "After I finished adding on to the cabin and modernizing things like the kitchen and bathrooms, I turned the house over to my mom for the decorating. She has a real knack for that kind of thing."

"Marlene did a wonderful job," Fee said, smiling. "She should have been a professional interior decorator."

"She was too busy chasing a houseful of kids." Before she could ask what he meant, he nodded toward the stairs. "Would you like to see your room?"

"Absolutely," she said as they started upstairs. She couldn't believe how eager she sounded about the bedroom, considering the moment they had just shared out by the truck. To cover the awkwardness, she added, "I can't wait to see what your mother did with the bedrooms."

When they reached the second floor, Chance directed her toward a room at the far end of the hall and opened the door. "If you don't like this one, there are four more you can choose from."

"I love it," Fee said, walking into the cheery room.

The log walls were the same honey color as the ones downstairs, but the room had a more feminine feel to it with the yellow calico curtains and bright patchwork quilt on the log bed. An antique mirror hung on the wall above a cedar-log dresser with a white milk glass pitcher and bowl on top. But her favorite feature of the room had to be the padded window seat beneath the double windows. She could imagine spending rainy afternoons curled up with a good book and a cup of hot peach tea on that bench.

"Your private bathroom is just through there," he said, pointing toward a closed door as he set her luggage on the hardwood plank floor.

"Thank you, Chance." She continued to look around. "This is just fine."

"I'll be downstairs in the kitchen if you need anything. When you get your things unpacked, come on down and we'll see what there is for supper." He stepped closer and lightly touched her cheek with the back of his knuckles. "And just so you know, I am going to do what both of us want."

"W-what's that?" she asked, wondering why the sound of his voice made her feel warm all over.

Her heart skipped a beat when his gaze locked with hers. But when he lightly traced her lower lip with the pad of his thumb, a shiver of anticipation slid up her spine and goose bumps shimmered over her skin.

"I'm going to kiss you, Fee," he said, his tone low and intimate. "And soon." Without another word, he turned and walked out into the hall, closing the door behind him.

Staring after him, she would have liked to deny that he was right about what she wanted. But she couldn't. She had thought he was going to kiss her when he came to get her at the rental house this afternoon and then again when they arrived at the ranch. Both times she'd been disappointed when he hadn't.

With her knees wobbling, she crossed the room to sit on the side of the bed. What on earth had gotten into her? She had a job to do and a promotion to earn. She didn't need the added distraction of a man in her life—even if it was only briefly.

But as she sat there wondering why he was more tempting than any other man she'd ever met, Fee knew without a shadow of doubt that the chemistry between herself and Chance was going to be extremely hard to resist. Every time he got within ten feet of her, she felt as if the air had been charged by an electric current, and when he touched her, all she could think about was how his lips would feel on hers when he kissed her. She could tell from the looks he gave her and his constant desire to touch her that he was feeling it, as well.

But she had her priorities straight. She was focused on her goal of becoming Lassiter Media's first vice president in charge of public relations under the age of thirty. She wasn't going to risk her career for any man and especially not for a summer fling— even if the sexy-as-sin cowboy had a charming smile and a voice that could melt the polar ice caps.

* * *

"Did you get the little lady squared away?" Gus Swenson asked when Chance entered the kitchen.

Too old to continue doing ranch work and too ornery to go anywhere else, Gus had become the cook and housekeeper after the renovations to the homestead had been completed. If it had been left up to him, Chance would have just had Gus move into the homestead and that would have been that. After all, Gus had been his dad's lifelong best friend—he was practically family. But Gus's pride had been at stake and that's why Chance had disguised his offer in the form of a job. The old man had grumbled about being reduced to doing "women's work," but Chance knew Gus was grateful for the opportunity to live out the rest of his days on the ranch he had worked for the past fifty years.

"Yup. She's in the room across the hall from mine," Chance answered, walking over to hang his hat on a peg beside the back door.

Reaching into the refrigerator, he got himself a beer and popped off the metal cap. He needed something to take the edge off the tension building inside him.

In hindsight, it might not have been the smartest decision he'd ever made to put Fee in the room across from the master suite. If touching her smooth cheek was all it took to make him feel as restless as a bull moose in mating season, how the hell was he going to get any sleep? He tipped the bottle up and drank half the contents. Just the thought of her lying in bed within feet of where he would be, wearing something soft and transparent, her silky blond hair spread across the pillow, had him ready to jump out of his own skin.

"You still got the notion you're gonna talk her outta makin' you a movie star?" Gus asked, drawing him out of his unsettling insight.

"I told you she wants me to be the spokesman for her PR campaign," Chance said, finishing off the beer. "That's a far cry from being in a movie."

"You're gonna be in front of a camera, ain't ya?" Gus asked. Before Chance could answer, the old man went on. "I've got a month's pay that says you'll end up doin' it."

Chance laughed as he tossed the empty bottle in the recycling container under the sink. "That's one bet you'll lose."

The old man grunted. "We'll see, hotshot. You ain't never asked a woman to come stay here before and that's a surefire sign that she's already got you roped. It's just a matter of time before she's got you fallin' all over yourself to do whatever she wants."

Deciding there might be a ring of truth to Gus's observations and not at all comfortable with it, Chance changed the subject. "Did Slim check on the north pasture's grazing conditions today?"

He didn't have to ask if Gus had seen the ranch foreman. The old guy made a trip out to the barn every afternoon when the men came back to the ranch for the day, to shoot the breeze and feel as if he was still a working cowboy.

Gus shook his head. "Slim said they couldn't get to it today. He had to send a couple of the boys over to the west pasture to fix a pretty good stretch of fence that last storm tore up and the rest of 'em were movin' the herd over by the cutbank so they can start mowin' for hay next week."

"I'll take care of it tomorrow," Chance said. He had intended to show Fee around the ranch anyway; he could include the northern section of pasture as part of the tour.

"Something smells absolutely wonderful," she said, walking into the kitchen.

"Thank you, ma'am." Bent over to take a pan of biscuits out of the oven, Gus added, "I don't fix anything real fancy, but I can guarantee it'll taste good and there's plenty of it."

"Fee Sinclair, this is Gus Swenson, the orneriest cowboy this side of the Continental Divide," Chance said, making the introductions.

When Gus straightened and finally turned to face her, Chance watched a slow grin appear on the old man's wrinkled face. "Real nice to meet you, gal." He stood there grinning like a damned fool for several moments before a scowl replaced his easy expression. "Where's your manners, boy? Don't just stand there blinkin' your eyes like a bastard calf in a hailstorm. Offer this little lady a seat while I finish up supper."

"Thank you, but I'd be more than happy to help you finish dinner," Fee offered, smiling.

"I got it all under control, gal," Gus said, reaching into the cabinet to get some plates.

"Could I at least set the table for you?" she asked, walking over to the butcher block island, where Gus had set the plates. "I really do want to help."

Gus looked like a teenage boy with his first crush when he nodded and handed her the dinnerware. "I appreciate it, ma'am."

"Please call me Fee," she said, smiling as she took the plates from the old man.

When she turned toward the table, Gus grinned like a possum and gave Chance a thumbs-up behind her back. "Why don't you make yourself useful, boy? Get some glasses and pour up somethin' for all of us to drink."

As Chance poured three glasses of iced tea and carried them to the table, he couldn't get over the change in Gus. Normally as grouchy as a grizzly bear with a sore paw, the crusty old cowboy was downright pleasant to Fee—at least as close to it as Gus ever got. If he didn't know better, Chance would swear that Gus was smitten.

Twenty minutes later after eating a heaping plate of beef stew, homemade biscuits and a slice of hot apple pie, Chance sat back from the table. "Gus, you outdid yourself. I think that was one of the best meals you've ever made."

"Everything was delicious," Fee agreed, reaching over to cover the old man's hand with hers. "Thank you, Gus."

The gesture caused Gus's cheeks to turn red above

his grizzled beard. "You're more than welcome, gal. Can I get you anything else? Maybe another piece of pie? We got plenty."

Smiling, Fee shook her head. "I couldn't eat another thing. I'm positively stuffed."

Chance rose to take his and Fee's plates to the sink. If anyone was falling all over themselves to do whatever Fee wanted, it was Gus. The old guy was practically begging her to let him do something—anything—for her.

"Would you like to go for a walk after I help Gus clear up the kitchen?" Chance asked, wanting to spend a little time alone with her.

"That would be nice," she said, getting up from the table. "But I want to help with the cleanup first."

"You kids go on and take your walk," Gus said as he got to his feet. "There ain't nothin' much to do but put the leftovers in the refrigerator and load the dishwasher."

"Are you sure, Mr. Swenson?" Fee asked, her voice uncertain.

"The name's Gus, little lady," the old geezer said, grinning from ear to ear. "And I don't mind one bit."

Chance turned to stare at Gus to see if the old man had sprouted another head and a new personality to go with it. He'd never in his entire thirty-two years heard Gus sound so amiable. What was wrong with him?

"Are you feeling all right?" Chance asked, frowning.

"I'm just fine," Gus answered, his smile warning

Chance to drop the matter. "Now, you kids go ahead and take that walk. I'm gonna be turnin' in pretty soon. I'll see you both at breakfast in the mornin'."

Chance shook his head as he reached for his hat hanging on the peg and opened the door. He suddenly knew exactly what was wrong with Gus. Damned if the old fart wasn't trying to play matchmaker.

As they left the house, Fee looked confused. "It's not that late. Is Gus really going to bed this early?"

Chance shook his head. "No, but he's got a set of priorities and in the summer it's baseball. The Rockies are playing the Cardinals on one of the satellite TV channels tonight and he wouldn't miss that for anything. He's going to hole up in his room watching the game."

They fell silent for a moment as they started across the yard toward the barn. "Do you mind if I ask you something, Chance?"

"Not at all. What do you want to know?" he asked, barely resisting the urge to put his arm around her.

To keep from acting on the impulse, he stuffed his hands into the front pockets of his jeans. She had only been on the ranch a couple of hours and he didn't want her to feel as if he was rushing things.

"Earlier this afternoon, you said your mother didn't have time to become an interior decorator because she was too busy chasing after a houseful of children." She paused as if she wasn't sure how to word her question. "I was under the impression that the only sibling you had was your sister."

He nodded. "She is. But up until a couple of months ago, I thought I was an only child."

Fee's confusion was written all over her pretty face. "Am I missing something?"

"Hannah is the product of an affair my dad had when he was out on the rodeo circuit," Chance admitted, still feeling a bit resentful. Although he loved and accepted his half sister, he still struggled with the fact that his father had cheated on his mother. "My mom, dad and uncle J.D. knew about her, but the rest of the family didn't find out until a couple of months ago."

"Okay," Fee said slowly. "But if all your mother had was you, who were the other kids she was running after?"

"Working for Lassiter Media, you've probably heard that Uncle J.D.'s wife died within a few days of having Angelica." When Fee nodded, he continued, "Uncle J.D. had his hands full trying to raise three little kids on his own. Mom helped out as much as she could, but she had me and Dad to take care of and was only able to do so much. Then after my dad got killed four years later, my uncle suggested that Mom and I move into the main house with him and his kids. By that time he had opened the Lassiter Media office in L.A. and traveled back and forth a lot. He needed someone he trusted to take care of his kids and my mom was the obvious choice. She knew and loved the kids and they all considered her a second mother anyway."

"That makes sense," she agreed. "Was your parents' home nearby?"

"We lived here at the homestead." He couldn't help but feel a strong sense of pride that he was the third generation to own this section of the ranch. "My dad was more of a cowboy than Uncle J.D. ever thought about being and when he wasn't riding the rough stock in a rodeo somewhere, Dad was working here at the ranch. After my uncle built the main house, Uncle J.D. gave this part of the Big Blue to us."

"No wonder the family is extremely close," Fee said thoughtfully. "Sage, Dylan and Angelica are more like your siblings than they are cousins."

As they walked into the barn, Chance gave in to temptation and casually draped his arm across her slender shoulders. She gave him a sideways glance, but he took it as a good sign that she didn't protest.

"The only time the four of us weren't together was at night when we went to bed," he explained. "Uncle J.D. gave my mom and me one wing of the house so that we would have our privacy, while he and his kids took the other wing."

"You must have had a wonderful childhood with other children to play with," Fee said, sounding wistful.

"I can't complain," he admitted. "What about your family? Do you have a brother or sister?"

She shook her head. "I was an only child."

When she failed to elaborate, Chance decided to let the matter drop. It was clear she didn't want to talk about it and he'd never been one to pry. If Fee wanted to tell him about her family, he would be more than happy to listen. If she didn't, then that was her call.

Walking down the long aisle between the horse stalls, Chance pointed to a paint mare that had curiously poked her head over the bottom half of the stall door. "That's the horse you'll learn to ride tomorrow."

Fee looked uncertain. "It looks so big. Do you have one in a smaller size?"

"You make it sound like you're trying on a pair of shoes," he said, laughing. "Rosy is about as small as we have around here."

"I'm not so comfortable with large animals," she said, shaking her head. "When I was little girl, my grandmother's next door neighbor had an overly friendly Great Dane that knocked me down every time I was around him. I know he wasn't trying to hurt me, but I ended up with stitches in my knee from his friendly gestures." She eyed the mare suspiciously. "She's bigger than he was."

He guided Fee over to the stall. "I promise Rosy is the gentlest horse we have on the ranch and loves people." Reaching out, he scratched the mare's forehead. "She'll be the perfect starter horse for you and she won't knock you down."

"Rosy likes that?" Fee asked.

He nodded. "You want to try it?" When she shook her head, he took her hand in his. "Just rub Rosy's forehead like this," he said, showing her how. "While you two get acquainted, I'll go get a treat for you to feed her."

"I don't think that's a good idea, Chance." He heard the hesitancy in her voice as he walked across the aisle into the feed room. "She looks like she might have pretty big teeth. Does she bite?"

He shook his head as he walked back to the stall with a cube of sugar. "Rosy might nip you unintentionally, but she's never been one to bite." He placed the cube on Fee's palm. "Just keep your hand flat and Rosy will take care of the rest."

When Fee tentatively put her hand out, the mare scooped up the sugar cube with her lips. "Oh my goodness!" Fee's expression was filled with awe when she turned to look at him. "Her mouth is so soft. It feels just like velvet."

Seeing the wonder in her eyes and her delighted smile, Chance didn't think twice about closing the gap between them to take Fee in his arms. "Do you remember what I told you this afternoon?"

The glee in her vibrant blue eyes changed to the awareness he'd seen in them earlier in the day. "Y-yes."

"Good." He started to lower his head and was encouraged when she brought her arms up to encircle his neck. "I'm going to give you that kiss now that we've both been wanting."

When he covered her mouth with his, Chance didn't think he had ever tasted anything sweeter. He took his time to slowly, thoroughly explore her soft lips. They were perfect and clung to his as if she was eager for him to take the kiss to the next level. When she sighed and melted into him, he didn't think twice about tightening his arms around her and deepening the caress.

The moment his tongue touched hers, Chance felt a wave of heat shoot from the top of his head all the way to the soles of his feet. But when she slid her hands beneath the collar of his shirt to caress the nape of his neck, it felt as if his heart turned a somersault inside his chest. The magnetic pull between them was more explosive than anything he could have imagined and he knew as surely as he knew his own name it was inevitable—they would be making love. The thought caused the region south of his belt buckle to tighten so fast it left him feeling lightheaded.

Easing away from the kiss before things got out of hand, he gazed down at the dazed expression on her pretty face. She was as turned on as he was and, unless he missed his guess, a little confused by how quickly the passion had flared between them.

"I think we'd better call it a night," he said, continuing to hold her.

"I-it would…probably be a good…idea," she said, sounding as breathless as he felt.

"Mornings around here start earlier than you're probably used to," he advised, forcing himself to take a step back.

When he put his arm around her and started walking toward the open doors of the barn, she asked, "How early are we talking about?"

He grinned. "Well before daylight."

"Is it that imperative to get up so early?" she asked, frowning.

"The livestock get breakfast before we do," he explained, holding her to his side. "Besides, in the summer we get as much done as we can before the hottest part of the day. The earlier we get up and get started, the better chance we have of doing that."

"I suppose that makes sense," she said as they climbed the porch steps and went into the house. "Why don't you wake me up when you get back to the house after you feed the livestock?"

"Hey, you're the one who's here to observe what a real cowboy is all about," he reminded, laughing. "That includes the morning chores as well as what I do the rest of the day."

"No, I'm here to talk you into being the spokesman for your family's PR campaign," she shot back. "It was your idea that I needed to see what you do."

Walking her into the foyer of the homestead and up the stairs, they fell silent and Chance cursed himself as nine kinds of a fool the closer they got to their bedrooms. After he had put her in the room across the hall from his, he'd realized that it probably hadn't been one of his brightest ideas. But now that he knew the sweetness of her lips and how responsive she was to his kiss, there wasn't a doubt in his mind that it was the dumbest decision he'd made in his entire adult life. But at the time, he'd thought she might like the room with the window seat. It was the only one of the six bedrooms that was the least bit feminine.

When they stopped at the door to her room, he barely resisted the temptation of taking her back into his arms. "Sleep well, Fee."

"You, too, Chance," she said, giving him a smile that sent his blood pressure skyrocketing.

He waited until she went into her room, then quickly entering his, he closed the door and headed straight for the shower. Between the kiss they'd shared in the barn and the knowledge that at that very moment she was probably removing every stitch of clothes she had on, he was hotter than a two-dollar pistol in a skid-row pawn shop on Saturday night.

He'd have liked nothing more than to hold Fee to him and kiss her senseless. But that hadn't been an option. If he had so much as touched her, he knew he wouldn't have wanted to let her go. And that had never happened to him before.

It wasn't as if he hadn't experienced a strong attraction for a woman in the past. But nothing in his adult life had been as passionate as fast as what he had felt with Fee when he kissed her. He hadn't counted on that when he asked her to stay with him. Hell, the possibility hadn't even been on his radar.

Quickly stripping out of his clothes, he turned on the water and stepped beneath the icy spray. Maybe if he traumatized his body with a cold shower, he'd not only be able to get some sleep, maybe some of his sanity would return.

As he stood there shivering uncontrollably, he shook his head. Yeah, and if he believed that, there was someone, somewhere waiting to sell him the Grand Canyon or Mount Rushmore.

Four

Fee yawned as she sat on a bale of hay in the barn and watched Chance saddle Rosy and another horse he'd called Dakota. She couldn't believe that after he'd knocked on her door an hour and a half before the sun came up, he'd gone on to feed all of the animals housed in the barns and holding pens and met with his ranch foreman to go over the chores for the day—all before breakfast.

Hiding another yawn with her hand, she decided she might not be as tired if she'd gotten more rest the night before. But sleep had eluded her and she knew exactly what had caused her insomnia. Not only had Chance's kiss been way more than she'd expected, it had caused her to question her sanity.

Several different times yesterday, she had practically asked the man to kiss her and when he finally had, she'd acted completely shameless and all but melted into a puddle at his big booted feet. Thank goodness he'd kept it fairly brief and ended the kiss before she'd made a bigger fool of herself than she already had.

Then there was the matter of the promise she'd made to herself years ago. She'd seemed to forget all about her vow to never put her career in jeopardy because of a man.

"You're not your mother," she whispered to herself.

Her mother had been a prime example of how that kind of diversion could destroy a career, and Fee was determined not to let that happen to her. Rita Sinclair had abandoned her position as a successful financial advisor when she foolishly fell head over heels in love with a dreamer—a man who chased his lofty ideas from one place to another without ever considering the sacrifices his aspirations had cost her. Maybe he'd asked her to marry him because she had become pregnant with Fee or maybe he'd thought it was what he wanted at the time. Either way, he had eventually decided that his wife and infant daughter were holding him back and he'd moved on without them.

But instead of picking up the pieces of her life and resuming her career, Fee's mother had settled for working one dead-end job after another that left her with little time for her daughter. Her mother had died ten years ago, still waiting for the dreamer to return to take her with him on his next irresponsible adventure. Fee suspected that her mother had died of a broken heart because he never did.

When she'd been old enough to understand the life her mother had given up for her father, Fee had made a conscious decision to avoid making the same mistakes.

Although he wasn't her boss, Chance's family owned the company she worked for and that was even worse. She could very easily end up getting herself fired.

She tried to think if she'd heard anything about Lassiter Media's policy on fraternization. Would that even apply in this situation? Chance wasn't an employee of the company, nor was he an owner. But he was closely related to those who were and she'd been sent to smooth over a scandal, not create another one.

"I don't know what you're thinking, but if that frown on your face is any indication, it can't be good," Chance said, breaking into her disturbing thoughts.

"I was thinking about the PR campaign," she answered, staring down at the toes of her new boots. "I should be working on ideas for the videos and print ads."

Technically it wasn't really a lie. She had been thinking about the reasons she'd been sent to Wyoming and how losing her focus when it came to him could very easily cost her a perfectly good job.

Squatting down in front of her, Chance used his index finger to lift her chin until their gazes met.

KATHIE DeNOSKY   75

"What do you say we forget about fixing the Lassiter reputation today and just have a little fun?"

The moment he touched her, Fee could barely remember her own name, let alone the fact that she had a job she might lose if she wasn't careful. "You think I'm going to have fun riding a horse?" she asked, unable to keep the skepticism from her voice.

"I promise you will," he said, taking her hands in his. Straightening to his full height, he pulled her to her feet, then picked up her hat where she had placed it on the bale of hay when she sat down. Positioning it on her head, he pointed to Rosy. "Now, are you ready to mount up and get started?"

"Not really," she said, wondering if workers' compensation would cover her falling off a horse since she was only learning to ride in an effort to get him to agree to be the Lassiter spokesman. Eying the mare, Fee shook her head. "Is it just me or did she get a lot bigger overnight?"

"It's just you," he said, laughing as he led her over to the mare's side. He explained how to put her foot in the stirrup and take hold of the saddle to pull herself up onto the back of the horse. "Don't worry about Rosy. She's been trained to stand perfectly still until you're seated and give her the signal you're ready for her to move."

"It's the after I'm seated part that I'm worried about," Fee muttered as she took a deep breath and barely managed to raise her foot high enough to place it in the stirrup. Grabbing the saddle as Chance had instructed, she tried to mount the horse but found the task impossible. "How is stepping into the stirrup any help when your knee is even with your chin?" she asked, feeling relief flow through her. If she couldn't mount the horse, she couldn't ride it. "I guess I won't be able to go riding. At least not until you get a shorter horse."

"It takes a little practice," he answered, grinning. "Besides, the horse isn't as tall as you are short."

She shook her head. "There's nothing wrong with being short."

"I didn't say there was," he said, stepping behind her.

Fee's heart felt as if it stopped, then took off at a gallop when, without warning, he placed one hand at her waist and the other on the seat of her new jeans. Before she could process what was taking place, Chance boosted her up into the saddle. Her cheeks heated and she wasn't sure if it was from embarrassment or the awareness coursing through her.

But when she realized she was actually sitting atop Rosy, Fee forgot all about sorting out her reaction to Chance. Wrapping both hands around the saddle horn, she held on for dear life. "This is even higher than I thought it would be. I really do think a shorter horse would work out a lot better."

"Try to relax and sit naturally," he coaxed. He reached up to gently pry her hands from the saddle. "You don't want to be as stiff as a ramrod."

When the mare shifted her weight from one foot to the other, Fee scrunched her eyes shut and waited for the worst. "I thought you said she would stand still."

"Fee, look at me," he commanded. When she opened first one eye and then the other, the promise in his brilliant green eyes stole her breath. "Do you trust me?"

"Yes." She wasn't sure why, given that she hadn't known him all that long, but she did trust him.

"I give you my word that I won't let anything happen to you," he assured her. "You're completely safe, sweetheart."

Her heart stalled and she suddenly found it hard to draw a breath. The sound of his deep voice when he used the endearment caused heat to fill her. Why did she suddenly wish he was talking about something besides riding a horse?

Unable to get her vocal cords to work, she simply nodded.

"Good." He checked to make sure the stirrups were adjusted to the right length. "Now I want you to slightly tilt your heels down just below horizontal."

"Why?" she asked even as she followed his instructions.

"Shifting your weight to your heels instead of the balls of your feet helps you relax your legs and sit more securely," he explained. "And it's more natural and comfortable for both you and Rosy." He took hold of the mare's reins, then reached for his horse's reins, as well. "Now are you ready to go for your first ride?"

"Would it make a difference if I said no?" she asked, already knowing the answer.

Grinning, he shook his head. "Nope."

"I didn't think so." Fee caught her breath when the mare slowly started walking beside Chance as he led both horses out of the barn. But instead of the bumpy ride she expected, it was more of a smooth rocking motion. "This isn't as rough as I thought it would be."

"It isn't when you relax and move with the horse, instead of against it," he said, leading them over to the round pen he had mentioned was used for training. Once he had his horse tied to the outside of the fence, he opened the gate and led the mare inside. "Hold the reins loosely," he said, handing Fee the leather straps. He walked around the pen beside Rosy until they had made a complete circle. "Now, I'm going to stand right here while you and Rosy go around."

A mixture of adrenaline and fear rose inside of Fee like a Pacific tsunami. "What am I supposed to do?"

"Just sit there and let Rosy do the rest," he said calmly. "I promise you'll be fine."

As the horse carried her around the enclosure, Fee noticed that the mare kept turning her head to look back at her. "Yes, Rosy, I'm scared witless. Please prove Chance right and don't do anything I'll regret."

To her surprise the mare snorted and bobbed her head up and down as if she understood what Fee had requested as she continued to slowly walk around the inside of the fence.

By the time Rosy had made her way back around to the gate for the second time, Fee began to feel a little more confident. "This isn't as difficult as I thought it would be."

"It's not," Chance said when the mare stopped in front of him. "Are you ready to take a tour of the ranch now?" he asked, patting the mare's sleek neck.

"I…guess so," Fee answered, not at all sure she was ready to ride outside of the enclosure. But Rosy seemed to be willing and Fee felt some of her usual self-confidence begin to return.

"Don't worry," Chance said, as if reading her mind. He opened the gate to lead the mare out. "Rosy is kid broke and you're doing great for your first time on a horse."

Fee frowned. "What does kid broke mean?"

"Her temperament and training make her safe enough to let a little kid ride her with minimal risk of anything happening," he said, mounting his horse. "And I'll be right beside you."

As they rode across the pasture and headed toward a hillside in the distance, she reflected on how far out of her element she was. Up until today, her idea of adventure had been a shopping trip to one of the malls in the San Fernando Valley the day after Thanksgiving.

But she had to admit that riding a horse wasn't as bad as she thought it would be. In fact, the more she thought about it, the more she realized she was actu-

ally enjoying the experience. And if that wasn't unusual enough, they were traveling across a deserted
expanse of land where wild animals roamed free and
she wasn't all that afraid of being something's next
meal. Unbelievable!

Fee glanced over at the man riding beside her.
What was it about Chance that could get her to do
things that were totally out of character for her and
without much protest on her part?

Staring out across the land, she knew exactly why
she was willing to step out of her comfort zone and
try new things. She trusted Chance—trusted that he
wouldn't ask anything of her that she couldn't do and
wouldn't allow anything to harm her.

The realization caused her heart to skip a beat.
She didn't trust easily and especially when it came
to men. The fact that she had already placed her faith
in Chance was more than a little disturbing. Why
was he different?

It could have something to do with the fact that
so far, he was exactly what he said he was—a hard-
working rancher who was more interested in drawing attention to the quality of the beef he raised than
being in the limelight himself. Or maybe it was the
fact that he was vastly different from any of the men
she knew in L.A. Although great guys, most of them
would rather sit behind a desk in a climate-controlled
office than be outside getting their hands dirty.

She wasn't sure why she trusted Chance, but one
thing was certain: she was going to have to be on

her guard at all times. Otherwise, she just might find herself falling for him and end up out of a job.

As they rode up the trail leading to the north pasture, Chance was proud of the way Fee had taken to horseback riding. At first, she had been extremely apprehensive about getting on a horse, but she'd at least had the guts to try. That was something he admired.

In fact, there were a lot of things about her that he appreciated. She was not only courageous, she was dedicated. He didn't know any other woman who would go to the lengths she had in her effort to do her job and do it right. Fee was willing to do whatever it took to get him to agree to be the spokesman in her ad campaign, even if that meant getting up at a time most city dwellers thought was the middle of the night and riding a horse for the first time. And from what Sage had told him, she was sensitive to others. Apparently, Colleen had tentatively offered to let Fee use their upcoming wedding as part of the PR campaign to improve the Lassiters' image, but she hadn't wanted to exploit their big day and had politely declined.

"Rosy and I seem to be getting along pretty well," Fee said, bringing him back to the present.

"So you're having a good time?" he asked, noticing how silky her hair looked as a light breeze played with the blond strands of her ponytail.

"Yes," she said, giving him a smile. "I didn't think

I would, but I really am. Of course, I might not feel the same way if I was riding a different horse."

"I was pretty sure you and Rosy were…a good match," he said, distracted by the faint sound of a cow bawling in the distance. Staring in the direction the sound came from, he spotted a large black cow lying on her side about two hundred yards away. It was clear the animal was in distress. "Damn!"

"What happened?" Fee asked, looking alarmed.

"I'm going to have to ride on ahead," he said quickly. "You'll be fine. I'll be within sight and Rosy will bring you right to me."

Before Fee had the chance to question him further or protest that he was leaving her behind, he kicked Dakota into a gallop and raced toward the cow. The bay gelding covered the distance quickly and when he reached the cow, Chance could tell that not only was she in labor, she was having trouble delivering the calf.

Dismounting, he immediately started rolling up the long sleeves on his chambray shirt. He could tell from her shallow breathing that the animal had been at this awhile and was extremely weak. He was going to have to see what the problem was, then try to do what he could to help. Otherwise there was a very real possibility he would lose both the heifer and her calf.

"What's wrong with it?" Fee asked when she and Rosy finally reached the spot where the cow lay.

"I'm pretty sure the calf is hung up," he said, taking off his wristwatch and slipping it into the front pocket of his jeans. He reached into the saddlebags tied behind Dakota's saddle and removed a packet of disinfectant wipes.

Fee looked genuinely concerned. "Oh, the poor thing. Is there anything you can do to help her? Should you call the veterinarian?"

"The vet will take too long to get here." Walking over to the mare, he lifted Fee down from the saddle and set her on her feet. "I'm going to need you to hold the heifer's tail while I check to see what the problem is," he said, taking several of the wet cloths from the packet to wipe down his hands and arms. "Do you think you can do that, Fee?"

He could tell she wasn't at all sure about getting that close to the animal, but she took a deep breath and nodded. "I'll do my best."

"Good." He couldn't stop himself from giving her a quick kiss. Then catching the cow's wildly switching tail, he handed it to Fee. "Hold on tight while I see if the calf's breech or it's just too big."

While Fee held the tail out of the way, Chance knelt down at the back of the animal. He wished that he had some of the shoulder-length gloves from one of the calving sheds back at ranch headquarters, but since that wasn't an option, he gritted his teeth and proceeded to do what he could to help the heifer. Reaching inside, he felt the calf, and sure enough, one of the legs was folded at the knee. Pushing the calf back, he carefully straightened its front leg, then gently but firmly pulled it back into the birth position.

"Will she be able to have the calf now?" Fee asked, her tone anxious as she let go of the tail and put distance between herself and the cow.

"I hope so," he said, rising to his feet. Using more of the wipes, he cleaned his arm as he waited to see if the heifer was going to be able to calve. "I'll have to check my records when I get back to the house, but I'm pretty sure this is her first calf."

When the cow made an odd noise, Fee looked worried. "Is she all right?"

"She's pretty tired, but we should know within a few minutes if she'll be able to do this on her own," he said, focusing on the cow to see if there were any more signs of distress. When he saw none, he walked over to Fee.

"And if she can't?" Fee asked.

"Then I become a bovine obstetrician and help her out," he answered, shrugging. "It wouldn't be the first time and it won't be the last."

"This is definitely one of those jobs you mentioned that most people would consider disgusting."

"Yup." He noticed the heifer was starting to work with her contractions and that was a good sign she at least wasn't too exhausted to try.

"Maybe a lot of people find something like this distasteful, but I think it's rather heroic," Fee said, thoughtfully. "You care enough about the animals on this ranch to make sure they're well taken care of and if that means getting your hands dirty to save one of them or to help relieve their suffering, then that's what you do."

He nodded. "I'm responsible for them and that includes keeping them healthy."

Chance had never really thought about his job the way Fee had just pointed out. Sure, he liked animals—liked working with them and being around them. He wouldn't be much of a rancher if he didn't. But he had never really thought about what he did as heroic. To him, taking good care of his livestock was not just part of the job description, it was the right thing to do.

"Oh my goodness," Fee said suddenly when the calf began to emerge from the cow. Her expression was filled with awe. "This is amazing."

Confident that the animal was going to be able to have the calf without further intervention on his part, he used his cell phone to call ranch headquarters. He needed to get one of his men to come out and watch over the heifer until she and the calf could be moved to one of the holding pens close to the barn.

When the calf slid out onto the ground, Chance walked over to make sure it was breathing and checked it over while the heifer rested. "It's a girl," he said, grinning as he walked back to Fee.

"Is the momma cow going to be all right?" Fee asked.

He nodded as he draped his arm across her shoulders. "I think she'll be just fine. But Slim is sending one of the boys out here to see that she gets back to the ranch, where we can watch her and she can rest up a little. Then she and her baby will rejoin the herd in a few days."

Fee frowned. "Why was she out here by herself to begin with?"

"Livestock have a tendency to want to go off by themselves when they're in labor," Chance explained.

"For privacy." She nodded. "I can understand that."

He watched the cow get up and nudge her baby with her nose, urging it to stand, as well. "She had probably done that yesterday when the men moved the herd and they just missed seeing her. Normally, our cattle calve in the spring, but she apparently got bred later than usual, throwing her having her calf to now."

"But they will be back at the ranch house and I'll be able to see the calf again?" she asked, looking hopeful as, after several attempts, the calf gained her footing and managed to stand.

"Sure, you'll be able to see her." He grinned. "But I somehow got the impression you didn't like big animals all that much and might even be a little afraid of them."

"This one is different," she insisted, her voice softening when the calf wobbled over to her mother and started to nurse. "It's a baby and not all that big yet. Besides, the fence will be between me and her momma."

Seeing the cowboy he'd called for riding toward them, Chance led Fee over to Rosy. "Our replacement is almost here. Are you ready to mount up and finish checking on the grazing conditions before we head back to the house?"

"I suppose," she said, lifting her foot to put it into the stirrup. "This would be a whole lot easier if Rosy was shorter."

As he stepped up behind her, Chance took a deep breath and got ready to give her a boost up into the saddle. Touching her cute little backside when she'd mounted the mare the first time had damn near caused him to have a coronary. He could only guess what his reaction would be this time.

The minute his palm touched the seat of her blue jeans, a jolt of electric current shot up his arm, down through his chest and straight to the region south of his belt buckle. His reaction was not only predictable, it was instantaneous.

Feeling as if his own jeans had suddenly gotten a couple of sizes smaller in the stride, he waited to make sure Fee was settled on Rosy before he caught Dakota's reins in one hand and gingerly swung up onto the gelding's saddle. He immediately shifted to keep from emasculating himself. Fee hadn't been on the ranch a full twenty-four hours and he was already in need of a second cold shower.

As they started toward the north pasture, Chance decided it was either going to be the most exciting two weeks of his life or the most grueling. And he had every intention of seeing that it was going to be the former, not the latter.

While Chance called his mother to make arrangements to take Cassie for ice cream the next day, Fee helped clean the kitchen after dinner. "Gus, it was the most amazing thing I've ever seen. He knew exactly what to do and everything turned out fine for the momma cow, as well as for her baby."

She still couldn't get over the efficiency and expertise Chance had demonstrated with the pregnant cow. What he'd had to do to help the animal was messy and disgusting, but he hadn't hesitated for a single second. He had immediately sprung into action and taken care of her and her calf to make sure they both survived.

It was hard to believe how many facets there were to Chance's job. He not only had to keep extensive records on all of the livestock, he had to be a land manager, an experienced horseman and an impromptu large-animal veterinarian. And she had a feeling that was just the tip of the iceberg.

"Don't go tellin' him I said so 'cause I don't want him gettin' bigheaded about it," Gus said, grinning. "But that boy's got better cow sense than even his daddy had. And that's sayin' somethin'. When Charlie Lassiter was alive there was none better at ranchin' than he was. He knew what a steer was gonna do before it did."

Fee remembered Chance telling her that his father had run the ranch when he wasn't out on the rodeo circuit. "How did Chance's father die? Was he killed at a rodeo?"

"It was one of them freak accidents that never shoulda happened." Gus shook his head sadly as he handed her a pot he had just finished washing. "Charlie was a saddle bronc and bareback rider when he was out on the rodeo circuit, and a damned good one. He always finished in the money and other than a busted arm one time, never got hurt real bad. But about three years after he stopped rodeoin' and went to ranchin' full time, he got throwed from a horse he was breakin'. He landed wrong and it snapped his neck. Charlie was dead as soon as he hit the ground."

"That's so sad," she said, drying the pot with a soft cotton dish towel before hanging it on the pot rack above the kitchen island.

"The real bad thing was Chance saw it all," Gus said, his tone turning husky.

"Oh, how awful!" Fee gasped.

Gus nodded. "After Charlie started bein' at home all the time, that little kid was his daddy's shadow and followed him everywhere. It weren't no surprise to any of us that Chance was sittin' on the top fence rail watchin' Charlie that day."

Fee's heart broke for Chance and it took a moment for her to be able to speak around the lump clogging her throat. "How old…was Chance?"

"That was twenty-four years ago," Gus answered. He cleared his throat as if he was having just as hard a time speaking as she was. "That would have made Chance about eight."

She couldn't stop tears from filling her eyes when she thought about Chance as a little boy watching the father he idolized die. Although she'd never really known her father and hadn't been all that close to her mother, she couldn't imagine watching someone she loved so much die in such a tragic way. That had to have been devastating for him.

"Well, that's taken care of," Chance said, walking into the room. He had called his mother to let her know what time they would be stopping by the main house tomorrow to take his niece to get ice cream. Marlene was keeping Cassie while Hannah and Logan were on their honeymoon, and she could probably use a break. "Mom said she would have Cassie ready tomorrow afternoon for us to come by and get her."

Without thinking, Fee walked over and wrapped her arms around his waist to give him a hug. She knew he would probably think she'd lost her mind, but she didn't care. The more she found out about Chance Lassiter the more she realized what a remarkable man he was. He'd suffered through a traumatic loss as a child, but that hadn't deterred him from following in his father's footsteps to become a rancher. And from what she'd seen at the wedding a few nights ago, he had gone out of his way to become close to the half sister and niece that he hadn't even known existed until just recently.

"Don't get me wrong, sweetheart," he said, chuckling as his arms closed around her. "I'm not complaining in the least, but what's this for?"

Knowing that if she tried to explain her actions, she'd make a fool of herself, she shrugged and took a step back. "I'm still amazed that you knew what to do today to save the momma cow and her baby."

He smiled. "How would you like to take a walk out to the holding pen to check on them?"

"I'd like that," she said, meaning it. "Gus and I just finished up the dishes."

Gus nodded. "I'll see you at breakfast. I've a baseball game comin' on the sports channel in a few minutes."

As Gus went to his room to watch the game, she and Chance left the house and walked across the yard toward the barn. She glanced up at him when he reached out and took her hand in his. It was a small gesture, but the fact that it felt so good to have him touch her, even in such a small way, was a little unsettling. Was she already in way over her head?

"Looks like we may have to cut our walk short," Chance said, pointing to a bank of clouds in the distance. "We might get a little rain."

"From the dark color, I'd say it's going to be a downpour," Fee commented as they reached the pen where the cow and calf were being held.

"Even if it is a downpour, it probably won't last long," he answered. "We get a lot of pop-up thundershowers this time of year. They move through, dump a little water on us and move on."

Noticing a covered area at one end of the enclosure, she nodded. "I'm glad to see there's shelter for them if it does start raining."

"Cattle don't usually mind being out in the rain during the summer months," he said, smiling. "It's one of the ways they cool off."

"What's another?" she asked, watching the little black calf venture away from her mother.

"If there's a pond or a river, they like to wade out and just stand there." He grinned. "Sort of like the bovine version of skinny-dipping."

"I can't say I blame them," she said, laughing. "I would think it gets rather hot with all that hair." When the calf got close to the fence, Fee couldn't help but feel a sense of awe. "She's so pretty. What are you going to name her?"

He chuckled. "We normally don't name cattle."

"I guess that would be kind of difficult when you have so many," she said, thinking it was a shame for something so cute not to have a name.

He nodded. "If they're going to be kept for breeding purposes, we tag their ears with a number. That's the way we identify them and keep track of their health and how well they do during calving season."

"I don't care," Fee said, looking into the baby's big brown eyes. "She's too cute to just be a number. I'm going to call her Belle."

"So before we take her and her mother to rejoin the herd, I should have her name put on her ear tag instead of a number?" he asked, grinning as he reached out and caught her to him.

She placed her hands on his chest and started to tell him that was exactly what she thought he should do, but she stopped short when several fat raindrops landed on her face. "We'll be soaked to the bone by the time we get back to the house," she said when it started raining harder.

Chance grabbed hold of her hand and pulled her along in the direction of the barn. "We can wait it out in there."

Sprinting the short distance, a loud clap of thunder echoed overhead as they ran inside. "That rain moved in fast," she said, laughing.

"Unless it's a big storm front, it should move through just as fast." He stared at her for several seconds before he took her by the hand and led her midway down the long center aisle to a narrow set of stairs on the far side of the feed room. "There's something I want to show you."

When he stepped back for her to precede him up the steps, she frowned. "What is it?"

"Trust me, you'll like it," he said, smiling mysteriously.

"I'm sure that's what a spider says to a fly just before it lures him into its web," she said, looking up the stairs to the floor above. She didn't know what he had up his sleeve, but she did trust him and smiling over her shoulder at him, climbed the stairs to the hayloft. When they stood facing each other at the top of the stairs, she asked, "Now, what is it you wanted to show me?"

He walked her over to the open doors at the end of the loft. "We'll have to wait until it stops raining and the sun comes back out," he said, taking her into his arms.

A shiver coursed through her and not entirely from her rain-dampened clothes. The look in Chance's eyes stole her breath and sent waves of goose bumps shimmering over her skin.

"Chance, I don't think this is a good idea," she warned. "I'm not interested in an involvement."

He shook his head. "I'm not, either. All I want is for both of us to enjoy your visit to the ranch."

"I need to talk to you about the PR campaign," she said, reminding him that she wasn't giving up on him being the family spokesman.

He nodded. "I promise we'll get to that soon. But right now, I'm going to kiss you again, Fee," he said, lowering his head. "And this time it's going to be a long, slow kiss that will leave both of us gasping for breath."

Fee's heart pounded hard in her chest when his mouth covered hers and a delicious heat began to spread throughout her body as she raised her arms to encircle his neck. True to his word, Chance took his time, teasing with tiny nibbling kisses that heightened her anticipation, and when he finally traced her lips with his tongue to deepen the caress, Fee felt as if she would go into total meltdown.

As he explored her slowly, thoroughly, he slid his hand from her back up along her ribs to the underside of her breast. Cupping her, he lightly teased the hardened tip with the pad of his thumb and even through the layers of her clothing the sensation was electrifying. A lazy tightening began to form a coil in the pit of her stomach and she instinctively leaned into his big, hard body.

The feel of his rigid arousal nestled against her

soft lower belly, the tightening of his strong arms around her and the feel of his heart pounding out a steady rhythm against her breast sent a need like nothing she had ever known flowing from the top of her head all the way to the soles of her feet.

Her knees wobbled, then failed her completely as he continued to stroke her with a tenderness that brought tears to her eyes. She had been kissed before, but nothing like this. It felt as if she had been waiting on this man and this moment her entire life.

The thought frightened her as little else could. Pushing against his chest, she took a step back to stare up at him. "I'm not good at playing games, Chance."

"I'm not asking you to play games, Fee." He shook his head. "We can have fun while you're here, and when you go back to L.A., you'll have the memory of the good time we had. As long as we keep that in mind, we should be just fine."

She stared at him for several long seconds as she waged a battle within herself. He wasn't asking for anything more from her than the here and now. But there was one problem with his reasoning. She wasn't entirely certain she could trust her heart to listen. Lowering his head, he kissed her again.

"I do believe, Fee Sinclair, that you have the sweetest lips of any woman I've ever known," he whispered close to her ear.

Another tremor of desire slid through her a moment before he pulled back and pointed toward the open doors of the loft. "This is what I wanted you to see."

Looking in the direction he indicated, Fee caught her breath. A brilliantly colored full rainbow arched across the bluest sky she had ever seen.

"It's gorgeous," she murmured.

"Did you know that in some cultures the rainbow symbolizes a new beginning or a new phase in a person's life?" he asked, kissing her forehead as he held her to him and they watched the vibrant prism fade away.

She swallowed hard as she turned her attention to the man holding her close. What was it about being wrapped in Chance's arms that made her feel as if she was entering a new phase in her life—one that she hadn't seen coming and was powerless to stop? And one that made her extremely uneasy.

Five

Standing at the ice-cream counter in Buckaroo Billy's General Store on the outskirts of Cheyenne, Chance glanced through the window at Fee and his niece seated under a big yellow umbrella at one of the picnic tables outside. Cassie was talking a mile a minute and it seemed that Fee was somehow keeping up. That in itself was pretty darned amazing. The kid usually had him confused as hell by the speed she changed subjects. He loved her dearly, but sometimes Cassie had the attention span of a flea and hopped from one topic to another faster than a drop of water on a hot griddle.

Paying for their ice cream, he juggled the three cones and a handful of paper napkins as he shouldered open the door. "A scoop of chocolate fudge brownie for you, princess," he said, handing Cassie the frozen treat. Turning to Fee, he grinned. "And mint chocolate chip for you."

"Uncle Chance!" Cassie exclaimed, pointing to his vanilla ice cream. "You were supposed to try something new this time."

"Where's your sense of adventure, Mr. Lassiter?" Fee asked, laughing.

"I like vanilla," he said, shrugging as he dropped the napkins onto the table and sat down. He should have known Cassie would remember he was supposed to try a new flavor. The kid had a mind like a steel trap. Grinning, he added, "But next week, I promise I'll leave what I get up to you two. How does that sound?"

Cassie's red curls bobbed when she nodded her approval. "I like that. I'll ask Momma what you should have when she gets home." True to form, she looked at Fee and took the conversation in another direction. "My mommy and daddy are on their moneyhoon. That's why I'm staying with Grandma Marlene."

"You mean honeymoon?" Chance asked, winking at Fee. He could tell she was trying hard not to laugh at Cassie's mix-up, the same as he was.

"Yeah. They went on a boat." Cassie shook her head. "But I don't know where."

"After much debate, Hannah and Logan went on a Caribbean cruise," Chance explained to Fee.

She smiled at his niece. "That sounds like a nice honeymoon."

"They're going to bring me back a present," Cassie added as she licked some of the chocolate dripping onto her fingers. When she started to touch her tongue to the ice cream in her usual exuberant fashion, the scoop dislodged from the cone and landed on the top of her tennis shoe. Tears immediately filled her big green eyes and her little chin began to wobble. "I'm sorry. It…fell…Uncle Chance."

"Don't cry, princess," he said gently as he reached over and gave her a hug. "It's all right. I'll get you another one."

While Fee used the napkins to clean off Cassie's shoe, he went back into the store to replace her ice-cream cone. By the time he returned a couple of minutes later, Cassie was all smiles and chattering like a magpie once again.

His mind wandered as his niece and Fee discussed the newest version of a popular fashion doll—and he couldn't help but notice every time Fee licked her ice cream.

"Chance, did you hear me?" Fee asked, sounding concerned.

"Oh, sorry." He grinned. "I was still thinking about doll accessories."

She gave him one of those looks that women were so fond of when they thought a man was full of bull roar. "I said I'm going to take Cassie to the ladies' room to wash her hands."

He nodded. "Good idea."

As he watched Fee and his niece walk into the store, he shook his head at his own foolishness and rose to his feet to walk over to his truck to wait for them to return. If he and Fee didn't make love soon, he was going to be a raving lunatic.

But as he stood there thinking about the danger to his mental health, he realized that making love with Fee wasn't all he wanted. The thought caused his heart to pound hard against his ribs. He wasn't thinking about an actual relationship, was he?

He shook his head to dispel the ridiculous thought. Aside from the fact that neither of them was looking for anything beyond some no-strings fun, he was hesitant to start anything long-term with any woman. His father had been the most honorable man he had ever known and from what he remembered and everything everyone said, Charles Lassiter had loved his wife with all his heart. If his father couldn't remain faithful, what made Chance think that he could do any better?

"Uncle Chance, Fee said we could play fashion show with my dolls the next time she's at Grandma Marlene's house," Cassie said, tugging on his shirtsleeve. "When will that be?"

He'd been so preoccupied with his unsettling thoughts that he hadn't even noticed Fee and Cassie had returned. "I'll talk to Grandma Marlene and see what we can work out," he said, smiling as he picked Cassie up to sit on his forearm. "How does that sound, princess?"

Yawning, Cassie nodded. "Good."

"I think someone is getting sleepy," Fee said when

Chance opened the rear passenger door and buckled Cassie into her safety seat.

"She'll be asleep before we get out of the parking lot," he said, closing the door and turning to help Fee into the truck.

When he got in behind the steering wheel and started the engine, Fee smiled. "After she goes to sleep, we'll have some time to talk."

"About the campaign?" he guessed, steering the truck out onto the road.

"I'd like to hear what your main objections are to being the spokesman," she said, settling back in the bucket seat.

"Being the center of attention isn't something I'm comfortable with and never have been," he said honestly.

"But it would only be some still photos and a few videos," she insisted. "We could even cut out the few personal appearances unless you decided you wanted to do them."

"Yeah, those are out of the question," he said firmly. As far as he was concerned those appearances she mentioned had been off the table from the get-go. "Like I told you the other day at lunch, I don't intend to be a monkey in a sideshow. What you see with me is what you get, sweetheart. I wouldn't know how to be an actor if I tried."

"What if we filmed the video spots on the ranch?" she asked, sounding as if she was thinking out loud. "I could have a cameraman take some footage of you riding up on your horse and then all you would have to do is read from a cue card." She paused for a moment. "We could probably even lift still shots from that."

He could tell she wasn't going to give up. "I'm by no means making any promises," he said, wondering what he could say that would discourage her. "But I'll have to think a little more about it."

"Okay," she said slowly. He could tell she wasn't happy that she hadn't wrangled an agreement from him.

Reaching over, he covered her hand with his. "I'm not saying no, Fee. I'm just saying I need more time to think it over."

When she looked at him, her expression hopeful, he almost caved in and told her he would be her spokesman. Fortunately, she didn't give him the opportunity.

"That's fair," she said, suddenly grinning. "But just keep in mind, I'm not giving up."

"It never occurred to me that you would," he said, laughing.

Fee sat in the middle of the bed with her laptop and an array of papers spread out around her on the colorful quilt. She was supposed to be working on the Lassiter PR campaign. But in the past hour, she had found herself daydreaming about a tall, handsome, green-eyed cowboy more than she had been thinking about ways to restore the public's faith in his family.

Watching him interact with his niece that afternoon had been almost as eye-opening as witnessing his skill at helping a cow give birth to her calf. Both times she had seen him interact with his niece, he had listened patiently when the child spoke and always made Cassie feel as if everything she said was of the utmost importance to him. Someday Chance was going to be a wonderful father and Fee couldn't help but feel a twinge of envy for the woman who would bear his child.

Her heart skipped a beat and she shook her head to dispel the unwarranted thought. What was wrong with her? Why was she even thinking about Chance having a child with some unknown woman?

It shouldn't matter to her. By the end of her month's stay, she would be back in Los Angeles scheduling commercial spots for the family campaign and working toward her goal of becoming Lassiter Media's first female public relations vice president under the age of thirty. And unlike being in Wyoming, she would enjoy the convenience of not having to drive forty miles just to reach a town where she could shop or dine out.

But as she sat there thinking about her life back in L.A., she couldn't seem to remember what the appeal of living there had been. Her condo building was filled with people she didn't know and didn't care to know. And for reasons she couldn't put her finger on, the job promotion didn't seem nearly as enticing as it had a week ago.

As she sat there trying to figure out why she was feeling less than enthusiastic about her life in California, there was a knock on her closed door. Gathering the papers around her to put back in the file folder, she turned off her laptop and walked over to find Chance standing on the other side of the door.

"It's a clear night and the moon is almost full," Chance said, leaning one shoulder against the door frame. "How would you like to go for a ride?"

"On a horse? Surely you can't be serious." She laughed as she shook her head. "I'm not that experienced at riding during the day. What makes you think I would be any better at night? Besides, don't wild animals prowl around more in the dark? There's probably something out there with sharp teeth and long claws just waiting for me to come riding along."

"Slow down, sweetheart. You're sounding a lot like Cassie," he said, laughing. "We won't be going far and other than a raccoon or a coyote, I doubt that we'll see any wildlife. Besides, you won't be riding Rosy. You'll be on the back of Dakota with me."

She gave him a doubtful look. "And you think that's an even better idea than me riding Rosy?"

He grinned as he rocked back on his heels. "Yup."

"I'll bet you even have a cozy little saddle made for two stashed in the tack room," she quipped.

"You're so cute." Laughing, he straightened to his full height and took her by the hand to lead her downstairs. "No, they don't make saddles for two people. We're going to ride bareback."

"Oh, yeah, that's even safer than me riding Rosy at night," she muttered as they left the house and started toward the barn.

"It is if you're a skilled horseman and you know your horse."

"Just remember, I'm counting on you to be right about that," she said, unable to believe she was going along with his scheme.

When they reached the barn, he led Dakota out of his stall and put a bridle on the gelding. Then turning, he loosely put his arms around her. "Thanks for going with me and Cassie today," he said, kissing her temple. "I know she enjoyed talking to you about her dolls."

"She's a delightful little girl. Very bright and outgoing," Fee said. "I had a wonderful time talking to her." Grinning, she added, "But I'm really surprised that you didn't join in the conversation when we were discussing the latest doll accessories."

"I'll be the first to admit I don't know diddlysquat about dolls." He chuckled. "But if you want to talk toy trucks or action figures, I'm you're guy."

"I'll take your word for that, too," she said, staring up into his eyes. "But all joking aside, I really did have fun chatting with your niece."

"What about me?" he whispered, leaning forward. "Did you have a good time talking with me?"

A quivering excitement ran through her body at the feel of his warm breath feathering over her ear and she had to brace her hands on his biceps to keep her balance. The feel of rock-hard muscle beneath his chambray shirt caused heat to flow through her veins.

"Yes, I always enjoy talking to you," she answered truthfully.

"I like spending my time with you, too." Lowering his head, he gave her a kiss so tender her knees threatened to buckle before he stepped back, took hold of the reins and a handful of Dakota's mane, then swung up onto the horse. "Turn your back to me, Fee."

When she did as he instructed, he reached down and effortlessly lifted her to sit in front of him on the gelding. Straddling the horse, she was glad Chance was holding on to her. "Whoa! This is a lot higher than sitting on Rosy."

Chance's deep chuckle vibrated against her back as he tightened his arm around her midsection and nudged the gelding into a slow walk. "I promise you're safe, sweetheart. I won't let you fall."

She knew he was talking about a fall from the horse, but what was going to keep her from falling for the man holding her so securely against him?

Fee quickly relegated the thought to the back of her mind as Dakota carried them from the barn out into the night and she gazed up at the sky. Billions of stars created a twinkling canopy above and the moon cast an ethereal glow over the rugged landscape.

"This is gorgeous, Chance." She shook her head. "I've never seen so many stars in the night sky before."

"That's because of smog and too many lights in the city to see them all," he answered, his voice low and intimate. He tightened his arms around her. "Are you chilly?"

She could lie and tell him that she was, but she suspected that he already knew her tiny shiver was caused by their close proximity. "Not really," she admitted, leaning her head back against his shoulder. "It's just that something this vast and beautiful is humbling."

They rode along in silence for some time before she felt the evidence of his reaction to being this close to her against her backside. So overwhelmed by the splendor of the night, she hadn't paid attention to the fact that her bottom was nestled tightly between his thighs. But it wasn't his arousal that surprised her as much as her reaction to it. Knowing that he desired her caused an answering warmth to spread throughout her body and an empty ache to settle in the most feminine part of her.

"Chance?"

"Don't freak out," he whispered, stopping Dakota. "I'm not going to deny that I want you. You're a desirable woman and I'm like any other man—I have needs. But nothing is going to happen unless it's what you want, too, sweetheart."

Before she could find her voice, Chance released his hold on her and slid off the horse to his feet. He immediately reached up to help her down, then wrapping his arms around her, gave her a kiss that caused her toes to curl inside her boots before he set her away from him.

Disappointed that the kiss had been so brief, she

tried to distract herself by looking around. Something shiny caught her attention and taking a few steps closer, she realized it was the moon reflecting off of a small pool of water. Surrounded on three sides by cottonwood trees, she could see wisps of mist rising from its surface and the faint sound of running water.

"Is that a natural spring?" she asked.

"It's actually considered a thermal spring even though the temperature never gets over about seventy-five degrees," Chance said, walking over to stand beside her. "I used to go swimming in it when I was a kid."

"It's that deep?" she asked, intrigued. Even with just the light from the moon, she could see a shadowy image of the bottom of the pool.

"It's only about four feet deep over by the outlet where it runs down to the river." He laughed. "But to a ten-year-old kid that's deep enough to get in and splash around."

Fee smiled as she thought of Chance playing in the water as a child. "I'm sure you had a lot of fun. I used to love going to the beach when I was young, and my grandmother's house had a swimming pool."

"We always had a pool up at the main house," he said, nodding. "But it's not as much fun as this. Have you ever been skinny-dipping?" he asked.

"No." She laughed. "Besides not really having the nerve to do it, I would have hated causing Mr. Harris next door to have a coronary, or scandalizing his wife to the point where she refused to go to the senior center with my grandmother to play bingo."

He gave her a wicked grin and reached down to pull off his boots and socks. "I will if you will."

"Skinny-dip? Here? Now?" She shook her head. "Have you lost your mind? Aren't you worried someone will see you?"

He tugged his shirt from his jeans and with one smooth motion released all of the snap closures. "Sweetheart, it's just you, me and Dakota out here. And since he's a gelding, all he's interested in is grass."

She glanced over at the horse. "What if he runs away and leaves us stranded out here?"

"He's trained to ground tie." He reached to unbuckle his belt and release the button at the top of his jeans. "As long as the ends of the reins are dragging the ground, he'll stay close." His grin widened. "Are you going to join me?"

"I don't think so." She wasn't a prude, but she wasn't sure she was ready to abandon years of her grandmother's lectures on modesty, either.

"Now who isn't being adventurous?" he teased.

"Trying a different flavor of ice cream is completely different than taking off all of your…" Her voice trailed off when Chance shrugged out of his shirt.

The man had the physique of a male model and she had firsthand knowledge of how hard and strong all those muscles were. She thought about how every time he helped her into his truck or lifted her onto one of the horses, he picked her up as if she weighed nothing.

Unable to look away when he unzipped his fly and shoved his jeans down his long muscular legs, Fee felt a lazy heat begin to flow through her veins. "I can't believe you're really going to do this."

"Yup, I'm really going to do this," he repeated as he stepped out of his jeans and tossed them on top of his shirt. When she continued to stare at him, he grinned as he hooked his thumbs into the waistband of his boxer briefs. "I'm not the least bit shy and don't mind you watching one little bit, but unless you want to see me in my birthday suit, you might want to close your eyes now."

"Oh!" She spun around. "Let me know when you're in the water."

"All clear," he announced. When she turned back, Chance was standing up in the pool. The water barely covered his navel. "You really should join me. The water is the perfect temperature."

"I can't," she said, shaking her head as she avoided looking below his bare chest. "It isn't deep enough."

"You know you want to," he said, grinning.

She didn't believe for a minute that he would keep his eyes averted as she was doing, but he was right about one thing. She was tempted to throw caution to the wind and go skinny-dipping for the first time in her life.

"I don't have a towel to dry off with." Her statement sounded lame even to her.

"We can dry off with my shirt," he offered.

"And you promise not to look?" she asked, knowing that his answer and what he would actually do were probably two different things.

"Scout's honor I won't look while you undress and get into the water," he said, raising his hand in a three-finger oath.

"Then close your eyes," she said decisively as she reached to pull the tail of her T-shirt from her jeans.

When he did, she quickly removed her boots and socks, then stripped out of her clothing before she had a chance to change her mind. Stepping into the water, she immediately covered her breasts with her arms and bent her knees until the water came up to her neck.

"I can't believe I'm actually doing this," she said between nervous giggles.

"Look at it this way," he said, opening his eyes. His low, intimate tone and the look on his handsome face as he moved through the water toward her made Fee feel as if he had cast a spell over her. "It's something you can check off your bucket list."

"I don't have a list," she said slowly.

"I'll help you make one." His gaze held hers as he reached beneath the water and lifted her to her feet. Taking her into his arms, he smiled. "Then I'll help you check off all of the new things you're doing."

Her arms automatically rose to encircle his neck and the moment her wet breasts pressed against his wide, bare chest a jolt of excitement rocked her. "You said you wouldn't look."

"I haven't…yet." His slow smile caused a nervous

energy in the deepest part of her. "But I never said I wouldn't touch you."

As he lowered his head, Fee welcomed the feel of his firm mouth covering hers. Chance's kisses were drugging and quickly becoming an addiction that she wasn't certain she could ever overcome.

The thought should have sent her running as fast as she could to the Cheyenne airport and the earliest flight back to L.A. But as his lips moved over hers with such tenderness, she forgot all the reasons she shouldn't become involved with him or any other man. All she could think about was the way he made her feel.

When he coaxed her to open for him, she couldn't have denied him if her life depended on it. At the first touch of his tongue to hers, it felt as if an electric current danced over every one of her nerve endings and a tiny moan escaped her parted lips. She wanted him, wanted to feel his arms around her and the strength of his lovemaking in every fiber of her being.

The feel of his hard arousal against her lower belly was proof he wanted her just as badly. The realization created a restlessness within her and she was so lost in the myriad sensations Chance had created, it took her a moment to realize he was ending the kiss.

"As bad as I hate to say this, I think we'd better head back to the house." His voice sounded a lot like a rusty hinge. "I have a good idea where this is headed and I don't have protection for us."

Covering her breasts with her arms, she nodded

reluctantly. There was no way she could deny that the passion between them was heading in that direction. Thank goodness he had the presence of mind to call a halt to it.

"Turn around."

He laughed. "Really? Our nude bodies were just pressed together from head to toe and you're worried about me seeing you?"

Her cheeks heated. "Feeling is one thing, seeing is entirely different."

"If you say so," he said, doing as she requested.

Hurriedly getting out of the water, Fee turned her back to him, used his shirt to quickly dry herself and then pulled on her panties and jeans. But when she searched for her bra, she couldn't seem to find it anywhere.

"Looking for this?" Chance asked.

Glancing over her shoulder, he was standing right behind her with her bra hanging from his index finger like a limp flag. "I thought you were supposed to stay in the water with your back turned until I got dressed," she scolded, taking her lacy brassiere from him to put the garment on.

"I stayed in the water right up until you started searching for your bra." She heard him pulling on his clothes. "After you dried off, you dropped my shirt on it when you reached for your panties."

"You watched me get dressed? You swore you wouldn't peek."

"Yeah, about that." He turned her to face him and the slow smile curving his mouth caused her to catch her breath. "I was never a Scout so that oath earlier didn't really count. But just for the record, I told you before I kissed you that I hadn't looked *yet*. I didn't say I wasn't going to." He gave her a quick kiss, then bent to pull on his socks and boots.

While he walked over to where Dakota stood munching on a patch of grass, Fee picked up his damp shirt and waited for him to help her onto the gelding's back. She should probably call her boss at Lassiter Media and arrange for someone else to take over the PR campaign, then head back to L.A. to get her priorities straight before she committed career suicide. But she rejected that idea immediately. No matter how difficult the assignment, she had never bowed out of a project and she wasn't going to back down now.

She was just going to have to be stronger and resist the temptation of Chance Lassiter. But heaven help her, she had a feeling it was going to be the hardest thing she'd ever have to do.

Chance lay in bed and damned his sense of responsibility for at least the hundredth time since he and Fee had returned to the house. He hadn't taken her on the moonlight ride with the intention of seducing her. On the contrary, it had simply been something he thought she might enjoy and he'd been right. She'd loved seeing all the billions of stars twinkling in the night sky.

At least, that's the way things had started out. What he hadn't allowed himself to consider was the effect her body would have on his when they rode double. Her delightful little bottom rubbing against the most vulnerable part of him had quickly proven to be the greatest test of his fortitude he'd ever faced. Then, if he hadn't been insane enough, she'd noticed the spring and he'd had the brilliant idea of going skinny-dipping.

"Yeah, like that didn't have disaster written all over it," he muttered as he stared up at the ceiling.

If he'd just stayed on his side of the pool and hadn't touched her or kissed her, he wouldn't be lying there feeling as if he was ready to climb the walls. But the allure of her being so close had been more than he could fight and once he'd touched her, he couldn't have stopped himself from kissing her any more than he could get Gus to give up baseball.

But what had really sent him into orbit had been her response. The minute their lips met, Fee had melted against him and his body had hardened so fast it had left him feeling as if he might pass out. The feel of her breasts against his chest and his arousal pressing into her soft lower belly had damn near driven him over the edge and he'd come dangerously close to forgetting about their protection.

Fortunately, he'd had enough strength left to be responsible. But that hadn't been easy.

He punched his pillow and turned to his side. No two ways around it, he should have known better. But he'd been fool enough to think that he could control the situation and ended up being the victim of his own damned arrogance.

He'd known full well the moment he'd laid eyes on her at Hannah and Logan's wedding, a spark ignited within him and with each day since the fire had increased to the point it was about to burn him up from the inside out. He wanted her, wanted to sink himself so deeply within her velvet depths that neither of them could remember where he ended and she began. And unless he was reading her wrong, it was what she wanted, too. So why was he in bed on one side of the hall and she in bed on the other now?

With a guttural curse that his mother would have had a fit over, Chance threw back the sheet and sat up on the side of the bed. Two hours of tossing and turning had gotten him nowhere. Maybe a drink would help him calm down enough to get a few hours of sleep.

Pulling on a pair of jeans, he didn't bother with a shirt as he left the master suite and stared at the closed door across the hall. He'd like nothing better than to go into that room, pick Fee up and carry her back to his bed. Instead, he forced himself to turn and walk barefoot down the hall to the stairs.

When he reached the kitchen, he went straight to the refrigerator for a beer, and then walked out onto the back porch. Hopefully, the beer and the cool night air would work their magic and help him relax.

Chance took a long draw from the bottle in his hand and stared out into the night as he tried to forget about the desirable woman upstairs. He needed to make a trip into town tomorrow for some supplies, as well as to stop by Lassiter Media's Cheyenne office to pick up his tickets for Frontier Days at the end of the month. Because Lassiter donated the use of some of their audio and video equipment for the annual event, the rodeo organizers always gave the company complimentary tickets. He attended the finals of the event every year and he thought Fee might enjoy going with him, even if she was back at the rental house by then.

Lightning streaked across the western sky, followed by the distant sound of thunder. It appeared the weather was as unsettled as he was, he thought as he downed the rest of his beer and headed back inside.

As he climbed the stairs a flash of lightning briefly illuminated his way and by the time he started down the upstairs hall, a trailing clap of thunder loud enough to wake the dead rattled the windows and reverberated throughout the house. He had just reached the master suite when the door to Fee's room flew open. When she came rushing out, she ran headlong into him.

"Whoa there, sweetheart." He placed his hands on her shoulders to keep her from falling backward. "What's wrong?"

"What was that noise?" she asked breathlessly.

"It's getting ready to storm," he said, trying his best not to notice how her sweet scent seemed to swirl around him and the fact that she had on a silky red nightgown that barely covered her panties.

"It sounded like an explosion," she said, seeming as if she might be a little disoriented.

"It's just a little thunder." He should probably be

ashamed of himself, but he had never been more thankful for a thunderstorm in his life. "You have storms in L.A., don't you?"

Nodding, she jumped when another clap of thunder resounded around them. "Not that many. And I never liked them when we did."

Chance put his arms around her and tried to remind himself that he was offering her comfort. "I guess I'm more used to them because at this time of year we have one almost every day."

"Really? That many?" She was beginning to sound more awake.

He nodded. "Occasionally we'll have severe storms, but most of the them are a lot like Gus— more noise than anything else."

"I think I'm glad I live in L.A. The city noise masks some of the thunder," she said, snuggling against his bare chest. "I'd be a nervous wreck if I lived here."

Chance felt a little let down. He wanted her to love the Big Blue ranch as much as he did even if she was only in Wyoming for a short time. But it wasn't as if he had been hoping she would relocate to the area. All he wanted was a summer fling.

Right now, he didn't have the presence of mind to give his unwarranted disappointment a lot of thought. Fee was clinging to him as if he was her lifeline and her scantily clad body pressed to his wasn't helping his earlier restlessness one damn bit. In fact, it was playing hell with his good intentions, causing his body to react in a way that she probably wouldn't appreciate, considering the situation.

"I'm going to drive into Cheyenne tomorrow to pick up some supplies and rodeo tickets," he said in an effort to distract both of them. "I thought we could have lunch at Lassiter Grill. Dylan and Jenna are back from their honeymoon and I figured you might like to see them."

"I'd like that very much." Her long blond hair brushed against his chest when she nodded. "Jenna and I became pretty good friends when I worked on the ads for the grand opening," she added, oblivious to his turmoil. "I also helped her out when one of the reporters became obsessed with her at the opening of Lassiter Grill and started asking questions about her and her father."

Sage had told him about Jenna's father being a con artist and that the man had made it look as if she'd been in on one of his schemes. He'd also mentioned the incident with the reporter at the restaurant's opening and how effectively Fee had handled the situation.

"Then that's what we'll do," he said, finding it harder with each passing second to ignore the heat building in his groin.

Another crash of thunder caused Fee to burrow even closer and Chance gave up trying to be noble. He had reached his limit and he was man enough to admit it.

"Fee?"

When she raised her head, he lowered his and

gave in to temptation, consequences be damned. It wasn't as if he'd been able to sleep anyway. He was going to give her a kiss that was guaranteed to keep them both up for the rest of the night.

Six

When Chance brought his mouth down on hers, Fee forgot all about her vow to be strong and try to resist him. The truth was, she wanted his kiss, wanted to once again experience the way only he could make her feel.

As his lips moved over hers, a calming warmth began to spread throughout her body, and she knew without question that as long as she was in his arms she would always be safe. But she didn't have time to think about what her insight might mean before he coaxed her with his tongue.

When his arms tightened around her and he deepened the kiss, she felt as if her bones had turned to rubber. The taste of need on his firm male lips, the feel of his solid bare chest pressed against her breasts and the hard ridge of his arousal cushioned by her stomach sent ribbons of desire threading their way through her.

He brought his hand around from her back up along her ribs. When he cupped her breast, then worried the taut peak with his thumb, her silk nightie chafing the sensitive nub felt absolutely wonderful and she closed her eyes to savor the sensation.

"I know all you want from me right now is reassurance," he said, nibbling kisses from her lips down the column of her neck to her collarbone. "But I've wanted you from the moment I first saw you at my sister's wedding." He left a trail of kisses from her chest to the V neckline of her short nightgown before pulling away. "If that's not what you want, too, then now would be the time for you to go back into your room and close the door."

Opening her eyes, she saw the passion reflected in his and it thrilled her. Fee knew what she should do. She should return to her room, pack her things and have him take her back to the corporate rental house in Cheyenne the first thing tomorrow morning. But that wasn't what she was going to do. It could very well prove to be the biggest mistake she'd ever made, but she wasn't going to think about her job or the danger of doing something foolish that could cause her to lose it.

"Chance, I don't want to go back to my room," she said, realizing she really didn't have a choice in the matter. They had been heading toward this moment since she looked up and watched him escort the matron of honor back up the aisle at his sister's wedding.

He closed his eyes and took a long, deep breath before he opened them again and gazed down at her. "I'm not looking for anything long-term, Fee."

"Neither am I," she said truthfully.

She ignored the little twinge of sadness that accompanied her agreement. She wasn't interested in anything beyond her time in Wyoming. At the end of her stay, she would go back to her life in California and he would stay here on the Big Blue ranch. Other than a trip back to film the video for the Lassiter PR campaign, they wouldn't be seeing each other again. That's the way it was supposed to be—the way it had to be.

"Let's go into my room, sweetheart," he said, taking her by the hand to lead her across the hall to the master suite.

The lightning flashed and thunder continued to rumble loudly outside, but Fee barely noticed as Chance closed the door behind them and led her over to the side of his king-size bed. When he turned on the bedside lamp, she looked around. The furniture was made of rustic logs, and with the exception of a silver picture frame sitting on the dresser, the room was decorated in the same Western theme as the rest of the house. The photo inside was of a young boy and a man who looked a lot like Chance. Before she could ask if it was a picture of him and his father, Chance caught her to him for a kiss that sent waves of heat coursing through her and made her forget everything but the man holding her.

"Do you have any idea how many times I've thought about doing this over the past week?" he asked as he ran his index finger along the thin strap of her nightie. "Every time I've looked at you, it's all I can think about."

"I hadn't…really given it…a lot of thought." Did he expect her to form a coherent answer when the intimate tone of his voice and his passionate words were sending shivers of anticipation through every part of her?

Needing to touch him, she placed her palms on his chest. "I have, however, thought a lot about you and how much I've wanted to do this." She ran her fingertips over the thick pads of his pectoral muscles and a heady sense of feminine power came over her when she felt a shudder run through him. "Your body is perfect. I thought so when we were at the spring." She touched one flat male nipple. "I wanted to touch you then, but—"

"By the time the night is over, I intend for both of us to know each other's body as well as we know our own," he said, sliding his hands down her sides to the lace hem of her nightgown.

His sensuous smile caused an interesting little tingle deep inside her as he lifted the garment up and over her head, and then tossed it aside. He caught her hands in his, took a step back and held her arms wide. His eyes seemed to caress her, the need she detected in their green depths stealing her breath.

"You're absolutely beautiful, Fee."

"So are you, Chance."

He gave her a smile that curled her toes, then brought her hands back up to his broad chest. "Ladies first."

She realized that he wanted her to feel comfortable with him and was willing to allow her to explore him before he touched her. His concession caused emotion to clog her throat. She'd never known any man as thoughtful and unselfish as Chance Lassiter.

Enjoying the feel of his warm bare flesh beneath her palms, she ran her hands down his chest to the ripples of muscle below. When she reached his navel, she quickly glanced up. His eyes were closed and his head was slightly tilted back as if he struggled for control.

"Does that feel good?" she asked, kissing his smooth skin as she trailed her finger down the thin line of dark hair from his navel to where it disappeared into the waistband of his jeans.

"Sweetheart, if it felt any better, I'm not sure I could handle it," he said, sounding as if he'd run a marathon. When she opened the snap, he stopped her and took a step back. "I don't want you to get the wrong idea. I'd love nothing more than to have you take my jeans off me, but this time it's something I have to take care of myself."

Slightly confused, she watched him ease the zipper down and when his fly gaped open, she realized the reason for his concern. "If I had tried… Oh, my… That could have been disastrous."

Grinning, he nodded as he shoved his jeans down

his long, heavily muscled legs and kicked them over to join her nightgown where it lay on the floor. "When I got up to go get a drink, I just grabbed a pair of jeans. I didn't bother putting on underwear."

Fee had purposely kept her eyes above his waist in the pool, but as she gazed at him now, she realized how truly magnificent his body was. Chance's shoulders were impossibly wide, his chest and abdomen sculpted with muscles made hard from years of ranch work. As her gaze drifted lower, she caught her breath. She'd felt his arousal when they'd gone skinny-dipping, but the strength of his desire for her was almost overwhelming.

"Don't ever doubt that I want you, Fee," he said, taking her into his arms. He lowered his head to softly kiss her lips, then nibbled his way down to the slope of her breast. "You're the most desirable woman I've ever met."

Her pulse raced as he slowly kissed his way to the hardened peak. But the moment he took the tip into his mouth, it felt as if her heart stopped and time stood still. Never in her entire twenty-nine years had she experienced anything as exquisite or electrifying as the feel of Chance's soft kiss on her rapidly heating body. When he turned his attention to her other breast, her head fell back and she found it hard to draw in enough air.

"Does that feel good?" he asked.

Unable to speak, she merely nodded.

Taking a step back, he held her gaze with his as he hooked his thumbs in the waistband of her bikini panties and slowly pulled them down her legs. When they fell to her ankles and she stepped out of them, he smiled and wrapped his arms around her. The feel of her softer skin pressed to his hard flesh caused her to sag against him.

He swung her up into his arms to carefully place her on the bed and she didn't think she'd ever felt more cherished. She watched him reach into the bedside table to remove a foil packet, then tucking it under his pillow, Chance stretched out on the bed beside her. He'd no sooner taken her back into his arms when lightning flashed outside and a loud clap of thunder caused the windows to rattle.

When the lamp flickered several times, he gathered her to him. "It looks like we might lose power."

The feel of all of him against her caused a shiver of excitement to course through her. "I'd forgotten it was even storming."

"And I intend to make sure you forget about it again," he said, covering her mouth with his.

He kissed her tenderly and ran his hand along her side to her hip. The light abrasion of his calloused palm as he leisurely caressed her was breathtaking, but when he moved his hand to touch her intimately, Fee wasn't certain she would ever breathe again.

As he stroked her with a feathery touch, the ache of unfulfilled desire coiled inside her. She needed him more than she'd ever needed anything in her life, but she wanted to touch him—to learn about him the same as he was learning about her.

When she moved her hands from his chest and

found him, he went completely still a moment before he groaned. "You're going to ruin…all my… good intentions, Fee."

"What would those be?" she asked as she measured his length and girth with her palms.

"I'd like to make this first time last…a little longer than what it's going to…if you keep doing that," he said, taking her hands to place them back on his chest. He took several deep breaths, then reached beneath his pillow. "I want you so much, I'd rather not finish the race before you get to the starting gate, sweetheart."

When he arranged their protection, he took her back into his arms and kissed her as he nudged her knees apart. Then capturing her gaze with his, he gave her a smile that sent heat coursing through her veins. "Show me where you want me, Fee."

Without a moment's hesitation, she guided him to her and he joined their bodies in one smooth thrust. He went perfectly still for a moment and she knew he was not only giving her time to adjust to being filled completely by him, he was also struggling to gain control.

"You're so beautiful and perfect," he finally said as he slowly began to rock against her.

"So are you," she managed as her body began to move in unison with his.

Fee felt as if she had been custom-made just for him and as Chance increased the rhythm of his thrusts, she became lost in the delicious sensations of their lovemaking. Heat filled her as she started climbing toward the fulfillment they both sought.

Unable to prolong the inevitable, she reluctantly gave herself up to the tension building within her. As waves of pleasure coursed through every cell in her being, she clung to him to keep from being lost. A moment later, she felt his body stiffen and knew he'd found his own satisfaction.

Wrapping her arms around his shoulders when he collapsed on top of her, Fee held him tight. She had never felt closer to anyone in her entire life than she did to Chance at that moment and she didn't want the connection to end.

The thought that she might be falling for him crossed her mind and caused her a moment's panic, but she gave herself a mental shake. It was true that she cared for him more than she could remember caring for any man, but that didn't mean she was falling in love with him. Chance was intelligent, caring and the most selfless man she'd ever met, and any woman would be lucky to win his heart. But she wasn't that woman.

The next morning as Chance got dressed, he smiled at the woman curled up in his bed. Fee was sound asleep and he wasn't going to wake her. They had spent most of the night making love and she had to be every bit as tired as he was. But he had chores to do and a ranch to run. Otherwise, he'd crawl back in bed, make love to her again and then hold her while they both slept.

As he stepped out into the hall, he regretfully closed the door behind him. He had never met any woman who felt as good or as natural in his arms as Fee did. She was amazing in just about every way he could think of, and even though she was a good nine or ten inches shorter than his six-foot-one-inch frame, when they made love they fit together perfectly.

Yawning as he entered the kitchen, he smiled when he thought about why he was so tired. "Gus, Fee and I are going into Cheyenne later this morning," he said, walking straight to the coffeemaker to pour himself a cup of the strong brew. "Is there anything you need me to pick up while I'm there?"

"Can't think of a thing," Gus said, opening the oven. "Where's Fee?"

"The storm kept her awake most of the night," Chance answered, going over to sit down at the table. "I thought I'd let her sleep in this morning."

When Gus turned, he stared at Chance for several long seconds before he slammed the pan of biscuits he had just removed from the oven onto the butcher-block island. "What the hell are you thinkin', boy?"

"What do you mean?" He was used to Gus and his off-the-wall questions and normally managed to figure out what the old man was talking about. But Chance had no idea what he'd done to piss the old boy off this early in the morning.

"I wasn't born yesterday," Gus said, shaking his head. "That storm moved on just past midnight and if you hadn't been awake with her, how would you know she didn't sleep?"

With his coffee cup halfway to his mouth, Chance stopped to glare at his old friend, then slowly set it down on the table. "Watch it, Gus. You're about to head into territory that isn't any of your concern."

"That little gal up in your bed ain't the kind of woman you bed, unless you're willin' to change her name," Gus said, ignoring Chance's warning.

"When did you become an expert on the subject of women?" Chance asked, doing his best to hold his anger in check out of respect for Gus's age and the fact that he was more like family than an employee.

"I never said I was an expert." Gus walked over to shake his finger at Chance. "But there's women you have a good time with and the kind you court for a while and marry." He pointed his index finger up at the ceiling. "That little gal upstairs is the courtin' kind."

"She's not interested in getting serious any more than I am," Chance said defensively.

"That may be what she's sayin'," Gus insisted. "And she probably even believes it. But I've heard how she goes on about you and the look in her eyes when you walk in a room." He grunted. "Your momma wore the same look every time she looked at your daddy."

"Yeah and we both know how that turned out," Chance muttered.

"Boy, don't go judgin' a man till you walk a mile

in his boots," Gus advised. "Your daddy loved your momma more than life itself."

"Is that why I've got a half sister from the affair he had with Hannah's mother?" Chance shot back before he could stop himself. He loved that he finally had a sibling, but the truth of the matter was, Charles Lassiter had cheated on his wife and that was something Chance wasn't sure he could ever come to terms with.

"Your daddy made a mistake and till the day he died, he did everything he could to make it up to your momma." Gus shook his head. "She forgave him, but I don't think he ever did forgive himself."

"Well, that's something I'll never have to deal with," Chance said, shrugging. "You can't cheat on your wife if you never get married."

Gus stared at him for a moment before he sighed heavily. "I never took you for a coward, boy."

Before Chance could tell Gus to mind his own damn business, he heard Fee coming down the stairs. "We'll finish this later."

"There ain't nothin' to finish," Gus said stubbornly. "I've said all I'm gonna say about it."

"Chance, why didn't you wake me?" Fee asked, entering the kitchen. "I wanted to help you feed Belle and her mother this morning."

"I thought I'd let you sleep in." Rising to his feet, Chance walked over and got a cup from the cupboard to pour her some coffee instead of taking her into his arms and kissing her the way he wanted to. "I know the storm kept you up last night and thought you could use the sleep." When Gus coughed, he glared at the old fart a moment before he walked over to set her coffee on the table. "I'll go out to the barn and give Slim the list of things I want him and the boys to get done today. Then after breakfast we'll feed the cow and calf before we take off to go into Cheyenne."

Her smile sent his hormones racing. "Great! I'll help Gus finish breakfast while you go talk to your foreman."

As Chance walked out of the house and across the yard, he thought about what Gus had said and how irritated he'd been with the old guy. Gus had been best friends with Charles Lassiter for years and it was only natural that he would defend him. And Chance had to admit that being out on the rodeo circuit had probably been lonely for his father without his family with him. But as far as Chance was concerned there was no excuse for infidelity. When a man committed himself to a woman, he didn't go looking for relief in another woman's arms.

That's why Chance had made the decision to remain single. Finding out a couple of months ago that a man like his father hadn't been able to resist temptation was enough to make Chance question a lot of things about himself. With the exception of his college girlfriend, he'd never been in a relationship for any real length of time. He'd always thought that was because he hadn't met the right woman. But could it be a clue he was incapable of committing himself to one woman? He wasn't sure and until he knew the answer to that question, his best bet would be to avoid getting too deeply involved with anyone. He certainly didn't want to run the risk of causing any woman the emotional pain that he was certain his mother had gone through.

He shook his head as he walked into the barn. He didn't know why he was giving anything Gus said a second thought. Gus had never been married and to Chance's knowledge the old guy hadn't had a date in more than twenty-five years. That wasn't exactly a glowing recommendation for Gus's advice on matters of the heart.

Besides, there were too many differences between Chance and Fee for anything to work out between them. She was a city girl who loved spending a day at the spa or in a boutique on Rodeo Drive, while he would rather go skinny-dipping or attend a rodeo. And then there was the matter of their jobs. She had a nice clean office in a climate-controlled skyscraper in downtown L.A. and his job required being out in all kinds of weather, doing things that most people considered dirty and thoroughly disgusting.

He took a deep breath and faced the facts. When Fee had to go back to L.A., he would tell her to get in touch with him whenever she was in town, kiss her goodbye and let her go. That was just the way it would have to be. But what he couldn't figure out was why the thought of her leaving made him feel completely empty inside.

"Chance is amazing with animals," Fee said to Jenna Montgomery-Lassiter after they enjoyed lunch at her new husband's restaurant. Chance and Dylan had gone into the office to discuss an increase in the amount of beef the Big Blue supplied to the Lassiter Grill chain, giving the women time for a little girl talk.

"Colleen and I have come to the conclusion that all of the Lassiter men are pretty amazing," Jenna agreed, grinning. "They aren't necessarily easy to love, but they are more than worth the effort."

"I'm sure they are," Fee said, smiling. "But I'm not in love with Chance."

Jenna gazed at her for several long moments. "Are you sure about that?"

Fee nodded. "We're just friends. I'm trying to talk him into helping me with the PR campaign to improve the Lassiter public image." Laughing, she added, "And he's trying to talk me out of it."

She felt a little guilty about not applying more pressure in her arguments to get him to agree to be the spokesman. But she sensed that the "hard sell" approach wouldn't work with him. If anything, it would make him that much more determined not to take on the job. And then there was the distraction he posed. Much of her time had been taken up with thinking about how soft his kisses were and how his touch made her feel as if she was the most cherished woman in the world.

"I'm sure Chance has been *very* persuasive," Jenna commented, her smile indicating that she knew something Fee didn't.

"What do you mean?" Fee couldn't imagine what her friend was alluding to.

Without answering, Jenna reached into her purse, handed Fee a small mirror, then tapped the side of her own neck with her index finger.

Looking into the mirror, Fee gasped and immediately pulled her long hair forward to hide the tiny blemish on the side of her neck. "I… Well, that is… We…" She clamped her mouth shut. There wasn't anything she could say. The little love bite on the side of her neck said it all.

To ease her embarrassment, Jenna smiled as she reached over to place a comforting hand on Fee's forearm. "It's barely noticeable and I probably would have missed it completely if I hadn't had one myself when we were on our honeymoon in Paris."

Her cheeks feeling as if they were on fire, Fee shook her head. "I haven't had one of those since I was a sophomore in college."

"The Lassiter men are very passionate," Jenna said, her tone reflecting her understanding. "It's one of the reasons we love them so much."

"I told you, Chance and I aren't in love," Fee insisted.

"I know," Jenna interrupted. "But I've seen the way you look at each other." She smiled. "If you two aren't there yet, it's just a matter of time."

Fee wasn't going to insult Jenna's intelligence by trying to deny that she was having to fight to keep herself from falling head over heels for Chance. "We're so different. I'm completely out of my element on the ranch, the same as he would be in a city the size of L.A."

"Differences are what makes things interesting," Jenna replied. "Heaven only knows, Dylan and I had our share. But if you really care deeply for someone, you work through the issues." She paused a moment. "I was certain that the implications of my father's illegal activities were going to tear Dylan and I apart. But we worked through that and our relationship is stronger than ever. If we can get past something like that, a little thing like distance between you and Chance should be a piece of cake to work out." She smiled. "You could always move here."

Fee stared down at her hands folded on top of the table for several seconds before she met Jenna's questioning gaze. "It's not just the distance of where we live that we'd have to work around," she said slowly. "I have a career that I won't give up." She sighed. "I won't bore you with the details, but my mother gave up a very promising career as a financial adviser because she fell in love with my father. After he left us, she'd been out of her field for so long, she decided it would be impossible to catch up." She shook her head. "I don't intend to give history the opportunity to repeat itself."

"I can understand wanting to maintain your independence," Jenna said, nodding. "But I don't think Chance would ever ask you to give up your career. He just doesn't impress me as being that type of man."

They both fell silent before Fee decided it was

time to lighten the mood. "Enough about that. Tell me about your honeymoon. I've never been to Paris. I've heard it's beautiful."

"It is," Jenna said, her eyes lighting up with enthusiasm. "Dylan spent a lot of time there when he was traveling through Europe and couldn't wait to show me all the little-known places he had discovered."

While her friend talked about the sites her husband had shown her in Paris, as well as the delectable French cuisine, Fee's thoughts strayed to Jenna's observations. If others could see how she felt about Chance, she probably was beginning to fall for him. He was a wonderful man and no matter how much she might deny it, she cared more deeply for him with each passing day and especially after making love last night.

But she couldn't allow herself to fall *in love* with Chance. Besides the fact that he had made it clear he wasn't looking for a relationship, she had far too much to lose. Not even taking into account the loss of her career, Fee could very easily end up facing a lifetime of heartache for a love that he could never return.

"Chance tells me you want him to be the family spokesman for the campaign," Dylan said, when he and Chance walked back to the table.

Fee nodded. "I believe he could be very convincing in getting the message across to the stockholders, as well as the public, that Lassiter Media is as solid as ever."

Dylan grinned as he and Chance took their seats. "I agree."

"Only because you're afraid she'll ask you to do it *if* I decide against it," Chance shot back.

"Well, there is that," Dylan said, laughing.

As she watched the two cousins' good-natured banter, Fee smiled. Of the three Lassiter men, she knew she had made the right choice. Chance wasn't as closed off as Sage and although Dylan was more open and outgoing than his brother, he had an air of sophistication about him that she didn't think would appeal to all demographics.

But she felt heartened by the exchange between Chance and Dylan. Chance hadn't said he wouldn't do the campaign; he had emphasized the word *if*. That had to mean he was considering the idea. Now all she had to do was get a firm commitment from Chance to be the family spokesman and she could start scheduling the video shoot.

A sadness began to fill her as she thought about what that meant. Once she had his agreement and the footage was filmed, she would go back to L.A. and he would stay on at the Big Blue. They might see each other occasionally at a Lassiter function, but eventually they would lose touch completely. Her chest tightened at the thought. No matter how many times she told herself that was the way it had to be, she knew it wasn't going to make their parting any easier. And she knew as surely as she knew her own name that she would be leaving her heart behind when she had to go.

Seven

Two days after their lunch with Dylan and Jenna, Chance watched Fee and his niece sitting cross-legged on the floor in the great room of the main ranch house having a good old time with Cassie's dolls. Fee was encouraging when the little girl wanted to try something different, listened attentively to everything Cassie said and wasn't the least bit put off by the child's constant questions.

No doubt about it, Fee was going to be a wonderful mother someday. The sudden thought that he wouldn't be the man giving her babies caused a knot to twist in his gut. Where had that come from? And why?

When he got up from the couch, Fee gave him a questioning look. "I think I'll go see if Mom needs help with dinner," he explained, thinking quickly. There was no way in hell he could tell her the real reason he was leaving the room.

"I should check to see if Marlene needs me to set the table," she said, starting to rise to her feet.

"No, you go ahead and have fun with your beauty pageant or fashion show or whatever it is you and Cassie are doing there," he said, forcing a laugh. "Mom loves to cook and probably already has everything under control. But I thought I'd offer just in case."

She smiled and the knot in his gut tightened painfully. "If I'm needed to do something, don't hesitate to come and tell me."

"I won't," he said, practically jogging from the room. The truth was, he needed to put some distance between them in order to come to terms with the fact that at some point in time another man was going to be holding her, loving her and raising a family with her. Up until two months ago when he learned about his father's failings, Chance had thought he'd have a shot at a family like that someday. Now he wasn't so sure that would ever happen.

Slowing his pace when he reached the hall, he walked into the kitchen, where his mother was getting ready to take a pot roast from the oven. If there was one thing Marlene Lassiter loved to do, it was cook, and even though the Lassiters could easily afford a world-class chef, she had always insisted on making the family meals herself. The only time he had ever known her to turn over the chore to someone else was when the ranch hosted a party or reception that required the hiring of a caterer.

"When are Hannah and Logan supposed to be back from the Caribbean?" he asked, walking over to take the pair of oven mitts from her. Opening the oven, he lifted the roast out and sat it on the counter for her. "I thought they were only going on a seven-day cruise."

"They got back from the cruise last night, but they are going to spend a few days in New Orleans seeing the sights before they fly back to Cheyenne," his mother said, smiling. He could tell that he and Fee had pleased her by accepting her dinner invitation when they'd brought Cassie back from her weekly trip for ice cream.

That only added a good dose of guilt to the feelings already twisting his gut. As he leaned against the counter and watched her arrange the roast on a platter with the potatoes and carrots around it, he decided there was no time like the present to get things out in the open and put them to rest once and for all. "Mom, I've been curious about something."

"What's that, dear?" she asked, turning to tear up lettuce for a salad.

"Why didn't you tell me about Hannah years ago instead of waiting until she showed up a couple of months back?" he asked point-blank.

He heard her soft gasp a moment before she stopped making the salad to turn and face him. "I know you feel cheated about not knowing you had a sister all these years, but it's the way it had to be, son. Hannah's mother didn't want her to know or have anything to do with the Lassiters. Whether I agreed with her decision or not, I respected those wishes because Hannah was her child, not mine."

"I know that's what you told me when we first met Hannah," Chance said slowly. "But why didn't she want Hannah to know about us?"

Marlene stared at him for a moment before she spoke. "I don't suppose it will hurt to tell you now." She sighed. "Ruth Lovell was a very bitter woman. She wanted your father to leave me and marry her. When he told her that wasn't going to happen, she refused to let Hannah have anything to do with any of us." She shook her head. "The ones who suffered the most from her decision were your father and Hannah. He didn't get to see his daughter more than a few times and she was too young to even know who he was."

"Did Dad ever try to get custody?" If he had been in his father's shoes, which he wouldn't have been in the first place, he'd have moved heaven and earth to be with his child.

Marlene nodded. "Your father consulted several lawyers, but back then a married man trying to gain custody of a child from an affair didn't have nearly the rights he has today."

Chance hesitated a moment, but since his mother brought up the subject of his father's affair, he was going to ask the question that had been bothering him since he learned about Hannah. "Why did you stay with him after he cheated on you with another woman? Weren't you angry and hurt by what he'd done?"

A faraway look entered his mother's eyes as if she might be looking back in time at the choices she'd made. "When Charles told me about his affair with Ruth Lovell, I was crushed," she admitted. "He was the love of my life and he'd betrayed me." She looked directly at Chance. "And don't think for a minute it was easy for me to stay with him or eventually forgive and start trusting him again. It wasn't. I struggled with that for quite some time before I accepted that your father had made a mistake he couldn't change, but one that he regretted with all of his heart."

"What finally convinced you to give him another chance?" he asked, still not fully comprehending her motivation to stay with a man who cheated on her.

"I finally realized that he was just as crushed by what he'd done as I was," she said, turning back to finish making the salad. "I only saw your father cry two times in his life—the day you were born and the day he told me about the affair."

"But how could he have done that to begin with?" Chance asked, unable to understand how a man could do something like that to the woman he loved.

"Back then, riders didn't fly home after a rodeo," Marlene said, setting the salad on the table. "They had to drive from one to another and that required them to be away from home for weeks at a time if they wanted to make any money at it. Your father got lonely and Ruth was there when I wasn't." She shrugged. "And I suspect alcohol was involved because after that I never saw your father take another drink."

"That's still no excuse for sleeping with another woman," Chance insisted.

"He was a man, Chance." She smiled sadly. "And men make mistakes. Some of the mistakes they make can be easily fixed, while others can't." Laying her hand on his arm, she looked him square in the eyes. "I know how much you worshipped your father and how disappointed in him you were when you learned that he wasn't perfect. But remember this, son. He had already ended the affair and I would have never known what he'd done if he hadn't told me right after it happened."

"Why did he tell you?" Chance frowned. "He could have kept his mouth shut and you wouldn't have had to suffer through all the emotional upset."

Marlene nodded. "That's true. But your father was an honorable man and if he hadn't told me and begged my forgiveness for what he'd done, it would have eaten him alive." She opened the cabinet, then handed him some plates to set the table. "I want you to think about the kind of courage it took for him to make his confession. He stood a very real chance of losing everything he loved. But he couldn't live with that kind of secret between us." She reached up to cup his cheek with her hand. "Don't let his one error in judgment distort your memories of him. He was every bit the good, upstanding man you've always thought him to be."

Chance realized that his mother was talking about more than just his father. In her way, she was telling him not to let his father's one failure affect the choices he made.

As he set the table, then went to tell Fee and Cassie that dinner was ready, he thought about what his mother had said. It was true his father had made a grievous mistake. But the man had been compelled to be truthful and make amends, even though it could have cost him his marriage. That did take a hell of a lot of courage. But it had also been the right thing to do.

Standing at the doorway of the great room, Chance watched Fee and his niece still playing with the dolls. Had he been too harsh in judging his father for simply being human? Had he used Charles Lassiter's transgression as an excuse to avoid falling in love?

When Fee looked up and smiled at him, his heart stalled. He could see his future in her eyes and he had a feeling that if he didn't find the answers to his questions, and damned quick, he could very well end up regretting it for the rest of his life.

When they returned to ranch headquarters after having dinner with Marlene and Cassie, Fee knew she should spend the rest of the evening going over her notes and at least make another attempt to get Chance's agreement to be the family spokesman. It had been days since she'd thought about improving the Lassiter family image, the job promotion she wanted or her life back in L.A.

Why didn't that bother her more? Just a couple of weeks ago, all she could think about was becoming the vice president in charge of public relations. Now, it didn't seem to matter as much as it once had.

"Thanks for being so patient with Cassie," Chance said as they entered the house. "I can't believe all the questions a five-year-old can come up with."

"I didn't mind at all. I enjoyed being with her." Smiling, Fee forgot all about her concerns regarding her lack of interest in the job promotion as she thought about his niece and the fun she'd had playing fashion show with the child. "Cassie's a bright, inquisitive little girl with a very active imagination."

He laughed as they walked down the dark hall toward the stairs. "That's a nice way of saying she's a handful."

"I could say the same thing about her uncle," Fee teased as they went upstairs.

When they reached his room, Chance led her inside, closed the door behind them and immediately took her into his arms. His wicked grin promised a night filled with passionate lovemaking, and the thought of what she knew they would be sharing caused her pulse to beat double time.

"I'll show you just how much of a handful I can be," he whispered. His warm breath feathering over her ear caused excitement and anticipation to course through her.

Lowering his head, he kissed her, and his desperation was thrilling. He wanted her as badly as she wanted him. His need fueled the answering desire deep inside her and stars danced behind her closed eyelids from its intensity.

"I thought I would go out of my mind this evening, watching you and not being able to touch you," he said as he nipped and kissed his way from her lips to the hollow below her ear. "All I could think about was getting you home."

"What did you intend to do when we got here?" she asked, feeling as if there wasn't nearly enough oxygen in the room.

"This for starters," he answered, tugging her mint-green tank top from the waistband of her jeans. Pulling it over her head, he tossed it aside, unhooked her bra and whisked it away. When he cupped her breasts with his hands, he kissed one taut nipple. "And this," he added, paying the same attention to the other tight peak.

Fee impatiently grasped the lapels of his chambray shirt, releasing all of the snaps with one quick jerk. Shoving the fabric from his shoulders, she placed her palms on his warm bare flesh.

"I love your body," she said, mapping the ridges and valleys of his chest and abdomen with her fingertips. "It's absolutely beautiful."

His hands stilled for a moment as he took a deep breath. "Guys have too many angles and hard edges to be beautiful," he said, his voice deep with passion. "But a woman's body is softer and has gentle curves that drive a man crazy with wanting," he added, gliding his hands down her sides to her hips. "That's true beauty, sweetheart."

As he unfastened her jeans, his heated gaze held hers and the promise in his dark green eyes stole her breath. He didn't need just any woman. He needed her. The knowledge sent a wave of heat washing over her and unable to remain passive, she unbuckled his belt and released the button at the top of his jeans.

Neither spoke as they stripped each other of their clothing. Words were unnecessary. They both wanted the same thing—to lose themselves in the pleasure of being joined together as one.

"I need you," Chance said as he kicked the rest of their clothing into a heap on the floor.

"I need you, too," she said, her body aching to be filled by him.

Without another word, Chance lifted her to him and Fee automatically wrapped her legs around his waist. Bracing the back of his shoulders against the wall, he lowered her onto him in one breathtaking movement. Fee's head fell back as she absorbed his body into hers, the feeling so exquisite it left her feeling faint.

He immediately began a rhythmic pace that sent a flash fire of heat flowing through her veins. All too quickly Fee felt herself climbing toward the culmination of their desire and she struggled to prolong the sensations, even as she raced to end them.

Her body suddenly broke free from the tension holding them captive and she gave herself up to the pleasure surging through every cell in her body. She heard Chance groan her name as he thrust deeply into her one last time, then holding her tightly against him, shuddered from the force of his own release.

As they slowly drifted back to reality, Chance suddenly went completely still for a moment before he cursed and set her on her feet. "I'm so sorry, Fee," he said, closing his eyes and shaking his head as if he'd done something he regretted.

"What are you sorry about?" she asked, becoming alarmed by his obvious distress.

When he opened his eyes and looked directly at her, she could see guilt in their emerald depths. "I was so hot and needed you so much, I forgot to use a condom."

Fee's heart came up in her throat and her knees threatened to give out as she made her way over to the side of the bed to sit down. She'd never had to face the possibility of becoming pregnant before. "I can't believe this."

Reaching for the folded comforter at the end of the bed, she wrapped it around herself as she tried to think. The possibility that she would become pregnant from this one time without protection had to be small. She remembered reading somewhere that there was only a 20 to 30 percent chance of success each month when a couple was trying to become pregnant. Surely that percentage went down significantly when a couple only had unprotected sex once. Of course, all of that meant absolutely nothing to the women who became pregnant after just one time in defiance of the statistics.

"Fee, look at me." Chance had put on his boxer briefs and was kneeling in front of her. Taking her hands in his, he shook his head. "I'm sorry, sweetheart. It's my fault and I take full responsibility."

Staring at him, it was her turn to shake her head. "I can't let you take all the blame. I didn't remember, either."

He looked as if he might be calculating the odds. "I doubt that you'll become pregnant from this one time." He took a deep breath and gently squeezed her hands in a comforting gesture. "But if you do, I swear I'll be at your side every step of the way."

"I'm sure the probability is small," she said, distracted.

What was wrong with her? Shouldn't she have a stronger reaction to the circumstances? Or was she simply in a state of shock?

Before she could sort out her feelings, Chance lifted her to the middle of the mattress, removed his boxer briefs, then stretched out beside her. Covering them both with the comforter, he pulled her into his arms and cradled her to his chest.

Kissing the top of her head, he ran his hands along her back in a soothing manner. "Fee, could I ask you something?"

Still trying to sort out her reaction to the turn of events, she simply nodded.

"I know our deal was for you to stay two weeks," he said slowly. "But I'd like for you to stay here with me until you go back to L.A. Maybe by that time we'll know for sure if you're pregnant."

"Okay," she said slowly.

She really didn't want to go back to the rental house Lassiter Media had provided for her. For one thing, she would miss Chance terribly. And for another, being alone while she waited to see if their carelessness had produced an unexpected pregnancy wasn't something she wanted to do.

"There's something else I'd like to know," he said, clearing his throat.

"What's that?" she asked.

"Would it be so bad if you did have my baby?" he asked quietly.

Leaning her head back, she searched his handsome features as she tried to formulate an answer. How could she explain what she didn't understand? Part of the reason she was struggling with the situation was the fact that she wasn't nearly as upset at the thought of being pregnant as she would have been just a couple of weeks ago.

"I'd rather not be pregnant," she finally said, trying to be as honest as possible. "But if I am, the answer is no. I wouldn't mind at all for you to be the baby's father."

Sitting on a bale of hay outside the feed room in the barn, Chance propped his forearms on his knees and stared down at the toes of his boots. He should be shot, propped up and shot again. Not even when he was a teenager with more hormones than good sense had he forgotten to use protection. It was something his uncle J.D. had stressed from the time he'd had "the talk" with Chance and his two cousins when they entered puberty until they all went off to college.

What had been different about last night? Why had he lost control with Fee when he'd never done that with any other woman?

If anything, he should have been more careful with her than he'd ever been. He'd fought against it—had even tried to deny it was happening—but she meant more to him than life itself.

His heart stalled and he felt as if he'd taken a sucker punch to the gut. It was the last thing he'd thought would happen, but he'd fallen in love with her.

As he tried to catch his breath, he realized he'd been a damned fool. Although Chance had no intention of telling Gus, the old cuss had been right. Fee wasn't a woman a man had a little fun with and then moved on from. She was the type of woman a man wanted in his life, his bed and his heart. Forever.

So what was he going to do about it? What could he do about it?

He knew she had feelings for him. Otherwise, she wouldn't have slept with him, nor would she have agreed to extend her stay with him. But she had made it clear she wasn't looking to get involved in anything long-term. Of course, if it turned out she was pregnant, he couldn't think of anything more long-term than raising a kid together. But that didn't mean she would marry him, nor would he expect her to. As far as he was concerned, marriage should be based on love, not because a baby was on the way.

"Whoa!" he said aloud. Was he really thinking about marriage?

As he turned the notion over in his mind, he wasn't certain that was something he wanted to do. He still hadn't completely forgiven his father's infidelity, even though his mother obviously had. If a man like Charles Lassiter could stray, what guarantees did Chance have that he wouldn't?

When he looked up to see Fee walking down the barn aisle toward him, Chance knew he had his answer. He would rather die than do anything to hurt her. If temptation presented itself, he had no doubt that he could walk away from it without so much as a backward glance.

But he wasn't going to spring the idea on her just yet. He needed to think things through and do a little planning.

"Did you finish helping Gus get everything cleared up from supper?" he asked, unable to stop grinning.

"He's already retired to his room for the Rockies game," she said, nodding. She tilted her head to one side. "You look happy. What happened?"

When she reached him, he patted his thigh. "Have a seat, sweetheart. I have something I want to ask you."

She gave him a suspicious glance, then sat down on his leg and put her arms across his shoulders. "What?"

"I intended to ask you the other day when I picked up the tickets, but forgot about it once we had lunch with Dylan and Jenna at Lassiter Grill." He gave her a quick kiss. "Would you like to go to the finals rodeo events at Cheyenne Frontier Days with me?"

"That sounds like a lot of fun," she said, smiling. "I've never been to a rodeo before."

Her delighted expression caused a warmth to spread from his chest throughout his body. She looked happy and he knew there wasn't anything he wouldn't do to please her.

Taking a deep breath, he placed his index finger under her chin to tilt it up until their gazes met. "We both know I'm not overly comfortable being in the public eye," he said, choosing his words carefully. "It's just not my thing. I'm happy staying right here on the ranch, doing what I do best—taking care of livestock and arguing with Gus. But I've been think-ing if you really want me to be the Lassiter family spokesman, I'll do it as long as we limit it to just a few pictures and a video or two."

Her excitement was palpable. "Really? You're going to do my campaign?"

"Yeah, I'll do it," he said, loving the way she threw her arms around his neck. When she gave him a kiss that left them both gasping for breath, he decided right then and there, he'd climb a barbed wire fence buck naked if that's what she wanted.

"Let's go back to the house," she said, standing up to take him by the hand.

"Why?" He hooked his thumb toward the horse stalls. "I thought you might like to go for a ride."

She gave him that look again—the one all women used when they thought men were being overly obtuse. "You're about to get lucky and you're going to stand here and tell me you want to go for a horseback ride?"

"No, ma'am."

"I didn't think so," she said, laughing as he hustled her toward the house.

Eight

A week after Chance told her he would be her spokesman in the ad campaign, Fee should have been elated. She had scheduled the first video shoot for the following week, had the first of the on-air spots reserved for the commercials and was well on her way to becoming the vice president of public relations at Lassiter Media. So why wasn't she thrilled?

She knew exactly why. Her time in Wyoming was drawing to a close and when the videographer left to go back to L.A. to edit the footage, she would be returning with him. A lump clogged her throat and for the first time in her life, Fee understood a little more about the choices her mother had made all those years ago. It was going to be the hardest thing she'd ever had to do to walk away from this man.

Blinking back tears, she decided not to think about it now. She would face that day at the end of next week. For now she was with him and she wasn't going to waste a single minute of what little time they had left together.

Seated in the huge covered grandstand with him, she turned her attention to the men on horseback as they roped calves. As soon as the animal had been stopped at the end of the rope, the cowboy would jump from his horse, tie three of the calf's legs together with lightning-fast speed, then wait to see if it stayed bound for a specified length of time. It was interesting to see how fast the cowboys accomplished the task and the level of skill they all possessed. She admired them all for their ability, but quickly decided if she had to do the task it might never get done.

Glancing over at Chance, she smiled. He had been wonderful telling her about the rich history of Frontier Days, explaining the way cowboys were awarded prize money and points toward qualifying for the National Finals Rodeo at the end of the year and patiently answering her questions about the different events. Fee found all of it fascinating and enjoyed every minute of what she'd seen thus far.

"What's next?" she asked, looking forward to more excitement.

"Saddle bronc riding," he answered, nodding toward horses that were being loaded into the bucking chutes. "This is one of the events my dad competed in."

"From what Gus told me, your father was very

successful at this and another event," she said while they waited for the action to begin.

Chance nodded. "He competed in the bareback riding as well as the saddle bronc riding." He smiled proudly. "Dad was world champion in both events several times before he retired."

"How old was he when he decided to quit?" she asked.

"He was thirty-six," Chance answered, staring at the media pit across the arena in front of the other grandstand.

She looked to see what he was so interested in all of a sudden. "Is something wrong?"

"No, I was just checking to see who was operating the cameras this year," he said, shrugging. "Lassiter Media donates the use of some of their audio and video equipment every year and I was just checking to see if any of the Lassiter technicians I'm acquainted with are helping out."

"I didn't realize those big screens belonged to Lassiter," she said, noticing for the first time the huge screens mounted on top of long trailers pulled by semis.

He nodded as he checked his watch. "We've donated the use of equipment for the rodeo as long as I can remember."

"I'll have to keep that in mind," she said thoughtfully. Even though she doubted she would need the information for publicity, it was nice to have it just in case.

When Chance checked his watch again, she frowned. "Do you have somewhere you need to be?"

"Not really." He grinned. "I was just thinking it's about time to get something else to eat."

"Where on earth do you put all that food?" she asked. They had stopped by the chuck wagon cook-off when they first arrived at the rodeo grounds and enjoyed heaping plates full of some of the delicious fare once fed to the men on cattle drives in the old West. "I'm positively stuffed."

"I've used a lot of extra calories the past few weeks," he said, his grin suggestive. "Especially at night."

"Forget I mentioned it," she said, laughing.

When one of the chutes opened and a cowboy on a horse burst into the arena, Fee turned her attention to the action in front of her. At times, all four of the horse's hooves were off the ground as the animal appeared to do aerial acrobatics in its effort to dislodge the rider. Well before the eight-second buzzer went off, the unfortunate cowboy landed on the ground in an undignified heap while the horse continued to buck its way around the arena.

"He doesn't get any points for that, right?" she turned to Chance and asked.

"Nope. He won't get a score, money or points," he answered, checking his watch before he rose to his feet. "While you watch the rest of the saddle bronc riding, I think I'm going to see about getting some food on a stick and maybe a basket of nachos. Do you want me to bring you a corn dog or something else?"

"No, thank you. But before you go, maybe you could explain something to me."

He nodded. "Sure, what do you want to know?"

"Why do men and children like their food on a stick?" she asked.

Laughing, he leaned down to kiss her cheek. "Sweetheart, fair food always comes on a stick and just tastes better that way. Same goes for food at a rodeo."

"I'll take your word for it," she said, unable to believe how many different foods had been put on sticks, dipped in batter and deep-fried at today's event. At one concession stand she'd even seen a sign for fried ice cream—on a stick, of course.

"Will you be all right?" he asked. "I'll only be a couple of minutes."

Smiling, she nodded. "I'll be right here when you get back."

As she turned her attention to the action in front of her, she marveled at the fact that most of the cowboys were able to stay in the saddle for even eight seconds. If she tried to ride a horse like that, she'd be lying on the ground after the first jump.

When the announcer informed the crowd that the saddle bronc event was over and the bareback riding was about to begin, she sat back in her seat to wait for Chance. What could be keeping him so long? Surely he wasn't visiting every concession stand in his quest for food on a stick.

"Dear, I'm sorry to bother you, but would you

mind letting me out?" an elderly woman asked, pointing to the aisle a few seats away.

"Not at all," Fee said, smiling. She stood up to allow the woman to pass in front of her.

"Thank you, dear." The older woman sighed. "My grandson decided he needs another soft drink."

Fee started to tell the woman it was no trouble at all when she heard her name over the public address system. She hadn't been paying attention as she spoke with the woman but now, when she looked up, she was riveted. There was Chance on the huge video screen across the arena, and he was asking, "…Will you marry me?"

She hadn't heard the beginning of his message, but she didn't need to. Chance was asking her to marry him? Why would he do that? And why did he have to do it in such a public way?

He'd made it perfectly clear weeks ago that he didn't want a permanent relationship. She knew he was fond of her and that he desired her, but he hadn't once told her that he loved her.

It suddenly dawned on her that the man who said he wasn't looking for anything permanent had only made the gesture because he thought she might be pregnant. She couldn't think of anything more humiliating than to be blindsided with a marriage proposal in a huge crowd when all Chance was trying to do was assuage his conscience.

The camera scanned the crowd, then zeroed in on her, and she gasped when she saw herself on the giant screens on either side of the grandstand. Her larger-than-life image wore the legendary deer-in-the-headlights expression and when the crowd started chanting "say yes," panic set in. She had to get out of there. She needed time to think and a rodeo arena filled with thousands of strangers wasn't the place to do it.

She felt as if she couldn't breathe as she quickly descended the steps of the grandstand. She'd fallen in love with Chance in spite of all her best efforts not to and if he loved her, his grand gesture would have been sweet and she would have seriously considered agreeing to be his wife. But she refused to marry a man who didn't return her love and only offered because there might be an unexpected pregnancy.

Fee wasn't her mother. She wasn't about to enter into a marriage because a man felt obligated to offer or because he was trying to rectify a mistake. She wanted him to love her as much as she loved him.

Digging through her purse, she managed to retrieve her cell phone. Her hands shook so badly she almost dropped it as she called and arranged for a cab to meet her on the street outside the rodeo grounds. As she made her way to the exit, she decided not to go back to the house Lassiter Media had rented. It was the first place Chance would look for her and at the moment, he was the last person she wanted to see.

No, she was going to the airport to buy a ticket on the first available commuter plane to Denver. From there she could take a flight back to L.A. It was where she could think and where she had the best chance of forgetting the cowboy who had broken her heart.

When Chance saw the look on Fee's face and watched her take off as if the hounds of hell were chasing her, his heart sank. She wasn't just getting away from the cameras. She was making a run for it. He didn't know exactly where she would go, but he knew as surely as he knew his own name that he wouldn't find her anywhere on the rodeo grounds.

Checking with the security office to make sure he was right about her leaving, one of the older guards recognized him as a Lassiter and, taking pity on Chance, showed him the surveillance tape of Fee hurrying through the east exit. Thanking the man, Chance went straight to his truck and climbed in. He felt like a damned fool. He'd gone against every one of his reservations about being the center of attention, told her he loved her and asked her to marry him in front of thousands of people, and she had thrown his proposal back in his face.

He'd told her how uncomfortable he was in front of a camera. Didn't she realize what his gesture meant—that he loved her and was sincere when he asked her to marry him?

He drove straight to the rental house. He knew better than to think Fee would go back to the ranch. The Big Blue was the last place she'd go because she knew he would be there.

The fact that she obviously didn't want to be

around him made Chance feel as if someone had reached in and ripped his heart from his chest. But as he navigated downtown Cheyenne and finally turned onto the street where the rental was located, he shook his head. What had he expected? Beyond great sex, they had very little in common. She was a city girl who had made it crystal clear she was more interested in climbing the corporate ladder than having a man in her life. And he was a country boy who would rather spend his nights gazing at billions of stars in the western sky than watch the moon rise over a skyscraper in L.A.

Parking his truck, he got out and walked up to knock on the door. The rental car was still in the driveway, but when Fee didn't answer, he walked back to the truck and sat there for several long minutes. She was either inside and just not answering the door or she was elsewhere. His money was on the latter.

As he started the truck and drove away, he decided that either way it didn't matter. She'd let him know in no uncertain terms what was important to her. And he wasn't it.

"Momma, Uncle Chance said Fee flew the car a few days ago," Cassie said, skipping ahead of Chance as they entered Hannah and Logan's house after their weekly trip for ice cream.

When his sister and brother-in-law walked into the foyer, Hannah gave Chance a questioning look. "Coop," he corrected. "Fee flew the coop."

"Yeah, that." Cassie frowned. "I was going to tell her today that I decided to call her Aunt Fee."

"Maybe you can tell her another time, sweetie," Hannah said, her gaze never leaving Chance's. "Logan?"

With his usual perceptiveness, Logan Whittaker nodded. "Cassie, why don't you and I go watch that new video cartoon Grandma Marlene got for you?" Logan suggested. "I think your mom wants to talk to your uncle Chance." He nodded at Chance as he led Cassie toward the media room. "My wife is amazing. If anyone can help you see the error of your ways, she can."

Chance frowned. "The error of *my* ways?"

Logan shrugged. "Take my word for it, ninety-nine percent of the time it's a man's fault."

"Let's go into the kitchen and I'll make us a cup of coffee," Hannah said, leading the way down the hall. "You look terrible. You haven't been sleeping well, have you?"

"Not really." When they entered the room, Chance sat down at the table in the breakfast nook while his sister started the coffeemaker. "There's really nothing to figure out, Hannah. I'm here and Fee isn't. End of story."

He appreciated his sister's concern, but he'd lain awake in his big empty bed for the past three nights, wondering how he could have been so wrong about Fee. He'd been sure she had started to care for him the way he cared for her. Obviously, he'd been wrong. Otherwise she wouldn't have left him standing at the rodeo looking like the biggest fool on the whole damned planet.

"Why don't you tell me what happened and let me decide if there's a way you might be able to turn this around?" She sat his coffee in front of him, then took a seat on the opposite side of the table. "Marlene said Gus told her you went to Frontier Days with Fee and came home without her."

Chance groaned. He should have known Gus would send out an alert to all interested parties. "Do you three have some kind of hotline to keep tabs on me now?"

"No, but that's a thought," Hannah shot back. "Now are you going to tell me what happened or am I going to have to get Logan in here to put his cross-examination skills to good use."

"You had to go and marry a lawyer, didn't you?" Chance said, stalling.

He had always been of the opinion that the more you picked at a wound the longer it took to heal. But as much as he wanted the aching in his chest where his heart used to be to end, he suspected the pain of Fee's rejection would be with him for the rest of his life.

"Yes, but don't hold Logan being a lawyer against him," Hannah said, grinning. "I had my doubts at first, but all in all he's turned out to be a pretty good guy. Now, tell me what happened."

Knowing his sister wasn't going to give up until she got to the bottom of what took place between him and Fee, Chance shrugged. "I asked Fee to marry me and she took off."

Hannah shook her head. "I know that. If Marlene hadn't told me, I would have read about it in the newspaper." She gave him a sympathetic smile. "It's not every day a Lassiter proposes and gets turned down in front of a crowd of people."

"Yeah, it wasn't pretty," he said, still disgusted with himself.

"So start over. You've left out some important details. What happened between our wedding reception and you asking Fee to marry you?"

When he told her about the deal he had come up with for Fee to stay with him on the Big Blue, he had to admit it didn't sound all that good. "Looking back, it wasn't one of my better ideas."

"You think?" Hannah asked sarcastically. "If you weren't my brother I'd swear you were a snake in blue jeans and boots. It sounds like you were planning her seduction more than you were trying to talk her out of making you the Lassiter family spokesman."

"I realize that now." He ran his hand over his face as he tried to wipe away some of the regret. "But at the time, all I wanted was to keep things light. I wasn't looking for anything permanent and she made it clear she wasn't, either. I figured we could have a little harmless fun together and when the time came, I'd go my way and she'd go hers."

Hannah shook her head. "It backfired on you, didn't it? You fell in love."

Chance nodded and took a sip of the coffee Hannah had placed in front of him. He really didn't want it, but he didn't want to hurt her feelings. He'd caused enough of those lately. He didn't want to add more. For the past couple of months, his mother had been upset because he made it clear he resented her not telling him about Hannah years ago, Cassie was upset that Fee had left and he'd obviously upset Fee when he asked her to marry him. Hell, he was beginning to think he couldn't win with females.

"So you fell in love, but Fee didn't?" Hannah prodded when he remained silent.

"To tell you the truth, I'm not sure," he admitted. "I thought she felt the same as I do. At least, she acted like she cared for me. But that obviously isn't the case."

"Trying to get something out of you is like trying to pull teeth." His sister sighed. "What gave you the idea she loves you? And did you actually tell her you love her?"

"I didn't tell her until just before I proposed," he answered, staring at his coffee cup.

"Well, what did she say?" He could tell Hannah was getting frustrated, but he didn't particularly care to share the most embarrassing moment of his entire life.

"I don't know what she said because we weren't together," he admitted.

"Okay, you're going to have to tell me how that works," Hannah said, looking confused a moment before her eyes narrowed. "Don't tell me you called her or sent her a text."

"No. I'm not that boneheaded." As he explained about telling Fee he loved her and proposing on the big screen at Frontier Days, he realized he should have told her sooner and in a more private way. "That might not have been the right timing." He'd figured that out on the lonely drive back to the Big Blue that same day.

"Oh, my God, Chance," Hannah gasped. "You seriously didn't do that, did you? I assumed you had told her you love her previously. I wasn't aware that was the first time."

Nodding, he finished off his coffee. "Once again, not one of my better ideas."

"Having a man tell her for the first time that he loves her is a very tender moment for a woman," Hannah said slowly, as if choosing her words carefully. "She doesn't necessarily want an audience of thousands to intrude on that. Especially when they're chanting *say yes* to a marriage proposal she didn't expect."

"Yeah, I got that when she took off," he said, nodding. He shook his head as he decided that he might as well tell Hannah the entire story. "There's something else."

His sister nodded. "I thought there might be. What else happened?"

"Nothing. At least not yet." He took a deep breath. "It's probably remote, but there is the possibility that Fee might be pregnant."

"That's the real problem right there," Hannah said, her tone adamant. "I don't think it's that Fee doesn't love you, Chance."

"Yeah, what's not to love?" he asked sarcastically. "I'm the guy who can't even propose to a woman without screwing it up."

"Don't be so hard on yourself," she said, placing her hand on his. "It really was a sweet gesture and if circumstances were different, everything might have worked out the way you intended. But I wouldn't be the least bit surprised if Fee thinks you proposed only because of the possible pregnancy."

The thought had crossed his mind, but that wasn't the case at all. Unfortunately, Fee didn't know that. "To tell you the truth, that had nothing to do with my decision to propose."

He had realized he loved her the night they had dinner at his mother's. But Fee didn't know that and if there was even the slightest possibility he could convince her, they might still have a chance.

When he remained silent, Hannah's eyes sparkled with excitement. "You're going to Los Angeles, aren't you?"

"I'm thinking about it," he said, feeling more hopeful than he had in the past three days.

Hannah got up and rounded the table to give him a hug. "I realize we haven't known about each other for more than a couple of months, but you're my brother and I want you to be happy. Take that leap of faith, Chance. You'll never know if you don't."

"Thanks for the advice, Hannah." He hugged her

back. "At first I had a real hard time with the fact that our dad had an affair with your mother. But if he hadn't, I wouldn't have you and Cassie in my life. And that's something I wouldn't trade for anything."

"I know what you mean," she said, nodding. "It took me a while to forgive my mother for not letting me know that I had a family who wanted me in their life. But letting go of the past has a way of making way for the future." Hannah gave him a pointed look. "And speaking of the future, you have something you need to do."

"Yeah, I guess I do," he said slowly.

Hannah took the cordless phone from its charger on the wall and handed it to him. "Now, call the Lassiter hangar and make arrangements for the corporate jet to take you to Los Angeles. You have some serious groveling to do." Laughing, she added, "And if you can refrain from making any more grand declarations in front of thousands of people, you might get another chance with Fee."

Chance shook his head. "You just had to bring that up, didn't you?"

"Of course." She smiled. "I've heard sisters are supposed to do that."

"Do what?" he asked, frowning.

She laughed as he dialed the phone. "Remind their brothers when they've been real boneheads."

Nine

"Hi, Becca," Fee said as she closed the door behind her friend. "Thanks for coming over."

"What's up, Fee?" Her friend looked concerned. "You sounded stressed when you called. Is everything all right?"

Fee shook her head. "Not really."

"Since you asked me to come over instead of meeting you somewhere for lunch, I assume you need a shoulder," Becca said, sitting in the chair flanking Fee's couch.

The director of the Lassiter Charitable Foundation, Becca Stevens had asked for Fee's help with publicity on several different occasions for the charity events put on by the Lassiters. Over the years, they had become good friends and frequently shared the highs and lows of their careers—and of their personal lives from time to time.

"Actually, I was going to tell you that there's a very good possibility I'll be leaving Lassiter Media within the next few weeks," Fee said, curling up in one corner of the couch.

"Why?" Clearly shocked, Becca sat forward in the chair. "I thought you love your job."

"I do," Fee admitted. "But after my trip to Wyoming, I think it's time for me to move on."

"What happened in Wyoming?" Becca's eyes narrowed suddenly. "You met a man, didn't you?"

"Yes." Fee shrugged one shoulder. "But I broke the rules."

Her friend looked confused. "What rules are you talking about?"

"Mine," Fee answered. "I got close to someone… and…it's just time for a change." She didn't want to go into details because it was simply too painful to explain.

Sitting back in her chair, Becca shook her head. "But you're in line for vice president of public relations—a position that I know you wanted."

"With my work experience, I don't think I'll have a problem finding another position elsewhere," Fee said, knowing she didn't sound at all enthusiastic about it. She loved working for Lassiter Media and would have continued to work there indefinitely if she hadn't met a ruggedly handsome cowboy who stole her heart.

"Before we talk about where you'll look for an-

other job, tell me about the man you got close to,"
Becca said gently. When Fee didn't say anything,
Becca's eyes grew wide and Fee knew her friend
had figured it out. "You got involved with one of
the Lassiters."

Tears filled her eyes as Fee nodded. "He's J.D.'s
nephew."

"So he doesn't work for Lassiter Media?" Becca
asked. When Fee shook her head, she continued,
"Then I don't see the problem." She frowned. "Actually, even if he did work for Lassiter there shouldn't
be an issue. As far as I know there isn't any kind of
company policy on dating another employee."

"It's…complicated," Fee said, sniffing back her
tears.

Becca seemed to consider her answer. "I take it
that things didn't work out between you?"

"No." Fee closed her eyes for a moment in an effort to regain her composure. "I know it wouldn't
happen often, but I don't want to risk running into
him at one of the corporate functions or one of your
fund-raisers. And I've handed over the Lassiter family PR campaign to someone else for the same reason."

"I can understand that." Becca smiled sadly. "But
I'm really going to miss working with you on the
publicity for the foundation."

Fee dabbed at her eyes with a tissue. It was completely out of character for her, but for the past few
days, everything made her cry.

"Enough about me and my problems," she said,

trying to lighten the mood. "Tell me what's been going on with you for the past month."

"Aside from the fact that donations for the foundation are way down and it's Jack Reed's fault, not a lot," Becca answered.

"He's a corporate raider," Fee commented. "Don't tell me he's started setting his sights on raiding charity foundations now."

"Not exactly," Becca said, her pretty face reflecting her anger. "He's been buying up blocks of Lassiter Media shares in an attempt at a hostile takeover. In light of the way he chops up companies and sells them off piece by piece, our contributors have backed off and haven't been nearly as generous with their donations. Some of the recipients of our funding are shying away from the association with Lassiter Media, too, especially with what's going on with Angelica. She seems to be in cahoots with Jack and that makes everyone nervous. I'm just glad her father isn't alive to see the way she's acting. I don't think he would be overly pleased."

"That's terrible," Fee said, upset by the news. "The Lassiter Charitable Foundation does so much good for so many people. How bad is it?"

"If something doesn't change—and soon—I'm going to have to start making cuts." Becca shook her head. "But I'm not going down without a fight. I'm going to pay Mr. Reed a visit and try to make him see reason."

"I hope you're successful," Fee said, meaning it.

"I've heard he's quite ruthless and doesn't care about anything that doesn't serve his own interests."

Becca took a deep breath. "He hasn't met me. I can be just as cutthroat as the next person when it's something I've worked hard to build and truly believe in."

"Something tells me Mr. Jack Reed has met his match," Fee said, managing a smile.

When Becca checked her watch, she rose to her feet. "I hate to run, but I need to get some things together for that meeting."

Fee rose to give her a hug. "Thanks for stopping by. Good luck and please let me know how it goes. I know if anyone can make Jack Reed see reason, you'll be the one to do it."

"And good luck to you, Fee," Becca said, hugging her back. "I wish you would change your mind, even if you aren't going to do the campaign or get the vice president job. I'm going to miss you terribly."

"We'll still be able to get together for lunch or dinner," Fee offered. "I'll let you know when I get another job."

Opening the door to see her friend out, Fee's breath lodged in her throat and she felt the blood drain from her face. Chance was coming up the walk. Dressed in a white Western-cut shirt, jeans, boots and his ever-present wide-brimmed black hat, he looked more handsome than any man had a right to look.

"Who is that?" Becca asked, sounding impressed.

When Fee remained silent, understanding dawned

on Becca's face. "That's him, isn't it?" She glanced from Fee to Chance and back again. "No wonder you broke your rule. He's gorgeous." Giving Fee another quick hug, Becca whispered, "Good luck working this out with him, too."

Watching Chance tip his hat as Becca passed him on the sidewalk, Fee felt tears threaten. How could she simultaneously be so happy to see him and feel as if her heart was breaking all over again?

"Hi, Fee," he said when he reached her door.

"What are you doing here, Chance?" she managed, thankful that her voice didn't sound as shaky as she felt.

"We need to talk."

"I don't think that would be a good idea," she said, her heart pounding hard against her ribs. Why couldn't he leave her alone to salvage what was left of her heart?

"I do," he said calmly. "Now are you going to ask me in or are we going to discuss this right here on your doorstep?"

Before she had a chance to answer, he placed his hands on her shoulders, guided her back into her condo and shut the door behind them. Her skin tingled from the warmth of his hands even through her clothing and she walked over to put the coffee table between them. If she didn't, she couldn't be sure she wouldn't turn to him and make a complete fool of herself by throwing herself into his arms.

"Why are you here?" she asked again.

"I'm here for your answer," he said simply.

"I thought you would figure out what my answer was when I left Cheyenne," she said, feeling tears fill her eyes.

"Oh, I figured it out right about the time I watched you run down the steps of the grandstand. It was kind of hard to miss on a JumboTron. But I want you to tell me face-to-face," he insisted, taking a step toward her. "You're going to have to look me in the eyes and tell me that you don't love me and don't want to be my wife."

She held out her hand to stop him. "Chance, please don't do this. Please don't…make me…say it."

He held up a DVD case she hadn't noticed before. "Maybe we should go back and replay my proposal so you can see the look in my eyes when you ran away. Then you can give me your answer."

"Why are you doing this?" she asked brokenly. "You don't love *me*. You only asked me to marry you because you think I might be pregnant."

"That's where you're wrong, sweetheart. I told you I love you before I asked you to marry me."

Her knees felt as if they had turned to rubber and she lowered herself onto the couch before they gave way. "No, you didn't. I would have remembered it if you had."

"I wondered if you might have missed that. That's why I brought this along—to prove it." He went to her television and put the disk in the DVD player, switching both machines on.

An image of Chance standing next to one of the rodeo announcers appeared on the screen. The man was saying that someone had a very special message for one of the ladies in the crowd. She watched Chance take a deep breath before he smiled and looked directly into the camera. "I love you, Felicity Sinclair. Will you marry me?"

Fee gasped as she remembered how she'd been distracted by the elderly woman trying to get past her in the grandstand. "I didn't hear you say you love me." She stared down at her tightly clasped hands in her lap. "All I heard was your proposal."

"Believe me, sweetheart, there's no way in hell I would have been on camera with all those people watching if I didn't love you," he stated.

As she thought about the sincerity in his eyes, as well as the number of times he'd told her he wasn't comfortable being the center of attention, she realized what he said must be true. He did love her. "I'm sorry, Chance," she said, wiping a tear from her cheek. "I panicked."

Chance walked over, squatted down in front of her and lifted her chin with his finger until their gazes met. "Just for the record, I'll admit that I'm a pretty traditional kind of guy. But I don't happen to believe that a man and woman should get married just because a baby is on the way."

"You don't?" she asked, loving the feel of his touch, even if it was just his finger on her chin.

He shook his head. "I believe two people should be in love and want to spend the rest of their lives together before they take that step."

"You want to spend the rest of your life with me?"

she asked, feeling hope begin to rise within her, even though the thought of marriage scared her as little else could.

"I do," he said firmly. "I never expected to find a woman I couldn't live without. A woman who invaded my dreams and made me burn for her by simply walking into the room. Then I saw you at Hannah and Logan's wedding and all that changed. I want to spend the rest of my life with you, Fee. I want to make love to you every night and wake up each morning with you in my arms. Is that what you want, too?"

She caught her lower lip between her teeth to keep it from trembling. "I'm…afraid, Chance."

Moving to sit beside her on the couch, he pulled her onto his lap and cradled her to him. "What are you afraid of, Fee?"

The gentle tone of his deep voice and the tender way he held her to him were so tempting. Did she dare trust that his love for her was as strong as hers was for him? Did she have the courage to reach for what she never thought she would ever have?

"I need to tell you why I'm so career driven and why the thought of being in love scares me to death," she said, wanting him to understand part of the reason she'd panicked.

"You can tell me anything," he said, kissing her temple. "There's nothing you can say that will ever stop me from loving you."

"When my mother met my father, she was a successful financial adviser in a prestigious firm in downtown L.A.," she explained. "She immediately fell in love with him and in no time was pregnant with me."

"They got married?" Chance guessed.

"Yes, but I have a feeling it would have never happened if my mother hadn't been pregnant." Fee shook her head. "From what my grandmother told me, my father wasn't the kind of man who stayed in one place for long and he eventually got tired of having a wife and baby in tow. When he decided to leave, he didn't even say goodbye. He just walked out and left us in a second-rate motel somewhere in eastern Arizona with no money and no way to get back to California."

"How did you get back home?" he asked, tightening his arms around her in a comforting gesture.

"Nana sent my mother enough money to pay for a train ticket and the outstanding motel bill." Sighing, she finished, "My mother never got over him, nor did she ever resume her career."

"I'm sorry, sweetheart," he said, gently stroking her hair. "Did he divorce her?"

"A few years after we went back to L.A., she received a set of divorce papers in the mail with instructions to sign them and return them to an attorney in Las Vegas." Fee shrugged. "She voluntarily gave up everything for him and would have followed him to the ends of the earth if that was where he wanted to go. And he couldn't even be bothered to come back and tell her it was over." She shook her head. "Even though they divorced, she held out hope that he would come back one day. She died ten years ago, still waiting for that to happen."

"And you've been afraid all these years that if you fell in love you would turn out like her?" Chance guessed, his voice filled with understanding.

"I know it sounds foolish, but I didn't want to be dependent on a man for my happiness, nor was I willing to give up my only means of support," she answered, nodding. "I didn't want to be like my mother."

"That's something you never have to worry about, Fee," Chance said, capturing her gaze with his. "I would never ask you to give up anything for me or change anything about yourself. I love you for who you are—the intelligent, independent, beautiful woman that took my breath away the moment I laid eyes on her."

Staring into his brilliant green eyes, she knew that she never really had a choice in the matter. She loved this man with all of her heart and soul and had from the moment their eyes met at his sister's wedding.

"I love you, Chance Lassiter," she whispered. Tears flowed down her cheeks as she released the last traces of her fear and embraced the only man she would ever love.

"I love you, too, Fee," he said, crushing her to him. "But I still need an answer, sweetheart."

A joy she'd never known before filled her entire being. "If you'll ask the question again, I'll be more than happy to give you an answer."

Setting her on the couch, he got down on one knee

in front of her. His smile was filled with more love than she ever dreamed of. "Felicity Sinclair, will you do me the honor of becoming my wife?"

Another wave of tears spilled down her cheeks as she nodded and threw her arms around his shoulders. "Yes, yes, yes."

He took her into his arms then and gave her a kiss that left them both gasping for air. "About your career," he said, holding her close. "Do you want me to move to L.A. or would you like to live on the Big Blue ranch and telecommute?"

"Chance, I would never ask you to leave the Big Blue," she said, shaking her head. "That ranch is your life."

He shook his head. "Nope. You are." Touching her cheek, he added, "I love the Big Blue ranch, but I love you more. If living in L.A. is what you want, I'll adjust. My home is wherever you are, Fee."

"I don't want you to give up being a cowboy— my cowboy," she said, kissing him. "I'll move to the ranch and telecommute if that can be arranged." She paused. "If I even have a job with Lassiter."

"Why do you think you wouldn't?" he asked, frowning.

"I handed the Lassiter campaign over to one of my colleagues and told Evan McCain that I might be looking for employment elsewhere," she said hesitantly. "I even mailed the keys to the rental house and the car to the Lassiter Media office in Cheyenne, instead of returning them myself."

"That's not going to happen. You're not going to

lose your job," he said, shaking his head. "I won't be the spokesman unless you're in charge of the campaign."

"But it's all set up with another PR executive," she argued. "They probably won't let me take it back."

"Don't be so sure. I think we can make that happen, as well as setting it up for you to telecommute," he said, laughing. "You're forgetting that your future husband has a little bit of pull with your bosses."

"I suppose you do, don't you, Mr. Lassiter?" she said, laughing with him. "It will make it easier to do the family-image campaign if I'm on the job site." She paused. "You are still going to be my spokesman, aren't you?"

"I'm anything you want me to be, Fee," he promised. "Name it and I'll do it, sweetheart." His expression turned serious. "Now that we have that settled, I have one more question for you."

"What's that?" she asked.

"Don't take this wrong… It really doesn't matter, but I was just wondering… Do you know if you're pregnant?" he asked cautiously.

"I'm not sure," she said honestly. "I haven't taken a pregnancy test."

He nodded. "If you're not pregnant now, you will be eventually."

"You think so?" she asked, grinning.

"Sure thing, sweetheart. The man you're going to marry has been in a perpetual state of arousal since he met you." Chance gave her a sensual grin that sent heat flowing through her veins. "Just say the word and I'll be more than happy to give you all the babies you want."

"Did you hear what I said?" she asked, unable to stop smiling.

Clearly confused, he frowned. "You said you're not sure—that you hadn't taken a test."

Nodding, she kissed him soundly. "The key words in that are *not sure,* cowboy."

As understanding dawned, his grin got wider. "Do you know something I don't?"

"I'm almost a week late," she said, nodding. "Since I'm as regular as clockwork, I would say there's the possibility that the first of all those babies you promised me is on the way."

He wrapped her in a bear hug. "I guess we beat the odds, sweetheart."

"It appears that the remote possibility wasn't so remote after all," she said, hugging him back.

"God, I love you," he said, kissing her cheeks, her forehead and the tip of her nose.

"And I love you, cowboy. With all my heart."

* * * * *

"A prince with benefits. That does sound intriguing."

She tapped her chin and pretended to think.

Adan had resisted her long enough—his last thought before he reeled her into his arms and kissed her. Piper didn't reject the gesture at all. She didn't push him away or tense against him. She simply kissed him back like a woman who had not been kissed enough.

Bent on telling her what she was doing to him, he brought his lips to her ear. "If we had no care in the world, and all the privacy we needed, I would lift up your dress, lower your panties and take you right here."

She pulled back and stared at him with hazy eyes. "I could think of worse things."

He could think of something much better. "You deserve a bed and champagne and candles our first time."

"You're certainly not lacking in confidence."

Subtlety had never been his strongest suit. "Provided we decide to take that next step."

"Provided we could actually find the time to do it while adhering to your son's schedule."

Right on time, the sound of a crying baby filtered out through the nursery's open window.

* * *

The Sheikh's Son
is part of the No.1 bestselling series from Mills & Boon® Desire™—Billionaires and Babies: Powerful men…wrapped around their babies' little fingers.

THE SHEIKH'S SON

BY
KRISTI GOLD

Published in Great Britain 2014
by Mills & Boon, an imprint of Harlequin (UK) Limited,
Eton House, 18-24 Paradise Road, Richmond, Surrey, TW9 1SR

© 2014 Kristi Goldberg

ISBN: 978-0-263-91472-6

51-0714

Harlequin (UK) Limited's policy is to use papers that are natural, renewable and recyclable products and made from wood grown in sustainable forests. The logging and manufacturing processes conform to the legal environmental regulations of the country of origin.

Printed and bound in Spain
by Blackprint CPI, Barcelona

Kristi Gold has a fondness for beaches, baseball and bridal reality shows. She firmly believes that love has remarkable healing powers and feels very fortunate to be able to weave stories of love and commitment. As a bestselling author, a National Readers' Choice Award winner and a Romance Writers of America three-time RITA® Award finalist, Kristi has learned that although accolades are wonderful, the most cherished rewards come from networking with readers. She can be reached through her website, at www.kristigold.com, or through Facebook.

To Bob…for giving me a quiet place to finish this book,
and for showing me that new beginnings do
happen when least expected.

One

If a woman wanted a trip to paradise, the gorgeous guy seated at the bar could be just the ticket. And Piper McAdams was more than ready to board that pleasure train.

For the past twenty minutes, she'd been sitting at a corner table in the Chicago hotel lounge, nursing a cosmopolitan while shamelessly studying the stranger's assets, at least those she could readily see in the dim light. He wore an expensive silk navy suit, a pricey watch on his wrist and his good looks like a badge of honor. His dark brown hair seemed as if it had been intentionally cut in a reckless—albeit sexy—style, but it definitely complemented the slight shading of whiskers framing his mouth. And those dimples. She'd spotted them the first time he smiled. Nothing better than prominent dimples on a man, except maybe…

The questionable thought vaulted into Piper's brain like a bullet, prompting her to close her eyes and rub her temples as if she had a tremendous headache. She chalked up the reaction to her long-standing membership in the Unintentional Celibacy Club. She wasn't necessarily a prude, only picky. She certainly wasn't opposed to taking sex out for a spin before saying, "I do," in the context of a committed relationship. She simply hadn't found the right man, though not from the lack of trying. But never, ever in twenty-six years had she considered ending her sexual drought with a complete stranger…until tonight.

The sound of laughter drew her gaze back to said stranger, where the pretty blond bartender leaned toward him, exposing enough cleavage to rival the Grand Canyon. Oddly, he continued to focus on Blondie's face, until his attention drifted in Piper's direction.

The moment Piper met his gaze and he grinned, she immediately glanced back to search for a bathroom or another blonde but didn't find either one. When she regarded him again and found his focus still leveled on her, she started fiddling with her cell phone, pretending to read a nonexistent text.

Great. Just great. He'd caught her staring like a schoolgirl, and she'd just provided a big boost to his ego. He wouldn't be interested in her, a nondescript, ridiculously average brunette, when he had a tall, well-endowed bombshell at his disposal. He could probably have any willing woman within a thousand-mile radius, and she wouldn't be even a blip on his masculine radar. She took the mirror out of her purse and did a quick check anyway, making sure her bangs were smooth and her mascara hadn't gone askew beneath her eyes.

And going to any trouble for a man like him was simply ridiculous. History had taught her that she more or less attracted guys who found her good breeding and trust fund extremely appealing. Nope, Mr. Hunky Stranger would never give her a second look....

"Are you waiting for someone?"

Piper's heart lurched at the sound of his voice. A very deep, and very British, voice. After she'd recovered enough to sneak a peek, her pulse started to sprint again as she came up close and personal with his incredible eyes. Eyes that were just this shade of brown and remarkably as clear as polished topaz. "Actually, no, I'm not waiting for anyone," she finally managed to say in a tone that sounded as if she was playing the frog to his prince, not the other way around.

He rested his hand on the back of the opposing chair, a gold signet ring containing a single ruby circling his little finger. "Would you mind if I join you?"

Mind? Did birds molt? "Be my guest."

After setting his drink on the table, he draped his overcoat on the back of the chair, sat and leaned back as if nothing out of the ordinary had occurred. Then again, this was probably the norm for him—picking up someone in a bar. For Piper, not so much.

"I'm surprised you're not keeping company with a man," he said. "You are much too beautiful to spend Saturday night all alone."

She was surprised she hadn't fainted from the impact of his fully formed grin, the sexy half-moon crescent in his chin and the compliment. "Actually, I just left a cocktail party a little while ago."

He studied her curiously. "In the hotel?"

She took a quick sip of her drink and nearly tipped

the glass over when she set it down. "Yes. A party in honor of some obscenely rich sheikh from some obscure country. I faked a headache and left before I had to endure meeting him. That's probably a good thing, since for the life of me, I can't remember his name."

"Prince Mehdi?"

"That's it."

"I happened to have left there a few moments ago myself."

Lovely, Piper. Open mouth, insert stiletto. "Do you know the prince?"

"I've known him for a very long time. Since birth, actually." He topped off the comment with another slow smile.

She swallowed around her mortification while wishing for a giant crevice to open up and swallow her whole. "I'm sorry for insulting your friend. I just have an aversion to overly wealthy men. I've never found one who isn't completely consumed with a sense of entitlement."

He rimmed his finger around the edge of the clear glass. "Actually, some would say he's a rather nice fellow."

She highly doubted that. "Is that your opinion?"

"Yes. Of the three Mehdi brothers, he is probably the most grounded. Definitely the best looking of the whole lot."

When Piper suddenly realized she'd abandoned her manners, she held out her hand. "I'm Piper McAdams, and you are?"

"Charmed to meet you," he said as he accepted the handshake, and then slid his thumb over her wrist before letting her go.

She shivered slightly but recovered quickly. "Well, Mr. Charmed, do you have a first name?"

"A.J."

"No last name?"

"I'd like to preserve a little mystery for the time being. Besides, last names should not be important between friends."

Clearly he was hiding something, but her suspicious nature couldn't compete with her attraction to this mysterious stranger. "We're not exactly friends."

"I hope to remedy that before night's end."

Piper hoped she could survive sitting across from him without going into a feminine free fall. She crossed one leg over the other beneath the table and tugged at the hem of her cocktail dress. "What do you do for a living, A.J.?"

He loosened his tie before lacing his fingers together atop the table. "I am the personal pilot for a rich and somewhat notorious family. They prefer to maintain their privacy."

A pretty flyboy. Unbelievable. "That must be a huge responsibility."

"You have no idea," he said before clearing his throat. "What do you do for a living, Ms. McAdams?"

Nothing she cared to be doing. "Please, call me Piper. Let's just say I serve as a goodwill ambassador for clients associated with my grandfather's company. It requires quite a bit of travel and patience."

He inclined his head and studied her face as if searching for secrets. "McAdams is a Scottish name, and the hint of auburn in your hair and beautiful blue eyes could indicate that lineage. Yet your skin isn't fair."

She touched her cheek as if she had no idea she even

owned any skin. "My great-grandparents were Colombian on my mother's side. My father's family is Scottish through and through. I suppose you could say I'm a perfect mix of both cultures."

"Colombian and Scottish. A very attractive combination. Do you tan in the summer?"

A sudden image of sitting with him on a beach—sans swimwear—assaulted her. "I do when I find the time to actually go to the beach. I'm not home that often."

"And where is home?" he asked.

"South Carolina. Charleston, actually." She refused to reveal that she currently resided in the guesthouse behind her grandparents' Greek Revival mansion.

He hesitated a moment as if mulling over the information. "Yet you have no Southern accent."

"It disappeared when I attended an all-female boarding school on the East Coast."

He leaned forward with obvious interest. "Really? I attended military academy in England."

That certainly explained his accent. "How long were you there?"

His expression turned suddenly serious. "A bloody lot longer than I should have been."

She suspected a story existed behind his obvious disdain. "An all-male academy, I take it."

"Unfortunately, yes. However, the campus was situated not far from a parochial school populated with curious females. We were more than happy to answer that curiosity."

No real surprise there. "Did you lead the panty raids?"

His smile reappeared as bright as the illuminated beer sign over the bar. "I confess I attempted to raid a few panties in my youth, and received several slaps for my efforts."

She was consumed by pleasant shivers when she should be shocked. "I highly doubt that was always the case."

"Not always." He leaned back again, his grin expanding, his dimples deepening. "Did you fall victim to the questionable antics of boarding-school boys?"

She'd fallen victim to playing the wallflower, though she hadn't exactly been playing. "My school was located in a fairly remote area, and the rules were extremely strict. The headmistress would probably have shot first and asked questions later if a boy ever dared darken our doorstep."

His eyes held a hint of amusement. "I'm certain a woman with your looks had no difficulty making up for lost time once you escaped the confines of convention."

If he only knew how far off the mark he was with that assumption, he'd probably run for the nearest exit. "Let's just say I've had my share of boys darkening my doorstep. Most had last names for first names and more money than sexual prowess, thanks to my grandfather's insistence I marry within his social circles."

"Not a decent lover among them?"

Only one, and he'd been far from decent. She imagined A.J. would be a seriously good lover. She'd seriously like to find out. "Since I'm not into kissing and telling, let's move off that subject. Do you have a significant other?"

"I did have an 'other' almost a year ago, but she is no longer significant."

"Bad breakup?"

"Let's just say it took a while to convince her we did break up."

His sour tone told Piper that topic was also off-limits. On to more generic questions. "When I first spotted you at the bar, I was sure you're Italian. Am I right?"

Luckily his pleasant demeanor returned. "No, but I am quite fond of Italy, and I do know Italian, courtesy of a former teacher."

"My second guess would be you're of French descent."

"Je ne suis pas français, mais je peux bien embrasser à la francaise."

A sexy devil with devastating dimples and a wry sense of humor—a deadly combination. "I'm sure the parochial girls appreciated your French-kissing expertise. But you didn't exactly answer my question about your heritage."

"I am not of French, but I am impressed you speak the language."

She laid a dramatic palm over her breast and pulled out her best Southern speak. "Why, sugar, we're not all dumb belles. I know French and German and even a little Japanese."

"Should you find yourself in need of an Italian translator, I would be happy to accommodate you."

She would be thrilled if he did more than that. "I've never been to Italy but I've always wanted to see Rome."

"You should make that a priority. I personally prefer Naples and the coast...."

As he continued, Piper became completely mesmerized by his mouth, and began to ridiculously fantasize about kissing him. Then her fantasies took major flight as she entertained thoughts of his mouth moving down her body. Slow and warm and, oh, so…

"…large pink salmon walk down the streets texting on their smartphones."

She rejoined reality following the odd declaration. "I beg your pardon?"

"Clearly I bored you into a near coma while playing the travel guide."

He'd inadvertently drawn her into a waking sex dream. "I'm so sorry," she said. "It must be the booze."

He reached over and without an invitation took a drink from her glass, then set it down with a thud. "That is bloody awful," he said. "What is in this unpalatable concoction?"

Piper turned her attention to the drink and momentarily became preoccupied with the fact his lips had caressed the glass. And that was probably as close to his lips she would get…unless she took the plunge and turned the good girl to bad. "Basically vodka and cranberry juice, but the bartender made it fairly strong. It's gone straight to my head." And so had he.

He pushed his half-full glass toward her. "Try this."

She picked up the tumbler and studied the amber liquid. "What is it?"

"Twenty-year-old Scotch. Once you've sampled it, no other drink will do."

She would really like to sample him, and if she didn't stop those thoughts in their tracks, she might derail her common sense. "I'm not sure I should. I don't want to have to crawl to the hotel room."

"If you need assistance, I'll make certain you arrive safely."

Piper returned his wily smile. "Well, in that case, I suppose I could have a small sip."

The minute the straight liquor hit her throat, she truly wanted to spit it out. Instead, she swallowed hard and handed the tumbler back to him.

"You don't like it?" he asked, sounding somewhat insulted.

"Sorry, but it's just not my cup of tea. Or cup of alcohol, I should say. But then, I can't claim to have good drinking skills."

"How are your kissing skills?" Right when she was about to suggest they find out, he straightened, looked away and cleared his throat again. "My apologies. You are too nice a woman to endure my habit of spewing innuendo."

"Why do you believe I wouldn't appreciate a little harmless innuendo?"

He streaked a hand over his jaw. "You have a certain innocence about you. Perhaps even purity."

Here we go again.... "Looks can be deceiving."

"True, but eyes do not deceive. I've noticed your growing discomfort during the course of our conversation."

"Have you considered my discomfort stems from my attraction to you?" Heavens, she hadn't really just admitted that, had she? Yes, she had. Her gal pals would be so proud. Her grandfather would lock her up and toss away the key.

"I'm flattered," he said without taking his gaze from hers. "I must admit I find you very attractive as well, and I would like to know you better. Because of that, I have a request. You are under no obligation to agree, but I hope you will."

The moment of truth had arrived. Would she be willing to hurl caution to the wind and sleep with him? Would she really take that risk when she knew so little about him, including his last name? Oh, heck yeah. "Ask away."

When A.J. stood and offered his hand, her heart vaulted into her throat. She held her breath and waited for the ultimate proposition, the word *yes* lingering on her lips.

"Piper McAdams, would you do me the honor of taking a walk with me?"

Sheikh Adan Jamal Mehdi did not take women on long walks. He took them to bed. Or he had before he'd taken that bloody vow of celibacy eight months before in order to be taken more seriously by his brothers. A vow that had suddenly lost its appeal.

Yet Piper McAdams wasn't his usual conquest. She was witty and outgoing, while he normally attracted sophisticated and somewhat cynical women. She was only slightly over five feet tall, he would estimate, were it not for the four-inch heels, when he usually preferred someone closer in height to his six feet two inches. She also had surprisingly long legs and extremely full breasts for someone so small in stature, and he'd had trouble keeping his eyes off those assets for any length of time. The oath of restraint had not silenced his libido in any sense, especially now.

They strolled along the walkway bordering the lake for a good twenty minutes, speaking mostly in generalities, until Adan felt strangely at a loss for words. Conversation had always been his forte, and so had kissing.

He thought it best to concentrate on the first. "Do you have any siblings?"

When a gust of wind swirled around them, she pulled her hem-length black cashmere sweater closer to her body. "One. A twin sister whose official name is Sunshine, but she goes by Sunny, for obvious reasons."

He was immediately struck by the familiar name. "Sunny McAdams, the renowned journalist?"

Her smile showed a certain pride. "That would be her. We're actually fraternal twins, as if you couldn't figure that out from our obvious physical differences."

Yet neither woman lacked in beauty despite the fact one was blond and the other brunette. "Piper and Sunshine are both rather unusual names. Did they hold some significance for your parents?"

Her expression turned somber. "It's my understanding my mother named Sunny. Unfortunately, we don't know our father. Actually, we don't even know who he is, and I'm not sure my mother does, either. You could say we were a thorn in her socialite side. Our grandparents basically raised us for that reason."

That explained her sudden change in demeanor. But due to his own questions about his heritage, he believed discussing family dynamics in-depth should be avoided at all costs. "You said your mother named your sister. Who named you?"

"My grandfather did," she said with a smile. "He adores bagpipes."

Her elevated mood pleased him greatly. "I learned to play the bagpipes at school, but I quickly determined the kilts weren't at all my style."

She paused to lean back against the railing. "Tell

me something. Is it true that men wear nothing under those kilts?"

"A man needs some reminder that he is still a man while wearing a skirt." Being so close to this particular woman served to remind him of his manhood at every turn.

She laughed softly. "I suppose that's true. Why did your parents send you to boarding school?"

He'd asked that question many times, and he'd always received the same answer that he'd never quite believed. "I was an incorrigible lad, or so I'm told, and my father decided I could use the structure a military academy provides."

"Guess he wasn't counting on the panty raids."

Hearing the word *panty* coming out of her pretty mouth did not help his current predicament in the least. "He never learned about them as far as I know." His father had never really been close to his youngest son, if the truth were known.

"I'm sure if you'd ask him today," Piper said, "he'd probably admit he knew everything. Fathers and grandfathers have an uncanny knack of knowing your business."

He moved to her side, faced the lake and rested his hands on the railing. "My father passed away not long ago. My mother died some time ago."

"I'm sorry, A.J.," she said. "I didn't mean to be so thoughtless."

"No need to apologize, Piper. You had no way of knowing." Nor did she know he hailed from Middle Eastern royalty, and that bothered him quite a bit. Yet she had clearly stated she loathed men with fortunes, and he had a sizable one. For that reason, he would continue to keep that information concealed.

Tonight he preferred to be only the pilot, not the prince. "Did you attend university?" he asked, keeping his attention trained on the less-interesting view in order to keep his desire for her in check.

"Yes, I did. In South Carolina. An all-women's university. Evidently my grandfather believed I couldn't handle the opposite sex. But since he was footing the bill, I put up with it long enough to get the dreaded business degree."

He shifted to face her, one elbow braced on the top of the railing. "Since business is apparently not your chosen field of expertise, what would you do if you weren't playing the ambassador?"

"Art," she said without the slightest hesitation. "Painting is my passion."

He knew all about passion, only his involved planes. "Then why not pursue that dream?"

She sighed. "I have several reasons, most having to do with obligation."

"To your grandfather?"

"Yes."

Not so unlike his obligation to his legacy. "What about remaining true to yourself and your own happiness, Piper?"

A span of silence passed before she spoke again. "It's complicated."

Family dynamics always were, especially in his case.

When he noticed Piper appeared to be shivering, Adan cursed his thoughtlessness. "Obviously you're cold. Do you wish to return to the hotel now?"

She shook her head. "I'm fine. Really."

"You're wearing little more than a glorified sweater, and I suspect your teeth are chattering behind that beautiful mouth of yours."

Her laugh drew him further into her lair, as did the pleasant scent of her perfume. "Maybe a tad. It's rather nippy for April."

"Let me remedy that for you."

When Adan began to slip the buttons on his overcoat, Piper raised both hands as if to ward him off. "Heavens, no. I don't want to be responsible for you freezing to death."

Her smile alone generated enough heat in Adan to fuel half the city of Chicago. "Are you sure? I am accustomed to extreme temperatures."

"Seriously, I'm okay."

Without waiting for another protest, he shrugged out of his coat, wrapped it around her shoulders and took a step back. "Better?"

"Much better, but now you're going to be cold."

Not likely. Not while she stood before him with her dark hair blowing in the breeze, her bright blue eyes reflecting the light above them and her coral-painted lips enticing him to kiss her. Answering the invitation was a risk he didn't dare take.

She inhaled deeply then released a slightly broken breath. "I need something else from you, A.J."

He hoped she meant something warm to drink, a good excuse to retire back inside the hotel before he hurled wisdom to the blustery wind. "What would that be?"

"I need you to kiss me."

Bloody hell, what could he to say to that? Should he answer "absolutely not" when he wanted to blurt out a resounding yes? He brushed away a strand of hair from her cheek and ran his thumb along her jaw. "I'm not certain that would be a banner idea." Many times he had heard that phrase, but never coming out of his own mouth.

Disappointment called out from her eyes. "Why not?"

"Because if I kiss you, I would not want to stop with only a kiss."

She sent him an angel's smile. "Do you have issues with maintaining control?"

He prided himself on control when it came to flying jets and yes, wooing women. Still, there was something about this particular woman that told him he could end up losing the war he now waged with his libido.

Before he could respond, she wrapped her hand around his neck and lowered his lips to hers. He immediately discovered the angel kissed like the devil, and he liked it. He liked the way she tasted and the silken glide of her tongue against his, and he definitely liked the way she pressed her entire body against him. He would like it better if they were in his hotel bed without the hindrance of clothing. He did not particularly care for the warning bells sounding inside his brain.

Gathering every ounce of strength he still possessed, Adan pulled away and stepped back before he did something they might both regret. The dejected look on Piper's face gave him pause, and the urge to come up with some viable excuse. "You, lovely lady, are too much of a temptation for even the most controlled man."

Her expression brightened. "No one has ever accused me of that before."

"Apparently you have not been with anyone who appreciates your finer points."

Now she looked somewhat coy. "But you appreciate them?"

If she could see the evidence of his appreciation, she would not have posed the question. "I more than appreciate them, as I also appreciate and respect you. Therefore I am going to escort you back to the hotel and bid you good night." Or crush his determination to refrain from sex for three more months.

Piper pretended to pout. "But the night is still young, and I'm still cold."

"All the more reason to deliver you safely inside the hotel."

"Your room or mine?"

She seemed determined to make this incredibly hard on him…in every sense of the word. "Your room, and then I will retire to mine."

She sighed. "All right, if that's what you really want."

If he said that, he would be lying. "It's not a question of if I want you. The question is, would it be wise to continue this?"

"And your answer?"

"Completely unwise."

"Maybe we should ignore wisdom and do what comes naturally. We're both of age and free to do as we please, so why not take advantage of the opportunity?"

Just as he opened his mouth to issue another unenthusiastic argument, she kissed him again. Deeper this time, more insistent. He slid his hand down her back, cupped her bottom and brought her up against his erection, hoping to discourage her. The plan failed. She made a move with her hips and sent him so close to the edge that he considered lifting her skirt, lowering his pants and dispensing with all propriety.

The last thread of his coveted self-control prevented him from acting on his desire. He refused to succumb to animal instinct. He could not discard the vow, or his common sense, for one night of unbridled passion with someone he was clearly deceiving. He would remain strong, stay grounded, ignore the fact that he had a beautiful, sensual woman at his disposal and…

Whom was he attempting to fool? "Let's retire to my room."

Two

She had always strived to be the good twin. Straight as an arrow. Boring as hell. Never before had she demonstrated such assertiveness toward a man.

Now remarkably Piper found herself alone in an elevator with that man, with only one goal in mind—ending her self-imposed celibacy in a virtual stranger's hotel room. Oddly A.J. kept his distance and remained silent as they traveled all the way to the top floor. After the doors sighed open and they stepped out of the car, she expected to see a corridor containing a line of rooms. Instead she noticed only one double mahogany door flanked by two massive, stoic guards. If a pilot warranted this much security, then he must work for an incredibly powerful family or some high-ranking politician.

A.J. lightly clasped her elbow to guide her forward

before stopping at the entry to mutter something in what she assumed to be Arabic. One of the men turned immediately, slid a card key in the lock and opened the doors. As soon as they were safely sequestered inside, Piper took a moment to survey the area—exquisite dark wood floors, towering windows revealing the Chicago skyline, even a baby grand piano in the corner. An opulent penthouse designed for the rich and infamous. Her current companion was one lucky employee.

Piper started to comment on that very thing, but her words never made it to her open mouth. A.J. did, and the kiss he gave her had the impact of a firebomb. Somehow she ended up with her back against one wall with A.J. pressed against her, her face bracketed in his palms. When he shrugged the sweater from her shoulders, slipped it away and tossed it behind him, her heart rate began to run amok. Any concerns flittered away on the heels of a heat she'd never felt before with any man. But this man knew what he was doing, right down to the way he brushed kisses along the line of her jaw and her neck before he brought his mouth to her ear. "The bedroom," he whispered. "Now."

Okay, that would be the next step. A daring step. A step Piper had never taken with a man she barely knew. "Lead the way."

No sooner had she said it than he clasped her hand and guided her toward another closed door where he paused to kiss her again. When his palms roved along her rib cage before they came to rest on her bottom, she found it very difficult to breathe.

He suddenly broke all contact and took a step back. "There is something I need to say before we go any further."

Piper managed to break through the sensual fog and back into reality. "You're married."

"Of course not."

That left only one scenario as far as she could see. "If you're worried that I'm making some alcohol-induced decision, you're wrong. Yes, I've had a couple of drinks, but I'm not drunk. And yes, this strangers-in-the night scenario is a first for me. In fact, I've only had one lover, and even calling him that is a stretch."

He seemed totally confused by that concept. "How is that possible for such an appealing woman?"

"Believe me, it is possible because I'm very particular."

"I am flattered, yet I still question whether you are giving this enough thought."

She didn't want to think, only do. "Look, in a perfect world, I'd suggest we spend a few days getting to know each other before we take this step. But unfortunately I was informed only a few hours ago that I'm traveling to some obscure Middle Eastern country to schmooze with sheikhs for the sake of trying to win a water conservation contract."

His expression went stone-cold serious. "Are you referring to the Mehdis?"

"Yes, and I realize they're your friends, but—"

"We need to talk."

That meant only one thing—party's over. "All right," she muttered, unable to mask the disappointment in her voice.

A.J. led her to the white sofa set out in the middle of the room. After they settled on the cushions side by side, he took both her hands into his. "You are one of the most beautiful, intelligent and intriguing women I have met in a very long time. Quite simply, you're special. For that reason, I do not want to take advantage of you."

Take advantage of me, dammit, she wanted to say, but opted for a more subtle debate. "I'm not special at all. However, I'm sure you normally require an experienced partner, and if it's that's your concern, I'm much more adventurous than I seem. I think my being in your hotel room is a sure sign of that."

He released her hands and leaned back. "As much as I would like to find out, I'd prefer not to complicate matters, which leads me to what I need to tell you. I pilot the Mehdis' plane."

Her eyes widened from sheer shock. "Why didn't you tell me this in the beginning?"

"It didn't matter until you said you'd be working with them. If the king learned I was bedding a prospective client, he would, simply put, go ballistic."

Figured. "Leave it to some well-heeled royal to spoil my good time. That's why I have no use for that kind of man."

His gaze wandered away. "He would be justified in his condemnation. I have a responsibility to the Mehdis and a need to be taken seriously by them."

"At all costs?"

"I'm afraid that is the case at this point in time."

In other words, thanks but no thanks, or at least that was what Piper heard. Feeling somewhat humiliated, she came to her feet. "It's been a pleasure to meet you, A.J. Thank you for a very lovely and eye-opening evening."

Before she had a meltdown, Piper headed away, only to be stopped by A.J. bracing her shoulders from behind before she could open the door.

He turned her to face him, his expression extremely solemn. "Piper, there are two things you must know about me. First, I have been taught that a man is only as good as his honor, and I am trying to honor you, even if I would like to take that black dress off you and carry you to my bed. Despite my concerns about my job, you also deserve the utmost respect and regard. And once you have time to consider my decision, you will thank me for saving you from a possible mistake."

For some reason that made Piper a little miffed. "Do you honestly believe I don't know my own mind?"

"I believe you're too trusting."

Now she was just plain mad. "I'm an adult, A.J., not some naive adolescent. And in case you're worried, I'm not a prude, I'm picky. Last, the only mistake I made tonight was thinking you could be the man who would be worth the wait. Obviously I was wrong."

He softly touched her face. "You are not wrong. When it comes to us—" he twined their fingers together, sending a message that wasn't lost on Piper "—making love, I assure you that would definitely be worth the wait. And that is what I'm proposing, waiting until we have the opportunity to know each other while you are in Bajul."

Piper's anger almost disappeared. Almost. "That would depend on whether you're everything you seem to be, because I believe honesty *and* honor go hand in hand. Now, what was the second thing you wanted me to know?"

A strange look passed over his face. "I still believe in chivalry. Will you allow me to walk you to your room?"

She shook her head. "No, thanks. I'm a big girl and I can find my way."

"As you wish." After he escorted her into the corridor, A.J. executed a slight bow. "If I don't see you tomorrow on the plane, Ms. McAdams, then I will make it a point to seek you out in Bajul."

She boarded the extremely large and lavish private plane less than five minutes before their scheduled departure, due to the rush-hour traffic and an apathetic cabdriver. When the five-man survey crew settled into the vacant beige leather seats at the front of the plane, she walked the aisle past what she assumed to be staff and press members. Despite the size of the plane, it appeared the back half had been cordoned off to passengers. Most likely it held a series of conference rooms and perhaps even living quarters. She might ask A.J. to give her the grand tour, provided she actually encountered him before they landed.

She paused in the aisle to address a middle-aged, professor-like man with sparse graying hair, wire-rimmed glasses and kind brown eyes. Hopefully he spoke English, and that the last remaining spot was available. "Is this seat taken?"

"It is reserved for Miss McAdams," he replied. "Is that you?"

Fortunately a language barrier wouldn't exist during the lengthy flight. "Yes, that's me."

"Then the seat is yours."

After sliding in next to the man and settling her red tote at her feet, she shifted toward him and stuck out her hand. "Hello, I'm Piper McAdams. I'm traveling to Bajul with the GLM engineers."

He gave her hand a soft shake. "Mr. Deeb."

Not a lot to go on there. Time for a fishing expedition. "Are you a friend of the sheikh's?"

"I am serving as his attaché on this trip."

"I'm sure that's a very interesting duty."

He pushed his glasses up on the bridge of his nose. "Managing Prince Adan's schedule can be challenging at times, evidenced by his absence at the moment."

A good thing, since she might have missed the flight if the guy had been punctual. "He has a habit of being late, does he?"

"He occasionally suffers from tardiness, among other things."

Piper wanted him to define "other things" but then she noticed a commotion toward the front of the plane. Assuming the mysterious monarch had finally arrived, she came to her feet along with the rest of the passengers and leaned slightly into the aisle to catch a glimpse. She spotted only A.J. dressed in a crisp, white shirt covered by a navy blue suit emblazoned with gold military-like insignias. Not a sheikh in sight.

She regarded Mr. Deeb again and lowered her voice. "He must be some kind of pilot to earn that reception."

He cleared his throat and glanced away. "Yes, he is quite the aviator."

After everyone settled into their seats, Piper followed suit, well aware that her pulse had unwittingly picked up speed as she noticed A.J. stopping in the aisle to speak to one man. A man who oddly addressed the pilot as Prince Adan.

Reality soon dawned, along with the sense that she might have been completely betrayed by blind faith. She turned a frown on Mr. Deeb. "He's not the plane's pilot, is he?"

Again the man refused to look at her directly. "Yes, he is the pilot, as well as commander in chief of Bajul's armed forces."

"And a Mehdi?"

Deeb gave her a contrite look. "The third Mehdi son in line to inherit the throne."

And a major liar, Piper realized as she watched the sheikh disappear into the cockpit. She thanked her lucky stars she hadn't made the mistake of climbing into bed with him. Then again, he'd been the one to put an end to that with his fake concerns over being only a royal employee, not a royal prince. And all that talk of honor. Honorable men didn't deceive unsuspecting women about their identities.

Fuming over the duplicity, Piper pulled a fashion magazine from her bag and flipped through the pages with a vengeance during takeoff. She didn't have to deal with the situation now, or ever for that matter. She didn't have to spend even one minute with A.J. or Adan or whatever his name was. He would be nothing more to her than a cute meet that had gone nowhere, a precautionary tale in the book of her life, a man she would endeavor to immediately forget....

"May I have a moment with you in the aft lounge, Ms. McAdams?"

She glanced up and immediately took in A.J.'s damnable dimples and his sexy mouth before visually traveling to his remarkable dark eyes. "Is the plane flying itself, *Prince* Mehdi?"

He tried on a contrite look. "I have turned the controls over to the copilot for the time being so we can converse."

And if she spent one second alone with him, she

might find herself caught up in his lair once more. "I do believe the seat belt sign is still on, and that means it's not safe to move about the cabin."

Of course said sign picked that moment to ding and dim, robbing her of any excuse to avoid this confrontation. Nevertheless, he happened to be resident royalty, not to mention he could hold the power to grant—or reject—her grandfather's bid. For that reason, she shoved the magazine back into the carry-on and slid out of the seat, putting her in very close proximity to the fibbing prince. "After you," she said in a tone that was borderline irritable, to say the least.

As the princely pilot started toward the rear of the plane, Piper followed behind him with her eyes lowered in an attempt to avoid the two female attendants' curious stares. He paused to open a sliding frosted-glass door and gestured her forward into a narrow corridor before he showed her into a lounge containing dark brown leather furniture.

"Make yourself comfortable," A.J. said as he closed the sliding door behind her.

Comfortable? Ha! Piper chose the lone chair to avoid inadvertent physical contact, while the sneaky sheikh settled on the opposing sofa.

He draped his arm casually over the back cushions and smiled. "Have you enjoyed your flight so far?"

In an effort to demonstrate some decorum, she bit back the harsh words clamoring to come out of her mouth. "Since it's been less than fifteen minutes into the flight, I prefer to reserve judgment until landing."

He gave her a lingering once-over. "You look very beautiful today, Piper."

She tugged the hem of her black coatdress down to

the top of her knees. Unfortunately she couldn't convert the open collar to a turtleneck. "Thank you, but if you believe compliments will put you in the clear after you lied to me, think again."

"I am being completely sincere in my admiration."

"Forgive me if I question your sincerity. And by the way, what am I supposed to call you?"

"What would you like to call me?"

He'd walked right into that one. "Jackass?"

He had the audacity to grin. "I believe I have been called that before."

She had the utterly stupid urge to kiss that grin off his face. "I don't doubt that a bit. And where did you come up with A.J.?"

"My given name is Adan Jamal. My classmates called me A.J., but as an adult I do prefer Adan."

"I would have preferred you explain all of this to me last night."

His expression turned serious. "When I discovered you were involved with the water project, I was completely thrown off-kilter."

Not a valid excuse, in her opinion. "And after learning that, did you seriously believe you could hide your identity from me indefinitely?"

He sighed. "No. I had hoped to speak with you before takeoff. Unfortunately, traffic detained our driver on the way to the airport and I had to adhere to the original flight plan."

She couldn't reject that defense when she'd experienced the same delays. Still… "You still should have told me before I left your room, at the very least."

He leaned forward, draped his elbows on his parted knees and studied the carpeted floor. "Do you know what it's like to be judged by your station in life even though it has nothing to do with who you really are?"

Actually, she did—the rich girl born to a spoiled, partying socialite and an unknown father. "I can relate to that in some ways."

He finally raised his gaze to hers. "Last night, I wanted you to see me as an average man, not a monarch."

There was absolutely nothing average about him. "I don't base my opinions on a person's social status."

He straightened and streaked a palm over his shadowed jaw. "I believe I recall you mentioning you have an aversion to wealthy men, and specifically, the Mehdis. Is that not so?"

Darned if he wasn't right. "Okay, yes, I might have said that. My apologies for making generalizations."

"And I apologize for deceiving you. I promise it will not happen again, as soon as I tell you something else I omitted last evening."

Just when she thought she might be able to trust him. "I'm listening."

"I've been celibate since my eldest brother's wedding."

"When was that?" she asked around her surprise.

"Eight months ago and approximately two months following the dissolution of my relationship."

Piper couldn't imagine such a vital, viral man could go that long without sex. "Your breakup must have been really devastating."

"Not exactly," he said. "My brothers have always seen me as being less than serious when it comes to my role in the family. I decided to prove to them that my entire life does not revolve around seeking the next conquest."

She so wanted to believe him, yet wasn't certain she could. "I admire your resolve, but I'm still having a hard time with the trust issue where you're concerned."

Adan came to his feet, crossed the small space between them, clasped her hands and pulled her off the chair. "I must see to my responsibility now as captain of this ship. But before I go, I have a request."

Who knew what that might entail? "Go ahead."

"If you will allow me to serve as your personal host in Bajul, I will prove to you that I am not only a man of my word, but I am an honorable man."

That remained to be seen. But right then, when Adan Mehdi looked at her as if she deserved his utmost attention, she couldn't manufacture one reason to refuse his hospitality. And if she didn't keep a cool head, she worried he could convince her of anything.

"Ms. Thorpe is here to see you, Emir."

Great. He'd barely walked into the palace with Piper at his side only to be greeted by an unwelcome visit from his past in the form of a persistent, self-absorbed ex-paramour.

The entire travel party scattered like rats on a sinking ship, including the turncoat Deeb. Only the messenger of doom remained, an extremely perplexed look splashed across his bearded face. "Did you know she was coming, Abdul?"

The man revealed his discomfort by wringing his hands. "No, Emir. I attempted to ask her to return tomorrow, yet she would not hear of it. She is currently in the study with…uh…those who accompanied her. It would be in your best interest to speak with her."

Leave it to Talia to bring an entourage. And if she created a scene, he would never earn Piper's trust. Therefore he had to find a way to keep the two women separated.

With that in mind, Adan turned to Piper and gestured toward the towering staircase leading to the upper floors. "This shouldn't take too long, Ms. McAdams. In the meantime, Abdul will show you to your quarters and I will meet you shortly in the third-floor sitting room. Abdul, put her things in the suite across from mine."

After Abdul picked up her luggage, she didn't make a move other than to give Adan a decidedly suspicious stare. "I have a room reserved at the inn in the village, so it's best I keep those arrangements, Your Highness," she said, prompting the houseman to set the bags back down.

He had to encourage her to stay at the palace, and he had limited time to do so. After signaling Abdul to gather the bags again, he regarded Piper. "The inn is small and will not allow you to have what you need in terms of your business. They currently do not have internet access or an office center. We have all that here."

Abdul bent slightly as if prepared to return the luggage to the floor while Adan tamped down his impatience over Piper's delay in responding. "I suppose you have a point," she finally said. "As long as it's not an inconvenience for your staff."

He would be inconvenienced if he didn't have her nearby, and in deep trouble if the old girlfriend suddenly made an appearance. "I assure you, the staff is accustomed to guests. So if you will follow Abdul—"

"It's about time you finally showed up, you inconsiderate arse."

Adan froze like an iceberg at the sound of the familiar voice. Trouble had definitely arrived.

He could pretend he hadn't heard her, or he could face the unavoidable confrontation like a man. Taking the second—and least palatable—option, he turned to discover Talia Thorpe standing at the entry to the hallway wearing a chic white dress, hands propped on her narrow hips and her green eyes alight with fury.

A compliment should help to diffuse the possible verbal bloodbath. Or so he hoped. "You're looking well, Talia."

She rolled her eyes. "Why haven't you returned my emails or calls? I've sent you at least a hundred messages over the past month alone."

He ventured a fast glance at Piper, who appeared to be somewhat taken aback, and rightfully so. "Might I remind you, Talia, we broke off our relationship a year ago."

Talia tossed a lock of her long platinum hair back over one shoulder. "*You* broke it off, and it's been ten months. If you hadn't ignored me, I wouldn't have been forced to disrupt my schedule and make this beastly trip."

When he'd told her they were done after their on-and-off six-year relationship, he'd meant it. "Perhaps we should continue this conversation somewhere more private."

She flipped a manicured hand in Piper's direction. "Are you worried your new chicky will be exposed to all the dirty details?"

As a matter of fact… "For your information, Ms. McAdams is here on business."

"Well, so am I," Talia said. "Serious business."

He wouldn't be at all surprised if she tried to sue him over the breakup. "I find that somewhat difficult to believe, Talia, yet I am curious. What business of yours would concern me?"

She turned around and clapped her hands. "Bridget, you may come in now and bring it with you."

Talia went through personal assistants as frequently as she went through money, so Adan wasn't surprised when he didn't recognize the name. He was mildly concerned over the "it" comment. But he was nothing less than astounded when the meek-looking plump brunette strolled into the room…gripping a baby carrier. Myriad concerns began rushing through his mind. Unthinkable possibilities. Unimaginable scenarios.

Yet when Talia took the carrier and turned it around, and he saw the sleeping baby with the tiny round face and the black cap of hair, he would swear his heart skipped several beats, and he began to sweat.

"Adan, meet Samuel, your new son."

Three

Piper wouldn't be a bit surprised if Adan Mehdi keeled over from shock. Instead, he assumed a rigid posture and a stern expression, hands fisted at his sides. "Talia, if you believe I will simply take you at your word about this, you are completely daft."

The woman swept her manicured hand toward the infant. "Just look at him, Adan. You can't deny he's yours. Dark hair and golden skin. He even has your dimples. Despite all that, I do have proof in the form of a DNA test."

"How did you get my bloody DNA?" he asked.

Talia crossed her arms beneath her breasts and lifted her chin. "It's all over my Paris flat, Adan. And you happened to leave your toothbrush the night you tossed me to the gutter."

The sheikh's defenses seemed to disappear right before Piper's eyes. "We were always careful to prevent pregnancy."

Talia tapped her chin. "I do recall that one night last year in Milan—"

"That was one blasted night, Talia," he replied, his tone fraught with anger.

"Once was quite enough." The woman handed the carrier off to a bewildered Bridget. "Anyway, I have a photo shoot in a remote location in Tasmania, which will give you an opportunity to get to know your kid. We'll discuss the custody particulars when I get back next month."

Adan narrowed his eyes in a menacing glare. "We will discuss this immediately."

Talia checked her watch. "My flight leaves in less than an hour."

"You will not take one step out this door until we talk," Adan demanded. "Into the study. Now."

After the sheikh and his former girlfriend exited, Piper looked around to find Abdul had disappeared, leaving her in a quandary over what to do next. She occupied her time by surveying the beige stone walls, the ornate gold statues and the unending staircase leading to the top of the massive structure. A baby's cry would definitely echo loudly throughout the building.

With that in mind, Piper sought out Bridget, who'd taken a seat on the gold brocade cushioned bench set against the wall, the carrier at her feet. She smiled at the woman, who managed a slight, albeit shaky return of the gesture. But when the baby began to fuss, the presumed au pair looked completely alarmed.

Not good. Piper launched into action, crossed to the carrier, unfolded the yellow blanket, picked up the

crying infant and held him against her shoulder. After
he quieted, she regarded the wide-eyed Bridget. "You
aren't a nanny, are you?"

"No, I am not," she finally responded, her tone hinting at a slight British accent and a lot of disdain. "I'm
Talia's personal assistant. The last nanny quit yesterday when she learned she'd have to make the trip here.
Traveling with Talia isn't pleasant under normal circumstances, let alone with a child in tow."

Piper claimed the vacant spot on the bench, laid the
swaddled baby in the crook of her arm and studied his
cherub face. "You're beautiful, little man, although you
don't look like a Samuel. Sam fits you better."

"Don't let Talia hear you call him that," Bridget
warned. "She fired the first nanny over that very thing."

That didn't exactly surprise Piper after what she'd
witnessed upon meeting the model. "Then she's very
protective of him, huh?"

Bridget frowned. "Not really. She hasn't held him
more than a handful of times since his birth."

Piper couldn't contain her contempt, a product of
her own experience. "Good mothers hold and care for
their babies. They certainly don't foist their children
off on someone else."

Bridget reached over and touched the infant's arm.
"You're right, but unfortunately Talia isn't maternal.
She's consumed by her modeling career and staying in
shape. All I've heard since his birth is how hard she's
had to work to regain her figure. I truly believe that's
why she waited four weeks to bring the baby here."

Vanity, thy name is Talia. She was beginning to like
her less and less. "At least now he'll have the opportunity to bond with his father."

"I am not prepared to raise a child, Talia."

So much for bonding, Piper thought at the sound of the sheikh's irritated tone.

The self-centered supermodel breezed into the room with one impatient prince following close on her heels. "At least you didn't have to suffer through thirteen hours of horrible labor last month. And just imagine pushing a soccer ball out your todger. Besides, you have a whole staff to assist you while I had to hire several useless nannies over the past month. Good help is hard to find."

"Perhaps that's because you have no idea how to treat the help," Adan muttered as he strode into the vestibule.

Talia turned and set an oversize light blue bag next to the carrier, affording Piper only a cursory glance. "Bridget gave him a bottle three hours ago, so no doubt he'll be hungry again very soon. There's enough nappies, bottles and cans of formula in here to get you by until tomorrow, plus a few outfits. After that, you're on your own. Let's go, Bridget."

Without giving the baby even a passing glance, much less a kiss goodbye, Talia headed for the door with poor Bridget cowering behind her. Piper practically bit a hole in her tongue against the urge to deliver a seething diatribe aimed at the woman's disregard for her child. Instead, she shifted Sam back to her shoulder and remained silent as Adan followed the two women to the entry and accompanied them out the door.

When the baby began to whimper again, Piper assumed he was probably in need of another bottle. Fortunately, feeding an infant wasn't an issue, even if it had been a while since her teenage babysitting days—the one job her grandparents had allowed her to accept, but only in a limited capacity, and exclusively for those parents who'd run in their social circle.

Piper laid Sam vertically in her lap, rummaged through the bag, withdrew a bottle and uncapped it. He took the nipple without hesitation and suckled with great enthusiasm, complete with soft, yummy noises that brought about her smile. After he drained the formula in record time, she set the empty bottle beside her, returned him to her shoulder and rubbed his back to successfully burp him. Then she cradled him in the crook of her arm and stroked his cotton-soft cheek. For a time he stared at her with an unfocused gaze before planting his right thumb in his rosebud mouth.

As his eyes drifted closed, Piper experienced sheer empathy for this precious little boy. She couldn't fathom how anyone would reject such a gift. Couldn't imagine how any mother worth her salt would simply drop off her child with a man who hadn't even known he had a son. Then again, why should she be surprised? Her very own mother had abandoned her and Sunny with their grandparents shortly after their birth. As far as she was concerned, women like Talia Thorpe and Millicent McAdams should not be allowed to procreate.

Despite her poor maternal example, Piper had always dreamed of having children of her own. So far she hadn't found a suitable candidate to father her future offspring, and she certainly wasn't going to settle for anything less than a loving relationship with a man who had the same wants and desires. A gentle, caring man. Grounded. Settled…

"I am officially moving to Antarctica."

After the declaration, Adan strode past Piper and disappeared into the nearby corridor adjacent to the

towering staircase. Again. Granted, she enjoyed holding baby Sam, but she hadn't signed on to be the royal
nursemaid. And apparently the sheikh hadn't signed up
for fatherhood, either.

A few moments passed before Adan returned with a
petite, attractive older woman wearing an impeccable
navy tailored blazer and skirt, her salt-and-pepper hair
styled in a neat bob. Yet when she caught sight of Piper
and the baby, her pleasant demeanor melted into obvious confusion. "May I help you, miss?"

"This is Piper McAdams," Adan said. "She has accompanied the survey crew, and while she's here, she
will be my guest. Piper, this is Elena Battelli, my former governess who now governs the entire household."

Piper came to her feet and smiled. "It's very nice to
meet you."

"And I, you." Elena leaned over and studied the baby.
"What a lovely child you have. Boy or girl?"

"He's Talia's child," Adan interjected before Piper
had a chance to respond.

Elena's initial shock melted into an acid look. "Is
that dreadful woman here?"

"She has departed for now," Adan said. "And she left
this infant in my charge before she left the premises."

Now the governess appeared completely appalled.
"She expects you to care for her child?"

The sheikh looked somewhat contrite before he re-
gained his commanding demeanor. "He is mine, Elena."

Piper really wanted to take the baby and bail before the verbal fireworks began. "If you two would like
some privacy—"

"You have no reason to leave," Adan said. "You have
already witnessed the worst of the situation."

Elena's features turned as stern as a practiced headmistress. "How long have you known about this child, *cara?* And how can you be certain that woman is being truthful?"

Adan streaked a palm over his neck. "I didn't know until today, and she provided the test results that prove I am his father. Now, before you begin the lecture, I have a few things I need you to do."

The woman straightened her shoulders and stared at him. "This is your bed, Adan Mehdi, and you will lie in it. So if you expect me to raise your son—"

"I do not expect that at all," Adan replied. "In fact, I intend to take complete control over his care until his mother returns."

Provided the missing model did come back, Piper's major concern. But at the moment, she had a more pressing issue that needed to be addressed. "Do you think you might like to hold your son first, Your Highness?"

Uncertainty called out from Adan's brown eyes as he slowly approached her. "I suppose that would be the most logical next step."

Piper turned the baby around and placed him in his father's arms. "I promise he's not going to break," she added when she noted his slight look of concern.

While the sheikh held his son for the first time, the former governess stood next to him, one hand resting on Adan's shoulder. "He looks exactly like you did at his age, *cara,*" she said in a reverent tone. "Such a *bella* baby. Does he have a name?"

"Sam," Piper chimed in without thought. "Actually, Samuel, but I think he looks more like a Sam. Or maybe Sammy." When she noticed Adan's disapproving glance, she amended that decision. "Sammy definitely doesn't work. Of course, what you call him is solely up to you."

"He will eventually be renamed in accordance with tradition," Adan said, sounding very authoritative and princely. "Right now I must see to his comfort, including finding him a suitable crib."

"The nursery is still in order," Elena said. "And since your brother and Madison are currently residing at their home in the States, you may use it. We still have several bottles in the pantry, and a few items in the cupboard in the nursery, but I'm afraid we have no diapers or formula since the twins have moved past that stage. But the cribs are still there and fully equipped with blankets and such."

Adan appeared somewhat perplexed. "The nursery is down the hall from my quarters. I will not be able to hear him if he needs me during the night."

The governess took the baby without permission, and without protest, from the fledgling father, a sure sign of her close bond with the youngest Mehdi son. "There is something known as a baby monitor, *cara*. You will be able to see and hear him at any time when you are in your suite."

"Have the monitor set up in my room," he said. "I will see to the supplies tomorrow. You mentioned Zain is in Los Angeles, but you have not said anything about Rafiq."

Rafiq Mehdi, the reigning king of Bajul, and reportedly a hard case, according to her grandfather. Piper would buy tickets to see his reaction to the current scandal. Then again, maybe not. She'd had enough drama for one day.

Elena continued to stare at the baby with the rever-
ence of a grandmother. "Rafiq has been with his wife
at the resort for the past week. They will not be returning for two more days."

Adan shrugged out of his jacket and hung it on an
ornately carved coat tree in the vestibule before returning to them. "Make certain Rafiq knows nothing about
this until I have the opportunity to speak with him."

When she recognized a serious problem with that
request, Piper decided to add her two cents. "Can you
trust the household staff to keep this quiet?"

"The staff knows to exercise complete confiden-
tially," Elena said.

"Or suffer the consequences," Adan added gruffly
before turning to the governess. "Please have Abdul deliver the monitor and our bags to our rooms, and watch
him while I show Ms. McAdams to her quarters."

Elena kissed the baby's forehead. "I have no reason to watch Abdul, *cara*. I trust he'll do as he's told."

After Adan muttered something in Arabic that didn't
sound exactly pleasant, Piper stifled a laugh and considered an offer. "I have no problem watching the baby
while you settle in, Your Highness."

"That will not be necessary, Ms. McAdams," Elena
said as she handed the baby back to Adan. "If you are
bent on being a good father to your son, then you should
begin immediately."

Adan looked slightly panicked. "But—"

"No buts, Adan Mehdi." The governess snatched the
empty bottle from the bench before addressing Piper
again. "Ms. McAdams, it was certainly a pleasure to
meet you, even under such unusual circumstances. I
shall go instruct Abdul while the royal pilot becomes

accustomed to paternity. Please let me know if you need any assistance with the boy."

Piper returned her smile. "Luckily I babysat quite a few times in my youth, so we'll be fine."

"Actually, I was referring to my former charge, the prince."

The two women shared a laugh before Elena walked away, leaving Piper alone with Adan and his son.

"She treats me as if I still wear knickers," he said, frustration evident in his tone.

Piper moved to his side and peeked at the still sleeping infant. "Evidently the two of you are very close, and I honestly believe she has your best interests at heart."

He released a rough sigh. "I suppose she does, at that. Now, if you're ready, I shall escort you to your room before I settle the baby into the nursery."

Piper almost insisted on returning to the inn, yet when she saw a trace of doubt in Adan's eyes, the touch of awkwardness as he held his child, the sympathy bug bit her. "Why don't we put him in the carrier while we climb the stairs?"

"No need," he said. "If you'll be so kind as to gather his things, I'll show you to the private elevator."

Piper couldn't help but smile over Adan's decision not to relinquish his son. Maybe she'd underestimated his ability to move into his new role after all.

He had untold riches at his disposal. He could fly jets at warp speed, navigate treacherous mountain slopes on skis and answer a woman's most secret fantasies with little effort. Yet he had no idea what to do with an infant.

As he studied the child in his arms, Adan's own paternal experience fueled his drive to succeed in this endeavor. He'd often wondered if the man who'd claimed him—and in many ways discarded him—had actually been his biological father. That question had always haunted him and always would. He vowed to give his son everything he would ever need, including his undivided attention.

His son. He'd never believed he would be in this position at this point in his life. Yet he was, and he had no one else to blame for his carelessness. No one to truly count on but himself.

"Is this where we get off, Your Highness?"

Until Piper had spoken, he hadn't noticed the car had come to a stop. "It is." After he moved through the open doors, he faced her in the corridor. "I respectfully request you call me Adan when we're in private."

She shifted the tote's strap to her shoulder. "All right, as long as you don't mind me referring to your son as Sam."

Clearly the woman was a born negotiator. "If that pleases you, I agree. I, however, will call him Samuel until he is renamed."

She sent him a satisfied smile. "It greatly pleases me, Adan."

Under different circumstances, he would definitely like to please her in other, more intimate ways. Then his son began to whimper, reminding him those carefree days were all but over. "Do you think he is hungry again?"

"I think he's probably wet," she said. "I also think we should stop by the nursery first and check it out."

A good plan. At least she could assist him when he took his first venture into diaper changing.

Piper followed behind him as he traveled the lengthy

hallway past several unoccupied guest suites. He stopped immediately right of the staircase landing and opened the door to the nursery that he had once occupied with his two brothers almost thirty years ago. The room had been left much the same, with two cribs and a small single bed set against the sand-colored walls, a large blue trunk holding the toys from his early childhood positioned in the corner. The miniature round table and chairs were still centered in the room, the place where Elena had taught the boys lessons as well as her native language, Italian. Where she had read to them nightly before bedtime in lieu of the mother Adan had never known. But that had lasted only until he'd turned six years old, when he'd been unceremoniously shipped off to boarding school.

The baby's cries began to escalate, thrusting the bittersweet memories away. He stepped aside to allow Piper entry, plagued by a sudden sense of absolute help-lessness when he couldn't think of a blasted thing to do to calm his son. He hated failure in any form, and he'd worked hard to succeed in nearly everything he'd en-deavored. Yet somehow this miniature human had left him virtually defenseless.

Piper crossed the room to the dressing table and set the tote and carrier at her feet. "Bring him over here."

"Gladly."

After he laid the infant on the white cushioned sur-face, Samuel continued to wail at a decibel that could possibly summon the palace guards. Piper seemed will-ing to speed up the process by sliding the yellow-footed pajama bottoms down the infant's legs. She then leaned down to retrieve a diaper that she set on the end of the table. "You can take it from here."

While the child continued to cry, Adan surveyed the plastic contraption and tried to recall a time when he'd watched his sister-in-law change one of the twins. Sadly, he could not. "I am not well versed in proper diaper-changing procedure."

Piper sighed. "First, you need to remove the wet diaper by releasing the tapes. But I need to warn you about something first."

He suspected it wouldn't be the last child-rearing caution he would hear. "Take care not to flip him on his head?"

She frowned. "Well, obviously that, and make sure you're ready to hold the diaper back in place if he's not done. Otherwise, you could find yourself being anointed in the face."

He certainly had never considered that. "How do you know these things?"

She withdrew a white container from the bag and opened it to reveal some sort of paper wipes. "I learned the hard way. I used to babysit for a family with three boys, and two of them were in diapers."

This woman—who had been a stranger to him twenty-four hours ago—could very well be his savior. After he lowered the diaper and didn't have to dodge, he readied for the next step. "Now what?"

"Gently grasp his ankles with one hand, lift his bottom, then slide the diaper from beneath him with your free hand."

Adan had earned a degree in aeronautics, yet this task seemed astronomical. Fortunately the boy found his thumb to pacify himself while his fumbling father figured out the process. And thankfully his hand easily circled both the infant's ankles, and raising his legs was akin to lifting a feather. Once he had the diaper removed and the baby lowered, he turned back to Piper. "Piece of cake."

She took the plastic garment from him and discarded it in the nearby bin. "True, but he's still little. Just realize there will soon come a time when he'll be much more mobile, and a lot less cooperative."

The image of his child vaulting from the dressing table assaulted him. "Will I need to strap him down?"

Piper laughed. "You'll have enough experience by then to handle him. And you'll probably want to change him in a place that's a little lower to the ground."

He shook his head. "I had no idea that caring for someone so small would require so much knowledge. I am ill equipped for the task."

"You're more than equipped, Adan." She handed him a damp paper cloth, set the container aside, then grabbed the clean diaper and unfolded it. "But right now your son requires that you finish this task. After you clean him up a bit, repeat the first step, only this time slide the diaper underneath him."

Piper displayed great patience as he followed her instructions to the letter. Once he had the infant rediapered and redressed, he noticed that his son had fallen asleep.

"Grab the bag and we'll put this little guy to bed," Piper said as she lifted the baby, crossed the room and placed him on his back in one of the two cribs.

Tote in hand, Adan came to her side. As he watched his child sleep, he experienced a strong sense of pride. "I must say he's quite something."

"Yes he is," she replied in a hushed tone. "Now let's

go so he can have a decent nap before it's feeding time again."

After one last look at his son, Adan guided Piper into the corridor, leaving the nursery room door ajar. "Do you think it's all right to leave him all alone in an unfamiliar place?"

She patted his arm and smiled. "He's going to be fine for the next hour or so. And I'm sure Elena will have the monitor in place very soon so you can track his every move. But you will need to send out for supplies tomorrow."

"I prefer to take care of the supplies myself," he said on a whim. "However, I could use some counsel on what to purchase, if you would be so kind as to accompany me into the village. I can also show you the sights while we're there."

"Aren't you afraid someone might recognize you?"

He was more afraid she would reject his plan to spend more time with her. "I have ways to disguise myself to avoid recognition. We would appear to be tourists exploring the town."

She hid a yawn behind her hands. "I could probably do that. But at the moment, I could use a nap. Jet lag has taken hold of me."

What an inconsiderate buffoon he'd become. "Of course. If you'll follow me, I will show you to your quarters."

Adan guided Piper toward the suite opposite his, situated two rooms down from the nursery. Once there, he opened the door and she breezed past him, coming to a stop at the end of the queen-size bed. He stepped inside and watched as she surveyed the room before facing the open windows that revealed the mountains in the distance.

"This is a beautiful view," she said without turning around.

"Yes, it is." And he wasn't referring to the panoramic scenery. She was beautiful. Incredibly beautiful, from the top of her hair that ruffled in the warm breeze, to her man-slaying high heels, and all points in between. What he wouldn't give to divest her of that black dress, lay her down on the purple silk bedspread and have his wicked way with her....

"That peak is really prominent."

She had no idea, and he was thankful she hadn't turned around to find out. After regaining some composure, he crossed the room and moved behind her. "The largest mountain is called Mabrúruk. Legend has it that it blesses Bajul with fertility."

She turned, putting them in close proximity. "Fertile as in crops?"

"Actually, livestock and village offspring. We've come to know it as the baby-making mountain."

She smiled. "Did its powers reach all the way to Milan?"

"Perhaps so."

Her smile disappeared, replaced by self-consciousness. "I'm sorry. I shouldn't have brought that up. Obviously you were shocked over learning you had a son."

An understatement of the first order. "Yes, but I am in part responsible. If I had answered Talia's messages, I would have known much sooner. But I frankly did not have the desire to speak with her after we broke off the relationship. Six years of Talia's antics had been quite enough."

"And that brings me to a question," she said, followed by, "if you don't mind me asking."

After all his talk of honor, she deserved to grill him as much as she would like. "Ask away."

"Why were you with Talia all that time if you found her intolerable?"

A very good question. "In all honesty, my attraction to her was purely physical. But in defense of Talia, she has not had an easy life. She practically raised herself in the back alleys of London after her mother died and her father drowned his sorrows in the local pubs. Beneath that tough and somewhat haughty exterior resides a lost little girl who fears poverty and a loss of pride."

Piper released a caustic laugh. "Sorry, but that doesn't excuse her for bringing a baby into the world and basically ignoring him after the fact."

He recalled the recent conversation he'd had with Talia in the study. "She told me she had considered giving Samuel up for adoption, but she also felt I had a right to decide if I wanted to be a part of his life."

"And she thought springing him on you was the way to handle that?"

"Talia is nothing if not spontaneous. And as I've said, I refused to answer any correspondence."

She sighed. "Look, I know it's really none of my business, but I suspect she could be using Sam as a pawn to get you back into her life."

"Or perhaps for monetary gain," he said, regretfully voicing his own suspicions.

Piper reacted with a scowl. "She wants you to buy your own son from her?"

"She did not exactly say that, but it is a possibility. And if that proves to be true, I would willingly give her any amount of money for the opportunity to raise my child without her interference."

Her features brightened. "I admire your conviction, Adan. Sam is lucky to have you as his dad."

She could have offered him an accommodation for bravery in battle and it would not have meant as much. "And I appreciate your faith in me, Piper. Yet I am well aware of the challenges ahead of me."

She favored him with a grin that traveled to her diamond-blue eyes. "Just wait until you have to give him a bath this evening."

That sent several horrific images shooting through his muddled mind. "Bloody hell, what if I drop him?"

She patted his cheek. "You won't if you're careful. And I'll be there to show you how it's done."

He caught her hand and brought it against his chest. "You have been a godsend, Piper McAdams. And you now hold the distinction of being the most attractive tutor I have ever encountered."

"Then we're even," she said, her voice soft and overtly sensuous.

He tugged her closer. "In what way?"

She wrested out of his grasp and draped her arms around his neck. "You happen to be the best kisser I've ever encountered to this point."

He wanted to kiss her now. Needed to kiss her now. And he did—without any compunction whatsoever, regardless of his responsibility to his sleeping son. With a bed very close at hand and her heady response to the thrust of his tongue, all reasoning flew out the open windows.

"Excuse me, Emir."

Abdul's voice was as effective as having ice water

poured down one's pants, thrusting Adan away from
Piper. He tried to clear the uncomfortable hitch from his
throat before facing the servant. "Yes, Abdul?"

"I have Ms. McAdams's luggage."

"Then bring it in."

The man set the bags at the end of the bed, then executed a slight bow before hurrying away and closing
the door behind him, something Adan should have done
to avoid the predicament.

He sent Piper an apologetic look. "I am very sorry I
did not see to our privacy."

She touched her fingertips to her lips. "We really
shouldn't be doing this."

The declaration sent his good spirits into a nose-
dive. "Why not?"

"Because I can't help but wonder exactly how much
you really knew about Talia's pregnancy."

This time when she called his honor into question,
he responded with fury. "I did not even remotely suspect she might be pregnant. Otherwise this issue would
have been resolved in the beginning. And it pains me
to know you hold me in such low esteem that you think
I would abandon my own child."

"I'm sorry," she said quietly. "That was an unfair
assumption since you seem so willing to care for your
son."

His anger diminished when he noted the sincerity
in her voice. "You do have every right to doubt me,
Piper, in light of my initial fabrications. But I swear
to you again that I will do everything in my power to
prove my honor."

She answered with a slight smile. "After meeting that

man-eater, Talia, I now understand why you might be driven straight into celibacy."

That vow was the last thing on his mind after he'd kissed Piper. "As I've said before, she had little to do with that decision. I am determined to demonstrate my ability to maintain control over baser urges."

"Then we should probably avoid situations where we're going to lose our heads and do something we both might regret."

He could not argue that point, but he would have no regrets when it came to making love to her should they arrive upon that decision. He might regret any emotional entanglement. "I suppose you're correct, but chemistry is very hard to control."

"We'll just have to learn to control it for the time being."

Easier said than done. "And let us both hope we can maintain control."

"Believe me, you'll have enough distractions taking care of Sam."

Perhaps while caring for his son that would be true, but she served as his primary distraction in private, the reason why he began backing toward the door—and away from these foreign feelings for Piper that had little to do with physical attraction. "Speaking of my son, I should go see about him. In the meantime, you should rest."

She yawned again and stretched her arms above her head. "A nap would be fantastic. So would a shower. Is there one nearby?"

Old habits reared their ugly heads when he almost offered his personal facilities—and his assistance—but instead he nodded to his right. "You have an en suite bathroom through that door. And my room is right across the hall, should you find you require anything else from me."

Her grin returned. "I'm sure I'll manage, but thank you for everything."

"My pleasure, and I do hope you get some much-needed sleep filled with pleasant dreams."

No doubt he would be having a few pleasant—and inadvisable—dreams about her.

Four

At the sound of a crying baby, Piper awoke with a start. She tried to regain her bearings only to discover the room was too dark to see much of anything, leading her to fumble for the bedside lamp and snap it on.

Since she hadn't bothered to reset her watch after she showered, she didn't know the exact time, nor did she know how long she'd been sleeping. She did know that her once-damp hair had dislodged from the towel and her pink silk robe was practically wrapped around her neck.

After pushing off the bed, she immediately strode to the dresser to untangle her hair with a brush and to select appropriate clothing before setting off to see about Sam. But the continuous cries had her tightening the robe's sash as she left the room and plodded down the hall on bare feet.

She paused at the nursery to find the door ajar and a disheveled sheikh pacing the area, a very distressed son cradled in his arms. She strolled into the room, feeling slightly uneasy over her state of dress—or undress as the case might be. While she wore only a flimsy robe, he was dressed in a white T-shirt and faded jeans, his feet also bare. He looked tousled and sexy and, oh, so tempting…and she needed to shift her brain back into an appropriate gear. "Having problems?"

Adan paused the pacing to give her a forlorn look. "I have fed him twice and diapered him more times than I can possibly count, and he still continues to cry at the top of his lungs."

Taking pity on the prince, she walked up to him, took Sam from his grasp and began patting the baby's back. "Did you burp him?"

He lowered his gaze. "Actually, no, I did not."

"Then it's probably just a bubble in his tummy." She sat down in a nearby rocker, draped the baby horizontally over her knees and rubbed his back. "Did Talia happen to mention anything about colic?" she asked, and when he seemed confused, she launched into an explanation. "It's an odd occurrence that happens to some babies at the same time every night. Basically a stomachache that can't quite be explained. On a positive note, it eventually resolves itself, usually when they're around three months old."

He slid his hands into his pockets and approached her slowly. "I highly doubt Talia would have known if he had this problem. Are you certain it's not dangerous?"

He sounded so worried her heart went out to him. "No, it's not dangerous. But it's probably wise to have him checked out by a doctor as soon as possible, just to make sure he's healthy and growing at the right rate. And please tell me Talia left some sort of medical records with you."

"That much she did," he said. "My sister-in-law, who also happens to be the queen and head of our ministry of health, is a physician. I will have her examine Samuel as soon as she returns at the end of the week."

Although Sam's sobs had turned into sniffles, she continued to gently pat the baby's back in hopes of relieving his tummy distress. "It's good to have a doctor in the family. How do you think the king will take the news about Sam?"

Adan leaned a shoulder against the wall. "He is no stranger to scandal, so he has no reason to judge me."

She recalled reading a bit about that scandal during a pretravel internet search. "I remember seeing something about him marrying a divorced woman."

"Maysa is a remarkable woman," he said. "And say what you will about Rafiq's reputation for being rigid, at least he has been willing to bring the country into the twenty-first century. He had the elevator installed."

Piper thanked her lucky stars for that modern convenience. She also experienced more good fortune when the baby lifted his little head and let out a loud belch. "I believe Sam could use a warm bath now that his belly problem's solved. I can do it if you're too exhausted to take that on."

Finally, he smiled. "As long as you are there to guide me, I am a willing student."

Piper shifted Sam to her shoulder, pushed out of the chair and nodded toward the cupboard angled in the corner. "Elena said there are still some baby things in there. Take a look and see what we have available."

Adan strode to the large cabinet and opened the double doors, revealing shelves that housed numerous infant outfits and supplies. "If we do not have what we need here, then it does not exist."

She crossed the room to survey the bounty. "You could be right about that. And I see exactly what we need on the top shelf. Grab that blue tub and two towels. And next to that you'll see a small container with all the shampoo and stuff. Get that, too."

After Adan complied, he turned around, the bathing provisions balanced precariously in his arms. "Anything else?"

"Just show me to the sink and we'll bathe your little boy."

"In here," Adan said as he opened a door to his immediate right.

Piper stepped into the adjacent bath that was right out of an Arabian dream. The large double sink, with ornate gold fixtures, appeared to be made of copper. The shower to her left was composed of rich beige stones, much like the one in her guest suite, only she had access to a deep marble soaking tub. For a nursery she would deem it way over the top, but functional enough to bathe an infant.

"Lay the towels out on the vanity and put the tub in the sink," she instructed Adan. "Always make sure you have everything within reach."

"In case he climbs out of the bath?"

This time she laughed. "He won't, at least not at this age. Once he's too big for this setup, you'll bathe him in a regular tub."

He frowned. "I greatly look forward to that time."

"And it will be here before you know it." After he

had the supplies set out, she handed Sam to him. "Now lay him down and undress him while I test the water."

With the bath moderately filled and the baby undressed, she slid her hands beneath Sam and laid him gently in the tub. "You're on, Daddy."

Sam seemed to be thoroughly enjoying the process. His father—not so much. Yet Piper admired the care in which he bathed his son, though at times he seemed somewhat tentative, especially when it came to removing the infant from the tub.

"He's soaking wet," he said. "What if I drop him?"

In consideration of his inexperience, she picked up Sam beneath the arms, careful to support his head with her fingertips, and wrapped him securely in the hooded towel. "See how easy that was?"

"Easy for you," he said. "I will definitely need more practice."

"You'll definitely get that."

After carrying the baby back to the dressing table, Piper outfitted him in one-piece white footed pajamas. Sam was wide-eyed and more awake than she'd seen him to this point, and she automatically leaned over to kiss his cheek. "You're a happy baby now, aren't you, sweetie? You smell so good, too."

"And you are a natural mother, Piper McAdams."

She straightened to find Adan staring at her, a soft smile enhancing his gorgeous face. "I don't know about that, but I do love kids."

Without any prompting, he picked up his son and set him in the crook of his arm. "And I would say this lad is fairly taken with you. I cannot say that I blame him."

Piper felt heat rise to her face over the compliment and his nearness. "You're a great father, Adan. The two of you will make a good team for many, many years to come."

The pride in his expression was unmistakable. "I am determined to do my best by him. Yet I already sense bedtime could be an issue. He does not appear at all ready to sleep."

Piper checked the clock on the wall and noted the time at half past nine. "I had no idea it was that late. I slept through dinner."

He gestured toward the door. "By all means, return to your quarters and I will have a tray sent up."

She truly hated to leave him all alone on his first night as a father. "Are you sure? I'm really not that hungry." A patent lie. Sam's half-full bottle of formula set on the table was starting to look appetizing.

"I have to learn to do this by myself eventually," he said. "You need food and sleep to sustain you during our shopping trip tomorrow."

She sincerely looked forward to the outing. "All right, but please let me know if you need help with Sam at any point during the night."

He reached over and pushed a damp strand of hair from her cheek. "You have done more than your share, Piper. I cannot express how much I appreciate your guidance."

He had no idea how much she appreciated his willingness to take on raising a baby on his own. "It was my pleasure. And before I turn in for the night, I'll make a list of things you'll need for the baby."

He grinned, showing his dimples to full advantage. "Perhaps I should purchase a pack mule while we're out."

She shrugged. "As long as you don't mind showing your ass all over town."

His laugh was gruff and extremely sexy. "I would rather show my son off all over town, so we will forgo the mule for the moment."

Piper wanted to argue against creating too much attention to his newly discovered child, but Adan seemed so proud of Sam, she didn't dare discourage him. In twenty-six years, her own mother had never expressed that devotion, nor would she ever.

Besides, the possibility of another scandal would fall on the royal family's shoulders, and they'd most likely dealt with those issues before. And if they played their cards right, no one would discover the prince in disguise in their midst.

Piper would swear the store clerk had recognized Adan, even though he wore a New York Yankees baseball cap covering his dark hair, sunglasses covering his amber eyes, khaki cargo pants, black T-shirt and heavy boots. Not to mention he hadn't shaved that morning, evident by the light blanket of whiskers along his chin, upper lip and jaw. She definitely liked that rugged, manly look. A lot. And maybe that was what had garnered the young woman's attention—Adan's sheer animal magnetism.

Yes, that had to be it. Why else would she giggle when Adan leaned over the counter and handed her the supply list? Unfortunately Piper couldn't understand a word they were saying, which left her to guess. And she'd begun to assume the sheikh might be making a date.

The baby began to stir in the stroller they'd purchased on their first stop, drawing Piper's attention and giving her a valid excuse to interrupt the exchange. "I believe Sam is going to want a bottle very soon."

He pushed away from the counter and glanced at Sam, who looked as if he might be in precrying mode. "I believe you are correct. We should be finished here soon."

After Adan spoke to the clerk again, she disappeared into a back room and returned a few moments later with a scowling, middle-aged man carrying three cardboard boxes. He set the boxes down hard on the counter, then eyed Adan suspiciously before he sent Piper a clear look of contempt. She had no idea what they had done to warrant his disdain, but she was relieved when he disappeared into the back area again. After the young woman placed the clothing, toys and other provisions they'd selected into several bags, Adan counted out cash—a lot of cash—then smiled when his admirer fumbled with the receipt before she finally set it in his open palm.

Ready for a quick escape before the love-struck clerk fainted, Piper flipped her sunglasses back into place—and immediately saw a problem with transporting the items since the driver had parked in an alley two blocks away to avoid detection. "Looks like we're going to have to make several trips to get all of this to the car."

"I'll take care of that," Adan replied as he headed out the exit, leaving her behind with a fussy baby and a smitten cashier.

Piper could easily remedy one problem by giving Sam a bottle. While she was rummaging through the diaper bag to do that very thing, she noticed the grumpy guy standing behind the counter, staring at her. She immediately glanced down to make sure the sundress hadn't slipped down and exposed too much cleavage. Not the case at all. And when she scooped the baby from the stroller to feed him, he continued to look at her as if she was a scourge on society.

Fortunately Adan returned a few moments later, three teenage boys dressed in muslin tunics and pants trailing behind him. He handed them each a few bills, barked a few orders, and like a well-oiled human machine, the trio picked up the supplies, awaiting further instruction.

After opening the door, Adan made a sweeping gesture with one hand. "After you, fair lady."

"Thank you, kind sir, and please bring the stroller and the bag."

With Sam in her arms and the secret sheikh by her side, they stepped onto the stone sidewalk and traveled past clay-colored artisan shops and small eateries. The luscious scents of a nearby restaurant reminded Piper they hadn't yet had lunch. The way people stared at them reminded her of the overly stern guy in the store. "Did you notice how that older man in the boutique kept looking at us?" she asked Adan as she handed him the empty bottle, then brought Sam up to her shoulder.

He dropped the bottle back into the bag resting in the stroller without breaking his stride. "Some of Bajul's citizens are not particularly fond of foreigners."

That made sense. Sort of. "He actually seemed angry."

"Perhaps he noticed you were not wearing a ring and assumed we are unmarried with a child."

"He would be wrong on all counts."

Piper experienced a sudden melancholy over that fact. She'd learned long ago not to chase unattainable dreams, and wanting more from Adan would definitely qualify. She still wasn't sure she could entirely trust him, although he seemed to be making an effort to earn it. Even so, she was clearly in danger of becoming too close to the baby—and the baby's father.

As they rounded the corner and entered the alley, a series of shouts startled the sleeping baby awake. Sam began to cry and Piper began to panic when a crowd of people converged upon them on the way to the car. Most members of the press, she surmised when she noticed the microphones being thrust in Adan's face. She hadn't been able to understand the questions until one lanky blond English-speaking reporter stepped forward. "Whose child is this, Sheikh Mehdi?"

Overcome with the need to protect Adan, Piper responded without thought. "He's mine."

She managed to open the car door as the driver loaded the trunk, escaping the chaos. But she'd barely settled inside before the reporter blocked the prince's path. "Is the baby your bastard child?"

Adan grabbed the journalist by the collar with both hands. "The child is not a bastard," he hissed. "He is my son."

Piper saw a disaster in the making and had to intervene. "Adan, he's not worth it."

The reporter cut a look in her direction. "Is this woman your mistress?"

Adan pointed in her direction. "That woman is… She is…my wife."

Your wife? What were you thinking, Adan?"

He hadn't been thinking at all, only reacting. But after spending a good hour sitting on the veranda outside the nursery, that was all he had been doing. "The bloody imbecile insulted my child, and then he insulted you."

Piper yanked the chair opposite his back from the table and sat. "Telling the press we're married was a bit extreme, don't you agree?"

That extreme stemmed from wrath over the circumstance. "Had you not begun this debacle by claiming to be Samuel's mother, then I would not have had to defend yours and my son's honor."

She sent him a withering look. "For your information, I was simply trying to protect you from answering questions you weren't prepared to answer. I had no idea you were going tell the world you're Sam's father, nor did I have a clue you were going to have us living in wedded bliss."

"I believe that would be preferable to confirming you're nothing more than a mistress who bore my *bastard* child."

"What would have been wrong with letting everyone believe he's mine and leave it at that?"

His anger returned with the strength of a tempest. "I will not deny my son to anyone. Under any circumstance."

She blew an upward breath that ruffled her bangs. "Okay, it's obvious we're not going to get anywhere by playing the blame game. The question is, what are you going to do now? I don't think moving to Antarctica is a viable option with a month-old child."

The trip was beginning to appeal to him greatly. "If I refuse to comment further, the rumors will eventually die down."

She leaned back and released an acerbic laugh. "By the time Sam turns twenty?"

He recognized the absurdity in believing any scandal involving the Mehdi family would simply go away. "You're right. I will have to come up with some way to explain the situation. But I will not retract my statement regarding my son."

She appeared resigned. "I understand that, but you have to be worried Talia might find out someone else is pretending to be your son's mother, not to mention your wife. If she decides to come forward, everyone will know Sam's the result of a relationship out of wedlock and you lied about our marriage."

Since his ex was the consummate publicity hound, handing her that bone could prove to be problematic eventually. "To my good fortune, she's unreachable at the moment. I highly doubt she will hear any of this until she returns to France."

"Possibly, but I'm sure the king has heard by now and—" she streaked both hands down her face "—if my grandfather finds out, he'll demand I board the next plane bound for the Carolinas."

Despite what had transpired an hour ago, he still did not want her to leave for many reasons. "As far as I know, you have not yet been identified."

"I saw camera flashes."

"And you were wearing sunglasses. You could be any number of women who've crossed my path." He regretted the comment the moment it left his stupid mouth.

"All your ex-lovers?" she asked, her voice surprisingly calm.

He grasped for anything to dig himself out of the hole. "I meant any woman, whether I've slept with her or not. When you are constantly in the spotlight, your reputation becomes completely overblown. My brother Zain could attest to that. His reputation preceded him before he married Madison."

"I recall Elena mentioning they're in Los Angeles," she said. "Is his wife from the States?"

"Yes, and she is unequivocally the best thing that has ever happened to him. I sincerely never believed he would settle down with one woman."

She leaned back against the seat and began to toy with the diamond pendant dangling between her breasts. "Well, since I'm apparently just any woman, I suppose I shouldn't be worried at all. However, if I know the press, it's only a matter of time before they learn who I am."

Adan pushed out of the chair and moved to the veranda's edge to stare at the mountainous panorama he had always taken for granted. "It would be better for Samuel if everyone believed you are his mother, not Talia. She has quite a few skeletons in her dressing room closet."

Piper joined him and folded her arms atop the ledge. "Haven't we all in some way?"

He turned and leaned back against the stone wall. "I would have a difficult time believing you have anything scandalous to hide."

She smiled. "Well, apparently I gave birth and I haven't been exposed to sex in quite some time. That would be some fairly heavy fodder for the gossipmongers."

He shook his head and returned her smile. "It's good to see your wit is still intact."

"Hey, if you can't immediately fix a terrible situation, you might as well find some humor in it."

A true optimist. He added that to his ever-expanding

list of her attributes. "Do you consider the thought of being wed to me so terrible?"

"Actually, I can think of a few perks being married to you would provide."

He inched closer to her. "What perks do you have in mind?"

She faced him and folded her arms beneath her breasts. "Living in a palace immediately comes to mind."

Not at all what he'd wanted to hear. "That's it?"

"Who wouldn't want to be waited on hand and foot?"

He reached out and tucked her hair behind her ear. "I'm disappointed that's the best you can do."

She frowned. "If you want me to include your expertise as a lover, I can't speak to that because I don't know. Not that I didn't try my best to convince you to show me in your hotel room."

He still wanted to be her lover. More than he'd wanted anything in quite some time, aside from being a worthy father to his son. "Since the rest of the world now believes we've conceived a child together, perhaps we should give lovemaking serious consideration."

Her grin rivaled the sun setting on the horizon. "Procreation in reverse. I kind of like the thought of that, but..." Her words trailed off along with her gaze.

"You still doubt my honor." He hadn't been able to mask the disappointment in his tone.

"You're wrong," she said adamantly. "I realize now only an honorable man would so obviously love a child he just met. I see it every time you look at Sam."

Every time he looked at her, he felt things he could not explain, and shouldn't be feeling. "Then what would stop you from exploring our relationship on an intimate level, particularly when you were so bent on doing so in Chicago?"

"I'm taking your need for celibacy into consideration."

That vow was quickly becoming the bane of his existence. "I do not believe that to be the case."

She sighed. "Fine. Truth is, I don't want to get hurt."

He slid a fingertip along her jaw. "I would never do anything to hurt you, Piper."

"Not intentionally," she said. "But if we take that all-important step, I worry it's going to be too hard to walk away. And we both know I'll be walking away sooner than later."

Letting her walk away wouldn't be one of his finest moments, either. But he could make no promises. "I propose we continue with our original plan and learn all we can about each other while you're here. Anything beyond that will happen only if we mutually decide it's beneficial for both of us."

She tapped her chin and pretended to think. "A prince with benefits. That does sound intriguing."

He had resisted her long enough was his last thought before he reeled her into his arms and kissed her. She didn't reject the gesture at all. She didn't push him away or tense against him. She simply kissed him back like a woman who had not been kissed enough. And as usual, his body responded in a way that would merit a serious scolding from his former governess.

Bent on telling her what she was doing to him, he brought his lips to her ear. "If we had no care in the world, and all the privacy we needed, I would lift up your dress, lower your panties and take you right here."

She pulled back and stared at him with hazy eyes. "I could think of worse things."

He could think of something much better. "You deserve a bed and champagne and candles our first time."

"You're certainly not lacking in confidence."

Subtlety had never been his strongest suit. "Provided we decide to take that next step."

"Provided we could actually find the time to do it while adhering to your son's schedule."

Right on time, the sound of a crying baby filtered out through the nursery's open window. "I shall go see about him," he said without removing his hold or his gaze from her.

"I'll do it," she answered without making a single move.

"I already have."

Adan glanced to his right to see Elena strolling onto the terrace, his son in her arms, sending him away from Piper. "We were on our way."

Elena rolled her eyes. "You were on your way, all right, but that had nothing to do with the *bambino*."

Caught by the former nanny like a juvenile delinquent stealing candy from the market. "We shall take charge of him now."

Elena moved in front of him and smiled. "I will watch him for a while until you and Miss McAdams return."

"Where are we going?" Piper asked before he could respond.

"Your presence is requested in the conference room. Both of you."

Perhaps the first information from the engineers, although he had a difficult time believing they'd have anything significant to report in such a short time. "Shouldn't we wait to meet with the conservation crew until after Rafiq returns?"

"Rafiq arrived a few minutes ago," Elena said. "He called the meeting."

Damn it all to hell. He'd been summoned to take his place in the king's hot seat. "Did he happen to mention anything about water conservation?"

"I would speculate he's interested in conserving the military commander in chief's reputation." Elena cradled the baby closer and patted Adan's arm. "Good luck, *cara*. You are absolutely going to need it."

Depending on what his brother had in store for him, he could very well need to call out the royal guard.

Five

Dead silence—Piper's first impression the minute she followed Adan into the conference room for the so-called meeting. And she had no doubt she knew exactly what was on the agenda—quite possibly her head delivered to her personally by the king of Bajul.

He wore a black silk suit, dark gray tie and a definite air of authority. His coal-colored eyes and near-black hair would qualify him as darkly handsome, and somewhat intimidating. *Very* intimidating, Piper realized when he pushed back from the head of the mahogany table and came to his feet. Adan might be an inch or so taller, but his brother's aura of sheer power made him seem gigantic.

The mysterious Mr. Deeb stood nearby, absently studying his glasses before he repositioned them over his eyes. "Please join us," he said, indicating the two chairs on each side of the stoic monarch.

Adan had already settled in before Piper had gathered enough courage to walk forward. She could do this. She could face Rafiq Mehdi with a calm head and feigned confidence. Or she could turn and run.

Choosing the first option for diplomacy's sake, she claimed the chair opposite Adan as the king sat and folded his hands before him on the tabletop. "It is a pleasure to meet you, Ms. McAdams," he began, "though I would have preferred to have done so under different circumstances."

She would have preferred not to meet him at all today, if ever. Sucking up seemed like a fantastic idea. "The pleasure is all mine, Your Excellency. My grandfather has said some wonderful things about your leadership. And you may call me Piper."

"And you may address me as Rafiq, since it seems you have become a part of the royal family without my knowledge."

Piper swallowed hard around her chagrin. "Actually, that's not—"

"Are you going to jump to conclusions without hearing our side of the story, Rafiq?" Adan asked, a serious hint of impatience in his tone.

The king leaned back and studied them both for a moment. "I am giving you the opportunity now."

"I have a son," Adan said. "That whole wife issue was simply a misunderstanding, and that is all there is to the story."

Rafiq released a gruff laugh. "I fear you are wrong about that, brother. I know this because I have heard the entire sordid tale. And I do believe that included you delivering the 'wife' proclamation yourself."

Piper noticed an immediate change in Adan's demeanor. He definitely didn't appear quite as confident as he had when they'd entered the room. She had to come to his defense due to her contribution to the mess. "Your Excellency, I'm in part responsible for—"

Adan put up a hand to silence her. "It was simply an error in judgment on both our parts. We were attempting to protect each other and my son."

"Yet instead you have created a scandal at a time when we are trying to convince our people this conservation project is worthwhile," Rafiq replied. "Their attention has now been diverted from the need to relocate some of the farms to an illegitimate child born to the man in charge of protecting our borders."

"Never use that word to describe my son again," Adan hissed. "I may not have known about him, but he is every bit a Mehdi."

Rafiq looked extremely surprised. "I never thought of you as being the paternal sort, Adan. That being said, it is my understanding his true mother is the narcissistic Talia Thorpe."

Evidently the royal family and staff held the model in very low esteem. "That's true," Piper interjected before she could be cut off again. "I was simply pretending to be the baby's mother to delay the questions over his parentage."

"Yet everyone now believes you are his mother," Rafiq replied. "That has created quite the dilemma."

"I promise you I will handle this," Adan said. "I will retract the marriage statement and explain that Samuel is my child from a previous relationship."

Rafiq straightened and scowled. "You will do no such thing."

Adan exchanged a look with Piper before bringing his attention back to his brother. "You would have us continue the lie?"

"As a matter of fact, that is exactly what you will do," Rafiq began, "until you find some way to be rid of the model, for both yours and your heir's sake. Naming her as the mother will only wreak more havoc. The woman is known for posing in the nude in several photographs."

The king's condescension ruffled Piper's artistic feathers. "Some do not find nudity offensive. It would depend on what the photographer was attempting to convey."

"Centerfold photos," Adan added. "She posed for several magazines, in print and online. Some of those publications are obscure and questionable at best."

That did change everything from an artistic stand-point. "Are they widely circulated here?"

Adan looked somewhat sheepish. "After word got out that we were involved."

The king turned his full attention to her. "Ms. Mc-Adams, if you would kindly continue the charade until your departure, then we will make certain you are compensated."

She could not believe someone was offering to pay her for a humongous fib that could alter her own life. "No offense, Your Excellency, but I can't in good conscience accept money for my silence."

"Temporary silence," the king added. "And I was not suggesting a bribe. However, I will award the contract to your corporation upon review of the bid. Once you have returned to the States, we will issue a statement saying you felt it best that the marriage be dissolved on the basis of irreconcilable differences, and that you feel your son should live in his homeland."

"And what do you propose we do with Talia?" Adan asked. "Bind and gag her before she leaks the truth to the media?"

"*She* we will have to pay," Rafiq stated. "I am certain it will cost a fortune to have her relinquish her rights as well as execute a legal document forbidding her to have any claim on the child. Fortunately, you have the means to meet her price, however high that might be."

Adan released a weary sigh. "Rafiq, this could all backfire no matter how carefully we plan. Talia could refuse to meet our terms, and furthermore, the truth may surface no matter how hard we try to conceal it."

"I trust that you and Ms. McAdams will see that does not happen."

The man was making too many impossible demands as far as Piper was concerned. "How do you propose we do that when you risk someone within these walls leaking that information?"

"The staff normally practices absolute discretion," Rafiq said, mirroring Adan's words from the day they discovered Sam existed. "Yet it would be foolish not to believe someone with lesser responsibility in the palace could sell the information to the highest bidder. Therefore it is paramount you both act as if you are a wedded couple at all times. We will issue a press release stating you were married at an undisclosed location prior to the pregnancy."

As she regarded Adan, Piper couldn't quite contain her sarcasm. "Would that be all right with you, dear?"

He shook his head. "None of this is right, but I do believe it is a viable plan, at least for the time being."

She saw her control over the situation begin to slip away. "Do I have any say in the matter?"

"Yes you do," Rafiq said. "You are free to refuse and leave immediately. With your company's crew."

A not-so-veiled threat. She mulled over a laundry list of pros and cons while Adan and the king waited for her answer. If she didn't agree, they would lose the contract, and that could send the struggling business into a free fall. If she did agree, she would have to stay on for at least a month immersed in a massive lie. And most important, she would be charged with contacting her grandparents to break the news before someone else did. She could only imagine her grandfather's reaction to either scenario. Then again, if she went along with the marriage pretense, she'd have the opportunity to stand up to him once and for all if he gave her any grief. She could finally be her own person and control her own life—for at least a month. Not a bad thing, at that.

A few more seconds ticked off while she weighed her options. The one bright spot she could see coming out of this entire debacle had directly to do with Adan. Being his make-believe spouse could come with some serious perks.

She drew in a deep breath, let it out slowly and said, "I'll do it."

Adan looked caught completely off guard. "You will?"

"I will." She rose from the chair and managed a smile. "Now, if you gentlemen would please excuse me, this pretend wife needs to make a call to her very real grandparents."

Adan stood and returned her smile. "Feel free to use my private study next door."

"Thanks. I believe I will."

Piper did an about-face, strode into the hall and prepared to lie.

"Have you totally lost your ever-lovin' mind, sweet pea?"

Oh, how she hated her grandfather's pet name for her. But Piper had to admit she was enjoying his shock. She'd never seriously shocked anyone in her sheltered life up to this point, at least not to this extreme. "No, Poppa, I'm quite sane. I would have told you sooner about the marriage but it was rather spontaneous." And pure fiction.

"When did you meet this character?"

Lie number one. "Quite a while ago, when I was in the U.K. last year."

"And you didn't bother to tell me this when you knew full well I was sending you to his country? That dog just don't hunt."

Lie number two. "We've kept our relationship quiet because we didn't want other contractors thinking I could influence the bidding process."

"And you don't have an influence over the bid now that you've gotten yourself hitched to him, sweet pea?"

Lie number three. "Not at all."

A span of silence passed before he responded. "I guess there's nothing I can do about it now, but at least it's good to know he's got royal blood and money to burn."

Of course that would be Walter McAdams's main concern when it came to her choice in a life partner. It always had been. "I'm sure when you met him back in Chicago you realized he's a very charming man."

"A charming snake," he muttered. "Of course, your grandmother's all atwitter over this. She wants to talk to you, so hang on a minute."

Piper heard him put down the receiver, followed by muffled conversation before someone picked up the phone again. "My little sugar plum is a married woman!"

Enough with the overly sweet endearments, she wanted to say, but kept her impatience in check. "Yes, Nana, I finally took the plunge." Headlong into a humongous fabricated fairy tale.

"I saw a picture of him on the internet, Piper. My, my, he's a good-looking young man. When did you two meet?"

Piper was frankly sick to death of fibbing, so she decided to try on the truth. "In a hotel bar. I attempted to seduce him but he didn't take the bait. He's quite the gentleman."

As usual, her grandmother giggled like a schoolgirl, a good indicator she didn't believe what she'd heard. "Oh, child, you are still such a cutup when it comes to boys. And you don't have to tell me any details right now."

But she did have to tell her more truths. "Nana, Adan is a very public figure, so you might hear a few rumors that aren't exactly accurate."

"What kind of rumors?" she asked with obvious concern.

She could trust her grandmother with some of the facts, even if the woman was a little too steeped in Southern society. "First, you have to promise me that whatever I tell you, it has to remain strictly confidential."

"Sugar, you know how I abhor gossip."

An advantage for Piper in this gossip game. "All right. You're probably going to hear that we've had a baby together."

Nana released an audible gasp. "Did you?"

Heavens, the woman wasn't thinking straight. "Do you recall me even remotely looking pregnant over the past few months?"

"Well, no."

"Precisely, because I wasn't. Adan does have an infant son, but obviously I'm not his mother. That said, as far as the world knows, Samuel is my baby. The biological mother's identity is a well-kept secret and has to remain so for reasons I can't reveal."

"Is she an actress? Maybe a singer? Oh, wait. Is she a call girl?"

Piper had no idea Drusilla McAdams even knew what that was. "Don't worry about it. I just need you to refuse to comment on anything if any reporters track you and Poppa down, and keep everything I've told you to yourself. Can you do that, Nana?"

"I certainly can, sugar plum," she said. "And I'm so proud of you, sweetie. It's admirable you're willing to take another woman's child and raise it as your own."

"I learned that from you, Nana."

A span of silence passed before her grandmother spoke again. "I have never regretted raising you and your sister, Piper. I do regret that Millie could never be a decent mother to you. But that's mine and your Poppa's fault. We spoiled her too much, maybe even loved her too much. She never had a care in the world aside from herself."

She still didn't as far as Piper could tell. She'd barely even seen her fly-by-night mother over the past few years, let alone established a relationship with her. "You were very good to me and Sunny, Nana. Millie is responsible for her behavior, not you. And I don't believe you can ever love anyone too much."

"Only if they can't possibly love you back, honey."

Her grandmother's words gave her some cause for concern. If she happened to stupidly fall in love with Adan, she wondered if he had the capacity to return her feelings. Probably not, and she certainly didn't intend to find out. Sadly, sometimes intentions went awry. "Look, Nana, I have a few things to do, but first, do you have any questions for me?" Piper held her breath and hoped for a no.

"Yes I do. How is the sheikh when it comes to… you know?"

Regretfully Piper hadn't experienced "you know"… yet. "Nana, a girl's gotta have her secrets, so I'll only say I'm not at all disappointed." Should she and Adan take that lovemaking step, she would wager she wouldn't be disappointed in the least.

"That's a good thing, sugar plum. What goes on between the sheets better be good if you want to sustain a relationship. Your grandfather and I have been happily going after—"

"I'd better go." Before they wandered into too-much-information territory. "I'll talk to you both real soon."

"Okay, but your grandfather told me to deliver a message before you hang up, the old grump."

Lovely. "What is it?"

"Married or not, you still have a job to do, and he expects a full report on the survey crew's progress within the next two days."

So much for spending time with father and son. For the time being, Adan would just have to go it alone.

"Congratulations, Dad. Your baby is the picture of health."

Adan turned from the crib to face Maysa Barad Mehdi—Arabian beauty, American-educated premiere physician and current queen of Bajul. "Are you absolutely certain? He seems rather small to me."

His sister-in-law sent him a sympathetic look, much to his chagrin. "He's not quite five weeks old, Adan, so he's going to be small. Fortunately Ms. Thorpe had the foresight to include copies of his medical records since his birth. He's gaining weight at a favorable pace and I expect that to continue." She paused and sent him a smile. "And before you know it, he will have a playmate."

Clearly the woman had taken leave of her senses. "I have no intention of having another child in the near future, if ever." First, he would have to have a willing partner, and his thoughts immediately turned to Piper. With her he wouldn't be seeking procreation, only practice. As much practice as she would allow, if she allowed any at all after being thrust into Rafiq's harebrained scheme.

"Let me rephrase that," Maysa said. "Samuel will have a new cousin in a little less than eight months."

Adan let that sink in for a moment before he responded, "You're pregnant?"

"Yes, I am."

He gave her a fond embrace. "Congratulations to you, as well. How is Rafiq handling impending parenthood?"

Her expression turned somber. "He is worried to death, though he tries not to show it."

"That's understandable considering the accident." The freak car accident that had claimed Rafiq's former wife and unborn child. A horrific event that had turned his brother into a temporary tyrant. "I'm certain he will relax eventually."

She frowned. "Did you only recently meet Rafiq, Adan? The man does not know the first thing about relaxing. I only hope he calms somewhat before the birth. Otherwise we'll have a fretful child."

He couldn't imagine Rafiq remaining calm under such a stressful situation. "Perhaps having Samuel around will demonstrate that tending to an infant isn't rocket science. If I can manage it, then certainly so will he."

She patted his cheek. "And you are doing very well from what I hear."

Curiosity and concern drove him to ask, "What else have you heard?"

"If you're wondering if I know about the presumed marriage, I do. My husband told me you could not have chosen a more suitable counterfeit wife." She accentuated the barb with a grin.

He found little humor in the current state of affairs. "This entire situation reeks of fraud, and I find it appalling that I've drawn Piper into that web of deceit. She's a remarkable woman and deserves much better."

Maysa inclined her head and studied him a few moments. "You sound as if you care a great deal for her."

More than he would ever let on—to Piper or to himself. "I've only known her a few days, yet I admittedly like what I do know."

"It shows," she said. "Your face lights up at the mention of her name."

A complete exaggeration. "Women always seem to imagine things that aren't there," he muttered. "Just because I am fond of her does not mean I see her as anything other than my unwitting partner in crime." But he could see her as his lover, as he had often in his fantasies. "I certainly have no plans to make this marriage real."

"We'll see," Maysa said as she covered the now-sleeping infant with the blanket. "One never knows what will transpire once intimacy is involved."

"I am not sleeping with her, Maysa," he said, a little too defensively. "And as it stands now, that is not on the to-do list." At least not on the one he wasn't hiding.

Maysa flipped a lock of her waist-length hair over one shoulder. "Adan, when you do not have an agenda that includes bedding a woman, then the world has truly spun on its axis."

If he had his way, someday people would see him as more than a womanizer. They would see him as a good father. "As always, dear queen, you are correct, at least partially. I would be telling a tale if I said I had not considered consummating our relationship. She's beautiful and intelligent and possesses a keen wit. She is also in many ways an innocent. For that reason I have vowed not to take advantage of her trusting nature."

"Perhaps you should explore the possibilities," she said. "And I do not mean in a sexual sense. You should take this time to get to know her better. You might be pleasantly surprised at what you learn."

Exactly as he had promised both himself and Piper—getting to know each other better before they took the next step. That was before he'd learned he had a son. "I see several problems with that prospect. Being charged with Samuel's care is taxing and time-consuming. Commanding the whole bloody Royal Air Force doesn't require as much attention."

Maysa began returning supplies to her black doctor's bag resting on the dressing table where she'd performed the examination on his son. "Then perhaps you will be happy to know my husband has instructed me to tell you to take your bride away for two days for a respite."

Adan firmly believed his brother had taken leave of his senses. "Why would he suggest that?"

She snapped the bag closed and turned toward him. "He's trying to buy more time, Adan. The media have already been hounding him for an interview with you, and it will only become worse once the palace releases an official statement later today. Rafiq feels that if he tells them you're away for a brief holiday, they'll let up for the time being. And considering Samuel's age, this would be the appropriate time for you to resume your husbandly duty."

He could not resume a duty he had yet to undertake. However, the prospect of spending more time with his presumed wife was greatly appealing, yet he could not ignore the obvious issues. "I cannot abandon Samuel."

"I am sure Elena would wholeheartedly step in while you're gone."

"Actually, she wouldn't," he said. "She's made it quite clear that she is handing all the responsibility to me."

"Then I will watch him until you return. And you are more than welcome to take your new wife to the resort."

He had his own secluded resort equipped with a pool where they could spend some quality time. Then again, swimming with Piper would involve very little clothing. Not a good scenario for a man who for months had engaged in sexual deprivation in order to build character. At the moment, he had enough character to rival philanthropists worldwide. "I certainly appreciate your offer, but I would not want to burden you with my responsibility."

"It's not a burden at all," Maysa said as she leaned over and touched the top of Samuel's head. "I consider it an opportunity to practice parenthood. Now, hurry along while you still have the better part of the day."

A plan began to formulate in Adan's brain. A good plan involving his favorite mode of transportation. Now all he had to do was convince Piper to come along for the ride of her life.

After the harrowing trip to the airbase, Piper would be out of her mind if she agreed to go on this little flying excursion in the miniplane built for two. "You don't really believe I'm going to climb into that sardine can, do you?"

Adan flipped his aviators up to rest atop his head and tried to grin his way out of trouble, which wasn't going to work on Piper. Much. "This happens to be a very solid aircraft," he said.

Solid, maybe. Too tiny. Definitely. "First, you make me wear a massive helmet, throw me onto the back of a motorcycle and travel at excessive speeds on skinny little back roads to get here—"

"That was designed to evade the press, and if my memory serves me correctly, you came along willingly."

Darn it, she had. "That's not the point. Now you want me to get into a plane equivalent to a golf cart with wings."

He moved in front of said wing and patted the white plane's belly as if it were a favored pet. "Do not let the propeller scare you away. This is a Royal Air Force training craft meticulously maintained by our best mechanics. And of course, you are in good hands with me as your personal pilot."

A personal pilot with great hands, and she sure would like to know how they would feel all over her body. Maybe today she might actually find out. Maybe squeezing into this plane would be well worth it. "Just show me to my seat."

He grinned and opened the miniature door. "Hand over your bag and I will assist you."

Piper relinquished the tote to Adan, as well as her coveted control. "Here you are, and be careful with it because it contains some breakable items."

His smile melted into a scowl. "This bag must weigh ten pounds. Did you pack all your worldly belongings?"

She playfully slapped at his biceps, well aware he had one heck of a muscle. "No, I did not. I just packed a swimsuit and a change of clothes, per your request. I also brought along a few toiletries and sunscreen and towels. And a small sketch pad and pencils, in case I want to immortalize our day together on paper."

His smile returned full force. "It is quite possible you will not have time to sketch."

That sounded very promising. "And why would that be, Your Highness?"

He leaned over and brushed a kiss across her cheek. "Well, my pretend princess, I have several activities planned to occupy our time."

She could think of only one activity at the moment that interested her. "Can you give me a hint?"

"No. I want you to be surprised." He executed a slight bow. "Now climb into my chariot, fair lady, and we will begin our adventure."

She managed a not-half-bad curtsy. "As you wish, good sir."

Luckily the step up into the two-seater plane wasn't all that steep, but the small space seemed somewhat claustrophobic once Adan took his place beside her.

After strapping himself in, he handed her a headset. "Put this on and we'll be able to hear each other over the engine noise."

Noisy engine—not good. "Are you sure this is safe?" she asked before she covered her ears.

"Positive. And don't look so worried. We'll barely be off the ground before it's time to land again."

"A planned landing, I hope," she muttered as she adjusted the bulky headphones.

From that point forward, Piper watched Adan in action as he guided the pitiful excuse for a plane to the airstrip adjacent to the fleet of high-powered jets. As he did a final check, the Arabic exchange between Adan and the air traffic controller sounded like gibberish to her. But once he began to taxi down the runway, she didn't care if the pilot was speaking pig Latin. She held her breath, fisted her hands in her lap, gritted her teeth and closed her eyes tightly.

During liftoff, her stomach dipped as if she were riding a roller coaster. She felt every bump and sway as they gained altitude, and even when the plane seemed to level off, she still refused to look.

"You are missing some incredible scenery."

Feeling somewhat foolish, Piper forced herself to peer out the window at the terrain now cast in the midmorning sun. She noticed only a few man-made structures dotting the landscape, but the approaching mountains looked as if she could reach out and touch them, and that did nothing for her anxiety.

As if sensing her stress, Adan reached over the controls and took her hand. "This is the best view of my country," he said. "And when I am flying, I feel completely at peace."

She wished she could say the same for herself. "I've got a swarm of butterflies in my belly."

"I had no idea you're such a nervous flier."

"Not usually," she said. "I've never been in an aircraft quite this small before."

"Try to think of this as being as close to heaven as you can possibly be."

"I'd prefer not to get too much closer."

He grinned and squeezed her hand. "I will have you earthbound in a matter of minutes. If you look straight ahead, you'll see where we are going to land."

She tried to focus on the horizon, and not the descent toward the ground. Or the fact Adan was guiding them toward what appeared to be no more than a glorified dirt road—and a rather large mountain not far away. Her stomach dipped along with the plane as they approached the makeshift runway, but this time she kept her eyes open. She still remained as tense as a tightrope when the wheels touched down and they bounced a time or two before coming to a stop.

Piper let out the breath she'd been holding and looked around to find a thick copse of odd-looking trees surrounding them, but no signs of human life. "Where are we?"

Adan removed his headset, then hers, and smiled. "I am about to show you my most favorite place on the planet, and an experience you will not soon forget."

Six

"Wow."

Piper's wide-eyed reaction to the mountain retreat greatly pleased Adan. He'd brought only one other woman there, and she'd complained incessantly about the lack of facilities. But then Talia wasn't fond of sacrificing creature comforts for nature's bounty.

"It's basically a simple structure," he explained as he led her farther into the lone living area. "It's comprised of native wood and powered by solar energy. The water comes from the nearby lake to the house through a filtering system."

She walked to the sofa and ran her fingertips along the back of the black leather cushion. "It's very comfortable and cozy."

Her code for small, he surmised. "It has all one would require in this setting. One loft bedroom and a bath upstairs, another bedroom and bath downstairs, and my study."

She turned and smiled. "No kitchen?"

He pointed to his left. "Behind the stone wall, and it's the most impressive part of the house. However, I rarely utilize the stove, but I do make good use of the refrigerator and microwave."

"No housekeeper available?"

"No, but I do have a caretaker. He and his wife look after the place when I'm away."

She dropped down onto the beige club chair and curled her legs beneath her. "What possessed you to build a place out in the middle of nowhere?"

"You will soon see." After setting her bag on the bamboo floor, Adan crossed the room and pushed aside the drapes, revealing the mountainous terrain.

"Wow again," Piper said as she came to his side. "A view and your own private pool. I'm impressed."

He slid double doors open, bringing the outdoors inside. "This greatly expands the living space. And you'll appreciate the scenery far better from the veranda."

She smiled. "Then lead the way."

When Piper followed him onto the deck containing an outdoor kitchen and several tables with matching chairs, Adan paused at the top of the steps leading to the infinity pool. "This glorified bathtub took two years to build."

"It's absolutely incredible."

So was this woman beside him. He sat on the first step and signaled her to join him. Once she complied, he attempted not to notice the way her white shorts rode up her thighs, or the cleavage showing from the rounded neck in her sleeveless coral top that formed to her breasts very nicely. "This has always been my sanctuary of sorts. A good place to escape."

She took her attention from the water and turned it on him. "Exactly what are you escaping, Adan?"

He'd asked himself that question many times, and the answers were always the same. "I suppose the drudgery of being a royal. Perhaps the responsibility of overseeing an entire military operation. At one time, my father."

The final comment brought about her frown. "Was he that hard on you?"

He sighed. "No. He wasn't particularly concerned with what I did. I once believed he'd never quite recovered from losing my mother." That was before he'd learned his father's secrets.

"You mentioned your mother when we were in Chicago," she began, "but you didn't say what happened to her. Of course, if it makes you uncomfortable to talk about it, I understand."

Oddly, he wanted to tell her about his mother, what little he knew of Cala Mehdi. He wanted to tell her many things he'd never spoken of to anyone. And eventually he would tell her their visit would be extended beyond the afternoon. "Her death was a mystery of sorts. She was found at the bottom of the mountain near the lake. Most believed she'd taken a fall. Some still wonder if she'd taken her own life due to depression following my birth. I've accepted the fact I'll never know the truth."

"Are you sure you've accepted it?"

It was as if she could see straight to his soul. "I have no choice. My father never spoke of her. But then, he rarely spoke to me. Perhaps I reminded him too much of her."

"At least you actually knew your real father."

"Not necessarily." The words spilled out of his stupid mouth before he'd had time to reel them back in.

She shifted slightly toward him and laid a palm on his arm. "Are you saying the king wasn't your biological father?"

He saw no reason to conceal his concerns now that he'd taken her into his confidence. "I only know I do not resemble him or my brothers. My hair is lighter and so are my eyes."

"That's not definitive proof, Adan," she said. "Maybe you look like your mother."

"I've seen a few photographs, and I see nothing of me in her. She had almost jet-black hair and extremely dark eyes, like Rafiq."

"If that's the case, then why would you think someone else fathered you?"

"Because my mother was reportedly very unhappy, and I suspect she could have turned to another man for comfort. Rafiq's former wife, Rima, did that very thing due to her own discontent with the marriage."

"Are you certain you're not speculating because of Rafiq's situation?"

He had valid reasons for his suspicions, namely his father's two-decade affair with the governess. Yet he had no intention of skewing Piper's opinion of Elena by revealing the truth yet. "My parents' marriage was arranged, as tradition ordained it. Marriage contracts are basically business arrangements, and in theory advantageous for both families. Unfortunately, when human emotions enter into the mix, the intent behind the agreement becomes muddled."

She frowned. "You mean emotions as in *love?*"

"Yes. The motivating force behind many of the world's ills."

"And the cure for many more."

She didn't sound pleased with his assessment. She had sounded somewhat wistful. "Spoken like a true romantic."

"Spoken like a diehard cynic," she said. "But your cynical days could soon be over now that you have a baby. There is no greater love than that which exists between parent and child, provided the parent is open to that love."

That sounded somewhat like an indictment to his character. "I have already established that bond with my son. But I have never welcomed romantic love for lack of a good example." And for fear of the inability to live up to unreasonable expectations.

She inclined her head and studied him. "Love isn't something you always have to work at, Your Highness. Sometimes it happens when you least expect it."

Piper sounded as if she spoke of her own experiences. "Have you ever been in love?" he asked.

"Not to this point." She glanced away briefly before bringing her attention back to him. "Do arranged marriages still exist in the royal family?"

Happily for him, the answer was no. "That requirement changed after Rafiq inherited the crown. Otherwise he would not have been able to marry a divorced woman. All the better. It was an illogical and worthless tradition, in my opinion."

She offered him a sunny smile that seemed somehow forced. "Well, I guess we really bucked tradition by arranging to have a fake marriage."

At the moment he'd like to have a fake honeymoon, yet he still had reservations. Piper had accommodated the king's wishes by joining in the ruse, and she'd self-lessly helped care for his son. He never wanted her to believe he would take advantage of the situation. "Quite frankly, all this talk of family dysfunction is making me weary." He stood and offered his hand. "Would you care to go for a swim?"

"Yes, I most definitely would," she said as she allowed him to help her up. "But are you sure you're up to it? You look tired, and I suspect that has to do with Sam."

"He was awake quite a bit last night and I had the devil of a time getting him back to sleep after the two o'clock feeding. Yet I grew accustomed to little sleep while training for my military duties."

"Why didn't you wake me? I would have taken a shift."

"Because my child is my responsibility, not yours." He immediately regretted the somewhat callous remark and set out to make amends. "I definitely appreciate all that you've done, but I do not want to take advantage of your generosity."

She attempted a smile that failed to reach her blue eyes. "I really don't mind, Adan. What are fake mothers for?"

He could always count on her to use humor to cover her hurt. Hurt that he had caused. "We'll worry about Samuel's care when we return in two days."

Her mouth momentarily dropped open. "Two days? I thought you said this was an afternoon outing."

He endeavored to appear guileless. "Did I?"

She doomed him to hell with a look. "You did."

"My apologies. As it turns out, we have been instructed by the king to remain absent from the palace for two days to avoid the media frenzy. I do think it's best we return tomorrow before sundown. I do not want to be away from Samuel two nights."

"But my grandfather ordered me to see that the engineers finalize the—"

"Bid, and that has been handled by Rafiq. He has accepted, and the contract will be couriered to your grandfather tomorrow. He has also arranged for the engineers to be transported to the States in the morning."

She threaded her lip between her teeth as she took several moments before speaking. "Then I guess everything has been handled."

"Yes, which frees you to relax and see to your own pleasure. Nonetheless, if you insist on returning early, we shall."

This time her smile arrived fully formed. "Where should I change to get this two-day party started?"

He caught her hands and brushed a kiss across her knuckles. "Never change, Piper McAdams. I like you exactly the way you are."

She wrested away, much to his disappointment. "I meant 'change' as in clothes. I need to put on my swimsuit."

He preferred she'd go without any clothes. "You may use the bath downstairs. You'll find it between my study and the guest room, immediately past the kitchen. Or if you prefer, use the one upstairs adjacent to my bedroom. It's much larger."

"Where are you going to change?"

"I hadn't planned on wearing anything at all." He couldn't contain his laughter when he noticed her shocked expression. "I'm not serious, so do not look so concerned. My swim trunks are upstairs."

She began backing toward the entry. "I'll use the downstairs bath while you go upstairs. And I'd better not find you naked in that pool when I come back."

The word *naked* put specific parts of his anatomy on high alert. "At one time that might have been the case, but I have turned over a new leaf."

She paused at the doors and eyed him suspiciously. "A leaf from the player tree?"

He supposed he deserved that. "Believe what you will, but there have not been that many women in my life. None since I ended my relationship with Talia."

"Ah, yes. The celibacy clause. How's that working out for you?"

Not very well at the moment. Not when he knew in a matter of moments he would see her with very little covering her body. Or so he hoped. "I will let you know by day's end."

As soon as she returned to the pool, Piper found Adan staring out over the horizon. She couldn't see his face or eyes, but she sensed his mind was on something else—or someone else, namely his child. Her mind immediately sank into the gutter when she shamelessly studied all the details from his bare, well-defined back to his impressive butt concealed by a pair of navy swim trunks.

She approached him slowly, overwhelmed by the urge to run her hands over the patently male terrain. Instead, she secured the towel knotted between her breasts. "I'm fairly sure that mountain won't move no matter how long you stare at it."

He turned to her, his expression surprisingly somber. "If only I had that power."

Once she moved past the initial shock of seeing his gorgeous bare chest, she found her voice. "Are you worried about Sam?"

"I'm worried that my position will prevent me from being a good father to him. I'm also concerned that perhaps I would be wrong to ask Talia to give up all claims on him."

"No offense, Adan, but I don't see Talia as the motherly type."

"Perhaps so, but isn't any mother better than no mother at all?"

"Not really," she said without thought. "My so-called mother never cared about her daughters. Her own needs took precedence over ours. Luckily for us, my grandmother willingly stepped in and gave us all the love we could ask for, and more. Otherwise I don't know how we would have turned out."

He brushed his knuckles over her cheek. "You have turned out very well. And now if you would kindly remove that towel, we'll spend the afternoon basking in the Bajul sun."

That would be the logical next step—revealing her black bikini that left little to the imagination. A step that required some advance preparation. "Before I do that, you need to know I'm not tall and skinny like Talia. I'm short and I haven't been blessed with a lean build and—"

He flipped the knot with one smooth move and the towel immediately fell to the ground. Then he gave her a lingering once-over before raising his gaze back to her eyes. "You have been blessed with a beautiful body, Piper. You have the curves this man desires."

He desired her curves? Incredible. "Your physique is the thing fantasies are made of. But the question is, how well do you swim? I have to warn you, I'm pretty darned good at it."

And without giving her any warning, he strode to the far end of the pool and executed a perfect dive. He emerged a few moments later, slicked back his hair and smiled. "Now it's your turn to prove your expertise."

If only she could stop gaping at his dimples and get her feet to move. Finally she willed herself to follow his lead by moving to the same spot he had and doing a little diving of her own. After her eyes adjusted, she sought Adan out where he now stood in the shallow end. She remained underwater until she swam immediately in front of him and came up for air. "How's that?"

"Perfect," he said as he put his arms around her. "As are you."

She laughed even though she could barely concentrate while being up close and personal. "Not hardly, Your Majesty. I can be stubborn and I do have a little bit of a temper at times. I'm also a picky eater and I speed when I drive—"

He cut off her laundry list of faults with a kiss. A kiss so hot it rivaled the sun beating down on her shoulders. A down-and-dirty, tongue-dueling kiss that had Piper heating up in unseen places on her person. When he streamed his palms along her rib cage and grazed the side of her breast, she thought she might melt. When he returned his hands to her shoulders, she thought she might groan in protest.

He studied her eyes with an intensity that stole what was left of her breath. "Before this continues, I need to say something."

She needed him to get on with it. "I'm listening."

"I want to make love to you, more than anything I have wished for in some time. But you are under no obligation to honor that request."

Was he kidding? "If I remember correctly, I went to your hotel room in Chicago with that one goal in mind. Of course, where I wanted to end my celibacy, you were determined to hang on to yours."

"Not anymore," he said. "Not since the day I met you, actually. You are different from any woman I have ever known."

"Is that a good thing?"

"A very good thing."

"Then let's put an end to doing without right here and now."

He gave her an unmistakable bad-boy grin. "Take off your suit."

"You go first," she said, suddenly feeling self-conscious.

"All right." He quickly removed the trunks and tossed them aside, where they hit the cement deck with a splat. "Your turn."

After drawing in a deep breath, she reached back and released the clasp, then untied the bow at her neck. Once she had that accomplished, she threw the top behind her, her bare breasts no longer concealed by the water. "Better?"

"Yes, but you're not finished yet."

Time to go for broke. Piper shimmied her bottoms down her legs and kicked them away. Right then she didn't care if they were carried away by the pool pump's current and ended up in another country. "Are you satisfied now?"

"Not quite, but I will be," he said as he pulled her close, took her hand and guided it down his belly and beyond.

When Adan pressed her palm against his erection, Piper blew out a staggered breath. "I do believe I've located an impressive sea creature down below."

"Actually, it's an eel."

"Electric?"

"Highly charged." He brought her hand back to his chest. "But should you investigate further, I fear I will not be able to make it to the bed."

She stood on tiptoe and kissed the cute cleft in his chin. "What's wrong with a little water play?"

"If you're referring to water foreplay, then I am all for that." He wrapped one arm around her waist, then lowered his mouth to her breast while slipping his hand between her thighs simultaneously.

Piper gripped his shoulders and grounded herself against the heady sensations. She felt as if her legs might liquefy with every pass of his tongue over her nipple, every stroke of his fingertip in a place that needed his attention the most.

As badly as she wanted the sensations to go on forever, the climax came in record time. She inadvertently dug her nails into his flesh and unsuccessfully stopped the odd sound bubbling up from her throat.

Once the waves subsided, Piper closed her eyes and sighed. "I'm so sorry that happened so fast," she murmured without looking at him.

He tipped her chin up with a fingertip. "You have no

need to apologize. It has been a while for you, by your own admission."

"Try never."

As she predicted, he was obviously stunned by the truth. "You've never had an orgasm?"

She managed a shrug. "Not with anyone else in the room."

"You clearly have encountered nothing but fools."

Fool, singular. "I've only been intimately involved with one man, and he basically treated me like a fast-food drive-through. In and out as quickly as possible."

Adan released a low, grainy laugh. "I am glad to know you find some humor in the situation. I personally find it appalling when a man has no concern for his lover's pleasure."

She draped her arms around his neck and wriggled her hips. "That goes both ways, and I do believe you are greatly in need of some pleasure. Why bother with a bed when we have a perfectly good pool deck and a comfy-looking chaise at our disposal?"

He kissed her lightly. "True, but we have no condoms."

"I see where that would be a problem."

"A very serious problem. I have already received one unexpected surprise with my son. I do not intend to have another."

Piper wasn't certain if he meant another surprise pregnancy or simply another child, period. Or he could mean he didn't care to have a baby with her. But she refused to let haywire emotions ruin this little tempo-rary piece of paradise, even if it was based on pretense. "Then I suggest you take me to bed, Your Machoness."

No sooner than the words left her mouth, Adan swept

her up into his arms and carried her into the house. She expected him to make use of the downstairs bedroom, but instead he started up the stairs with ease, as if she weighed no more than a feather. Far from the truth. Yet he had a knack for making her feel beautiful. She figured he'd probably earned pro status in the flattery department years ago.

Piper barely had time to look around before Adan deposited her in the middle of the bed covered in a lightweight beige spread. She did have time to assess all his finer details while he opened the nightstand drawer and retrieved a condom. He was evidently very proud to see her, and she was extremely happy to be there. But when he caught her watching, she grabbed the pillow from beneath her head and placed it over her fiery face.

She felt the mattress bend beside her right before he yanked the pillow away. "You're not growing shy on me, are you?" he asked.

No, but she was certainly growing hotter by the second. "I'm just feeling a bit exposed."

He smiled as he skimmed his palm down her belly and back up again. "And I am greatly enjoying the exposure." Then his expression turned oddly serious. "If you have any reservations whatsoever—"

She pressed a fingertip against his lips. "I want this, Adan. I have for a while now."

"Then say no more."

He stretched out and shifted atop her body, then eased inside her. She couldn't speak if she tried. His weight, his powerful movement, captured all her attention. The play of his muscles beneath her palms, the sound of his voice at her ear describing what he felt at that moment, sent her senses spiraling. His broken breaths, the way he tensed signaled he was barely maintaining control. When she lifted her hips to meet his thrust, he groaned and picked up the pace. Only a matter of time before he couldn't hold out, she realized. And then he shuddered with the force of his climax before collapsing against her breasts, where she could feel his heart beating rapidly.

Piper wanted to remain this way indefinitely—with a sexy, skilled man in her arms and a sense of pride that she'd taken him to the limit. She felt unusually brave, and incredibly empowered. Never before had it been this way with Keiler Farnsworth. And the fact that the jerk's name jumped into her brain made her as mad as a hornet. He couldn't hold a candle to Adan Mehdi. She suspected she'd be hard-pressed to find any man who would.

After a few blissful moments ticked off, Adan lifted his head from her shoulder and grinned. "I hope you don't judge me on the expediency of the act."

She tapped her chin and pretended to think. "I'll have to take a point off for that."

He frowned. "You are keeping score?"

"I wasn't until you mentioned it. However, I'm giving you back that point because you are just so darn cute. So no need to despair, because you've earned a perfect ten."

He rolled over onto his back, taking his weight away and leaving Piper feeling strangely bereft. "I will do much better next time," he said in a grainy voice.

Next time couldn't come soon enough for her.

Piper McAdams proved to be more enthusiastic than any woman before her. Adan had recognized that during their second heated round of lovemaking at midnight. And again a few hours ago, immediately before dawn, when she'd awakened him with a kiss before urging him to join her in the shower. They'd spent a good deal of time there bathing each other until he took her up against the tiled wall. Still he could not seem to get enough of her.

Making love to her a fourth time in twenty-four hours seemed highly improbable. He should be completely sated. Totally exhausted. Utterly spent.

"Smells like something good is cooking in the kitchen."

At the sound of her sensual morning voice, Adan glanced over one shoulder to find Piper standing in the opening, wearing his robe. The improbable became possible when his body reacted with a surprisingly spontaneous erection.

"I'm heating up the *ataif* that Ghania prepared." And attempting to hide his sins by paying more attention to the stove than his guest.

"What is *ataif?*" she asked.

Recipe recitation should aid in calming his baser urges. When goats sprouted wings. "*Ataif* is a Middle Eastern pancake dipped in honey and cinnamon and covered in walnuts. It is served with a heavy cream known as *kaymak.*"

"Thank you for such a thorough description, Chef Sheikh. Now, who is Ghania?"

He was somewhat surprised she hadn't asked that question first. "Ghania is Qareeb's wife. They're the caretakers. She was kind enough to bring the food by a few moments ago."

"How nice of her."

He afforded her another fast glance before returning to his task. "I received news about my son. According to Maysa, he only awoke one time."

"You have cell towers all the way out here?"

"No. The message arrived by carrier pigeon."

"Very amusing," she said before he felt something hit the back of his head.

He looked down to see a wadded paper napkin at his feet. "No need for violence. If you care to communicate with someone, you may use the phone in my study. It's a direct line to the palace that I had installed in the event a military crisis arises."

"That's good to know, and I'd also like to know why you refuse to look at me. I know my hair's still damp and I don't have on a scrap of makeup, but it can't be all that bad. Or maybe it could."

If she only knew how badly he wanted her, with or without the feminine frills, she would not sound so unsure of herself. "For your information, you are a natural beauty, and I am trying to retain some dignity since it seems I am unable to cool my engine in your presence."

"Still revving to go, are you?"

Piper's amused tone sent him around to face her. And if matters weren't bad enough, she was seated on the high-back bar stool facing him, her shapely thighs completely uncovered due to the split in the white cloth. "Are you naked beneath the robe?"

She leaned back against the stainless steel island, using her elbows for support. "Yes, I am. I forgot to bring panties into the bath before I showered."

He was seconds away from forgetting himself and the food preparation. "Perhaps you should dress before we dine."

She crossed one leg over the other and loosened the sash enough to create a gap at her breasts, giving him a glimpse of one pale pink nipple. "Perhaps we should forgo breakfast for the time being."

That was all it took to commit a culinary cardinal sin by leaving the pan on the burner. But if the whole bloody kitchen went up in flames, it could not rival the heat he experienced at that moment.

Without giving her fair warning, Adan crossed the small space between them and kissed her with a passion that seemed to know no bounds. He untied the robe, opened it completely, pushed it down her shoulders and then left her mouth to kiss her neck. He traveled down her bare torso, delivering more openmouthed kisses, pausing briefly to pay homage to her breasts before continuing down her abdomen. What he planned next could prompt her to shove him away, but he was willing to take a chance to reap the reward—driving her to the brink of sexual insanity. A small price to pay for ultimate pleasure, as she would soon see, if she allowed it.

When Adan parted her knees, he felt her tense and noted apprehension in her eyes. "Trust me, *mon ange*," he whispered.

She smiled weakly. "Considering I'm half-naked on a bar stool, that would indicate I'm no angel, Adan. But I do trust you. So hurry."

Permission granted, all systems go. He began by lowering to his knees and kissing the insides of her thighs until he felt her tremble. As he worked his way toward his intended target, she shifted restlessly and then lifted her hips toward his mouth in undeniable encouragement. He used gentle persuasion to coax her climax with soft strokes of his tongue, the steady pull of his lips. As she threaded her fingers through his hair and held on firmly, he sensed he would soon achieve his goal. He wasn't the least bit wrong. She released a low moan as the orgasm took over, yet he refused to let up until he was certain she'd experienced every last wave.

Only after he felt her relax did his own desires demand to be met, and so did the need to make haste. He quickly came to his feet, grabbed the condom she'd discarded on the island and ripped open the plastic with his teeth.

Adan had the condom in place in a matter of moments and then seated himself deep inside her. He tried to temper his thrusts, but when Piper wrapped her legs around his waist, restraint left the bungalow. He couldn't readily recall feeling so driven to please a woman. He could not remember the last time he had felt this good. His thoughts disappeared when his own climax came with the force of a missile and seemed to continue for an extraordinary amount of time.

Little by little, logic began to return, including the fact he'd probably turned the cakes into cinders. He lifted his head and sought Piper's gaze. "I fear I have failed in my chef duties."

She reached up and stroked his unshaven jaw. "But you didn't fail me in your lovemaking duties, and that's much more important than breakfast."

For the first time in his life, he'd needed to hear that declaration from a lover. He'd never lacked in confidence or consideration of his partners' needs, yet he had kept his emotions at arm's length with every woman—until now.

But as much as he wanted to please this beautiful woman in his arms, as much as he would like to give more of himself to her, he wasn't certain he could. And if his relationship history repeated itself, he would probably fail her, too.

Seven

After they arrived back at the airbase and boarded the blasted motorcycle again, Piper feared turning prematurely gray thanks to Adan's daredevil driving. Fortunately that wasn't the case, she realized when they entered the palace foyer and she sneaked a peek in the gold-framed mirror. Granted, her hair was a tangled mess, but she couldn't wait a minute longer to see baby Sam.

Adan obviously felt the same, evidenced by his decision to forgo the elevator and take the stairs instead. She practically had to sprint to catch up with him as Abdul, who insisted on carrying her bag, trailed behind them.

Once they reached the third floor, both she and the houseman were winded, while Adan continued toward the nursery as if he possessed all the energy in the world. He actually did, something she'd learned over the past forty-eight hours in his bed. In his shower. In his kitchen and the pool.

Before Adan could open the nursery door, a striking woman with waist-length brunette hair walked out, clearly startled by the sheikh's sudden appearance. "You took years off my life, brother-in-law."

"My apologies, Maysa," he replied, confirming she was the reining queen. "I'm anxious to see about my son."

Maysa closed the door behind her before facing Adan. "I have already put him down for the night and I advise you wait until he wakes. You seem as though you could use some rest." She topped off the comment with a smile aimed at Piper.

Taking that as her cue, she stepped forward, uncertain whether to curtsy or offer her hand. She opted to let the queen make the first move. "I'm Piper McAdams, and it's a pleasure to finally meet you, Your Highness."

"Welcome to the family," she said, then drew Piper into a surprising embrace. "And please call me Maysa."

Piper experienced a fraud alert. "Actually, I'm not really—"

"Accustomed to it yet," Adan interjected. "Given time she will take to the royal treatment as an electric eel takes to water."

Leave it to the prince to joke at a time like this. "I'm not in the market to be treated royally, but I have enjoyed my time in the palace so far."

"I am glad," Maysa said. "Now, if you will both excuse me, I am starving."

Adan checked his watch. "Isn't dinner later than usual?"

Maysa shrugged. "No, but Rafiq is waiting for me in our quarters."

He winked at Piper before regarding Maysa again. "Oh, you're referring to a different kind of appetite. Do not let us keep you from our king."

"You could not if you tried."

Following a slight wave and a smile, Maysa strode down the hallway and disappeared around the corner, leaving Piper alone with the shifty, oversexed sheikh. And she liked him that way. A lot.

He caught her hand and tugged her against him. "Have I told you how much I enjoyed our time together?"

"At least ten times, but I'll never grow tired of hearing it. I'm just sad it's over."

"It doesn't have to be, Piper. You can stay with me in my suite."

She could be entering dangerous emotional territory. "Maybe it should be, Adan. I'll be leaving in a few weeks."

"I know," he said, sounding somewhat disappointed. "All the more reason to spend as much time together before you depart. I am an advocate of taking advantage of pleasure at every opportunity."

How easy it would be to say yes. "I don't know if that's a good idea."

"Since we are to give the impression we are married, what better way than to share the same quarters?"

A false impression of holy matrimony. "We could do that without sleeping in the same bed."

He rimmed the shell of her ear with the tip of his tongue. "I don't recall mentioning sleep."

And she wouldn't get much if she agreed, for several reasons. "You have to consider Sam's needs over ours."

He pulled back and frowned. "Exactly as I intend to do, but he doesn't require all our time during the night."

"He requires quite a bit."

Framing her face in his palms, Adan looked as if his world revolved around her decision. "Stay with me, Piper. Stay until you must leave."

Spending time with this gorgeous Arabian prince, quality time, would be a fantasy come to life. Yet it could never be the real stuff fairy tales were made of. If she took wisdom into account, she'd say no. If she was willing to risk a broken heart, she'd say yes. And she suddenly realized this risk would be well worth undertaking now, even if it meant crying about it later.

"All right, Adan. I'll stay."

In the silence of his private quarters, the room illuminated by the soft glow of a single table lamp, Adan had never experienced such a strong sense of peace. He had the woman curled up next to him to thank for that. Granted, he still wanted Piper in every way imaginable—he'd proved that at his mountain retreat— yet he greatly appreciated the moments they'd spent in comfortable silence after retiring to his quarters.

That lack of conversation would soon end once he told her what he'd learned from his brother upon their arrival a few hours ago. "I have to go to the base tomorrow to oversee training exercises. It will require me to stay in the barracks overnight."

For a moment he'd thought she'd fallen asleep, until she shifted and rested her cheek above his heart. "Gee, thanks. You invite me to reside in your room and then promptly leave me for a whole night."

The teasing quality to her voice gave Adan some semblance of relief. "If I had to choose between sleeping in the barracks with twenty snoring men and sleeping with you, I would choose you every time. Unless you begin snoring—then I could possibly reconsider."

She lightly elbowed him in the rib cage. "If I did happen to snore, which I don't, you'd have no right to criticize me. I thought a freight train had come through the bedroom last night."

"Are you bloody serious?"

"I'm kidding, Adan," she said as she traced a path along his arm with a fingertip. "Your snore actually sounds more like a purr."

That did not please him in the least. "I prefer a freight train to a common house cat."

"Don't worry, Prince Mehdi. Snore or no snore, you're still as macho and sexy as ever."

He pressed a kiss against the corner of her smiling, sensual mouth. "You are now forgiven for the affront to my manhood."

She yawned and briefly stretched her arms over her head. "Have you ever been in live combat before?"

The query took him aback. "Yes, I have."

"Was it dangerous?"

He smiled at the zeal in her voice. "Does that prospect appeal to your daring side?"

"I'm not sure I actually have much of a daring side. I asked because we're presumed to be husband and wife, so I believe it might be prudent for me to learn all I can about you, in case someone asks."

That sounded logical, but not all his military experiences had been favorable. "I've been involved in a skirmish or two while protecting our no-fly zone."

"Bad skirmishes?"

This was the part he didn't speak of often, yet again he felt the need to bare his soul to her. "One turned out to be extremely bad."

"What happened?"

"I killed a man."

He feared the revelation had rendered her speechless, until she said, "I'm assuming it was justified."

"That is a correct assumption. If I hadn't shot down his plane, he would have dropped a bomb over the village."

"How horrible. Was he a citizen of Bajul?"

"No. He was a known insurgent from another country. Because the files are classified, I am not at liberty to say which country."

She lifted her head and kissed his neck before settling back against him. "You don't have to say anything else if you don't want to."

Oh, but he did, though he wasn't certain why. "It happened four years ago," he continued. "That morning I received intelligence about the threat, and I decided I would enter the fray. Later I found out my father was livid, but only because if I perished, he would be without a commander."

"He told you that?" Her tone indicated her disbelief.

"Rafiq informed me, but it doesn't really matter now. I assisted in thwarting an attack that could have led to war for the first time in Bajul's history, and that is what matters. But I never realized…"

"Realized what, Adan?"

He doubted she would let up unless he provided all

the details. "I never knew how affected I would be by sending a man to his death."

"I can imagine how hard on you that must have been."

"Oddly, I had no real reaction to the incident until the following day while briefing our governing council. Midway through the report, I felt as if I couldn't draw a breath. I excused myself and walked outside to regain some composure. That night I had horrible dreams, and they continued for several months."

"I'm so sorry," she said sincerely. "For what it's worth, I think you're a very brave and honorable man. Sam is very lucky to have you as his father."

He'd longed to hear her acknowledge his honor, but he didn't deserve that praise in this situation. "There is no honor in taking another life. And now that I have a son, I will stress that very thing to him."

"That attitude is exactly what makes you honorable," she said. "You were bothered by an evil man's demise to the point of having nightmares. That means you have compassion and a conscience."

If that were the case, he wouldn't have asked her to remain in his quarters for the duration of their time together. Yet he'd not considered anything other than his own needs. And he did need her—in ways he could not have predicted. Still, he couldn't get too close to her or build her expectations beyond what he could provide aside from being her lover. He wasn't suited for a permanent relationship, as his family had told him time and again. "We should try to sleep now. I suspect Samuel will be summoning me in less than two hours."

She fitted her body closer to his side. "I'll be glad to take care of Sam tonight while you get your rest."

"Again, that's not necessary."

"Maybe not, but I really want to do it, not only for you, but for me. We barely caught a glimpse of him tonight. Besides, I'll only have him a little longer, while you'll have him the rest of your life."

Piper's words filled Adan with unexpected regret. Regret that, in a matter of weeks, he would be forced to say goodbye to an incredible woman. In the meantime, he would make the most of their remaining hours together and grant her whatever her heart desired, not only as the provisional mother to his son, but as his temporary lover.

He rolled to face Piper, leaving nothing between them but bare flesh. "Since you have presented such a convincing argument, we will see to Samuel together. Before this, could I convince you to spend the next few hours in some interesting ways?"

She laughed softly. "I thought we were going to sleep."

Bent on persuasion, he skimmed his palm along her curves and paused at the bend of her waist. "We could do that if you'd like."

She draped her arm over his hip. "Sleeping is definitely overrated, so I'm willing to go wherever you lead me."

And she was leading him to a place he'd never been before—close to crashing and burning with no safe place to land. Tonight, he wouldn't analyze the unfamiliar feelings. Tonight, she was all his, and he would treat her as if she always would be.

What an incredible night.

A week ago, Piper would never have believed she

could find a lover as unselfish as Adan. She also couldn't believe her inhibitions had all but disappeared when they made love.

As she supported her cheek with her palm and studied him in the dim light streaming through a break in the heavy gold curtains, she wanted him desperately— even if she was a bit miffed he'd failed to wake her to help care for Sam. Apparently she'd been so relaxed in the postcoitus afterglow, she hadn't heard the baby's cries through the bedside monitor. Some mother she would make.

When Adan stirred, she turned her complete focus on him as he lay sleeping on his back, one arm resting above his head on the navy satin-covered pillow, the other draped loosely across his abdomen. She loved the dark shading of whiskers surrounding his gorgeous mouth, envied the way his long dark lashes fanned beneath his eyes and admired the intricate details of his hand as he slid his palm from his sternum down to beneath the sheet and back up again. The reflexive gesture was so masculine, so sexy, she fought the urge to rip back the covers and climb on board the pleasure express.

Then he opened his eyes and blinked twice before he presented a smile as slow as the sun rising above the mountains. "Good morning, princess."

Didn't she wish. "Good morning. Did you sleep well?"

"Always with you in my bed. How did you sleep?"

"Too soundly. I didn't even hear Sam last night, and evidently you either didn't wake me to help, or couldn't."

He frowned. "I didn't hear him, either."

Simultaneous panic set in, sending them both from the bed and grabbing robes as they hurried out of the bedroom. They practically sprinted toward the nursery and tore through the door, only to find an empty crib.

Piper's hand immediately went to her mouth to cover the gasp. "Someone took him."

"That is impossible," Adan said, a hint of fear calling out from his gold-brown eyes. "The palace is a virtual fortress. If someone kidnapped him, it would have to be an inside job. And if that is the case, I will kill them with my bare hands."

"No need for that, *cara*."

They both spun around to discover Elena sitting in the rocker in the far corner of the lengthy room, the baby cradled in her arms, her expression tinged with disapproval.

Weak with relief, Piper hung back and immediately launched into explanation overdrive. "We never heard him last night. We were both very tired and—"

"The bloody monitor must not be working," Adan added. "Is he all right?"

Elena continued to calmly rock Sam in a steady rhythm. "He is quite fine. And judging from the weight of his diaper when I changed him, I would guess he simply slept all night."

Adan narrowed his eyes and glared at her. "You should have said something the moment we walked into the room."

"You should learn to be more observant of your surroundings when it comes to your son, Adan," she replied. "A hard lesson learned, but one that needed to be taught. When he is toddling, you must know where he is at all times."

Piper, in theory, didn't disagree with the governess's assertions, but she did question her tactics. "We were both expecting to find him in the crib, and needless to say we were shocked when we didn't."

Adan clasped his hands behind his neck and began to pace. "I've been in treacherous military situations less harrowing than this."

Elena pushed out of the chair and approached him. "Settle down, Adan, and hold your baby."

He looked as though he might be afraid to touch him. "I have to prepare for my duties today, but I will return to check on him before I depart for the base."

And with that, he rushed away, leaving Piper alone with the former nanny.

"Well, I suppose I should put this little one to bed for a nap," Elena said, breaking the awkward silence.

Piper approached her and held out her arms. "May I?"

"Of course."

After Elena handed her Sam, Piper kissed his cheek before carefully lowering him to the crib. She continued to study Sam's sweet face slack with sleep, his tiny lips forming a rosebud. He'd grown so much in only a matter of days, and in only a few weeks, she would say goodbye to him—and his father—for good. "He's such a beautiful little boy."

The woman came to her side and rested her slender hands on the top of the railing. "Yes, he is, as his father was at that age."

She saw the chance to learn more about Adan from one of the biggest influences in his life and took it. "Was Adan a good baby?"

"Yes. He was very little trouble, until he turned two,

and then he became quite the terror. He climbed everything available to him, and I didn't dare turn my back
for more than a second or he would have dismantled
something. I would try to scold him over his bad behavior, and then he would give me that charming smile,
and all was forgiven."

Piper could absolutely relate to that. "He was lucky
to have you after losing his mother."

Some unnamed emotion passed over Elena's care-
worn face. "I was fortunate to have the opportunity to
raise him. All the brothers, for that matter."

Time to broach the subject of the paternal presence.
"Was the king involved in his upbringing?"

Elena turned and crossed the room to reclaim the
rocker, looking as if all the energy had left her. "He did
the best that he could under the circumstance. Losing
his wife proved to be devastating to him, yet he had
no choice but to postpone his grief in order to serve
his country."

Piper took the light blue club chair next to Elena.
"Adan has intimated the king was a strict disciplinar-
ian."

"He could be," she said. "He wanted his sons to be
strong, independent men, despite their wealth and their
station. Some might say he was too strict at times."

"Would you say that?"

"Perhaps, but it was not my place to interfere."

"I would think you had every right to state your opinion in light of your relationship."

Elena stiffened and appeared quite stunned by the
statement. "Has Adan spoken to you about myself and
the king?"

Piper smelled a scandal brewing. "Not at all. I only

meant that since you were in charge of the children, you should have had some say in how they were treated."

Elena relaxed somewhat, settled back against the rocker and set it in motion. "The king was stern, but fair."

"I'm not sure how fair it was for Adan when he shipped him off to boarding school at such a young age." And she'd probably just overstepped her bounds by at least a mile.

"He did so to protect him."

The defensiveness in her tone did not deter Piper. "Protect him from what?"

Elena tightened her grip on the chair's arms. "I have already said too much."

Not by a long shot, as far as she was concerned. "Look, I don't know what you know, and frankly I don't have to know it. But Adan deserves the truth."

"It would be too painful for him, and would serve no purpose at this point in time."

She wasn't getting through to the woman, which meant she would have to play the guilt card. "Have you ever asked Adan if he would prefer to be kept in the dark? I personally think he wouldn't."

"And you, Ms. McAdams, have not known him all that long."

Touché. "True, but we have spoken at length about his father. Even though he's reluctant to admit it, Adan has a lot of emotional scars, thanks to the king's careless disregard for his youngest son's needs."

She saw the first real hint of anger in Elena's topaz eyes. "Aahil...the king loved Adan. He gave him the very best of everything money could buy, and the opportunity to do what he loved the most. Fly jets."

A perfect lead-in to confront the crux of the matter, yet asking hard questions could be to her detriment. But if Adan could finally put his concerns to rest, it would be worth the risk. "I personally believe he failed to give Adan the one thing he needed most, and that would be a father who paid more attention to him, instead of shipping him far from his home. For that reason, Adan honestly believes the king isn't his biological father."

Elena glanced away, a very telling sign she could be skirting facts. "That is a wrongful assumption."

Piper wasn't ready to give up just yet. "Are you being absolutely honest with me, Elena? And before you speak, keep in mind Adan deserves to know so he could put that part of his past to rest."

"I swear on my papa's grave that the king was very much Adan's biological father."

Even though Elena sounded resolute, Piper couldn't quite help but believe the woman still had something to hide. "Then you need to tell him that, Elena. And you'll have to work hard to convince him, because he's certain something isn't right when it comes to his heritage."

Elena gave her a surprisingly meaningful look. "Do you care for Adan, Ms. McAdams?"

It was her turn to be shocked. "It's Piper, and yes, as one would care for a very good friend." Now she was the one hiding the truth.

"Then I suggest you not worry about things that do not concern you for Adan's sake."

Piper's frustration began to build. "But in some ways they do concern me. I want to see Adan happy and at peace. He can't do that when he knows full well people are protecting secrets from the past. And no offense, but I believe you're bent on protecting the king and his secrets."

"Are you not protecting Adan and Samuel by masquerading as his wife?"

She had her there. "That's true, but this pretense isn't causing either one of them pain."

"Give it time, Piper," Elena said in a gentler tone. "I can see in Adan's eyes that he cares for you, as well. Perhaps much more than he realizes at this point. But when the fantasy ends and you leave him, reality will be a bitter pill for both of you to swallow. Adan is not the kind of man to commit to one woman, or so he believes."

If Adan did care for her, but he could never be more than her lover, that would possibly shatter her heart completely. But she could still foolishly hope that the man she was dangerously close to loving might change his mind. All the more reason to give him the gift of knowledge, whether he came around or not. "Elena, if you ever cared for Adan at all, I'm imploring you to please consider telling him what you know. Isn't it time to put an end to the mystery and his misery?"

Elena sighed and stared off into space for a few moments before regarding Piper again. "This truth you are seeking will forever change him. He might never accept the mistakes the people in his life have made, even if those mistakes resulted in his very existence."

Finally they were getting somewhere. "Then it's true the queen had an extramarital affair that resulted in Adan's birth."

"No, that is not the case, but you are on the correct path."

Reality suddenly dawned on Piper. "The king had an indiscretion?"

She shook her head. "He had the desire to give the queen what she could not have. A third child. That decision required involving another woman."

"He used a surrogate?" Piper asked, unable to keep the shock from her voice.

"Yes. In a manner of speaking."

"And you know the mother," she said in a simple statement of fact.

Elena knitted her hands together and glanced away. "Very well."

She doubted she would get an answer, but she still had to ask. "Who is she, Elena?"

The woman turned a weary gaze to her and sighed. "I am."

Eight

Piper's brief time in Bajul had been fraught with misunderstanding and mysteries and more than a few surprises. But this bombshell trumped every last one of them. "Who else knows about this?" she asked when she'd finally recovered her voice.

Elena pushed slowly out of the rocker and walked to the window to peer outside. "No one else until now."

All these years, Adan had been living under the assumption that he was another man's child. A supposition that had caused him a great deal of pain, though he had downplayed his burden. But Piper had witnessed it firsthand, and now she wanted nothing more than to finally give him the answers he'd been silently seeking for years. "You have to tell him, Elena."

She turned from the window, a despondent look on

her face. "I have pondered that for many years. I still am not certain it would be wise."

Wise? Surely the former nanny wasn't serious. "Adan deserves to know the truth from the woman who gave him life."

"And he will hate me for withholding that truth for his entire life."

"Why did you withhold it?"

Elena reclaimed the chair and perched on the edge of the cushioned seat. "The king requested that Adan's parentage remain a secret, for both my sake and his."

"You mean for the king's sake, don't you?" She hadn't been able to tamp down the obvious anger in her tone, but she was angry. Livid, in fact.

"For all our sakes," Elena replied. "And for the benefit of the queen, who was already suffering from the decision Aahil made to give her another child."

"But I thought she wanted another baby."

"She did, yet after Adan was born, she could not hold him. In fact, she wanted nothing to do with him. What was meant to give her solace only drove her deeper into depression."

Piper was about to step out on a limb, even knowing it could break the revelations wide-open. "When Adan was conceived, was it through artificial means?"

Elena shook her head. "That process would have included medical staff, and we could not risk involving anyone who might reveal the truth."

"Then Adan was conceived—"

"Through natural means." Once again her gaze drifted away. "And after all was said and done, I am somewhat ashamed to say Aahil and I fell in love during the process, though he continued to be true to the queen until her demise. We remained devoted to each other until his death, and until last year, I kept our relationship a secret."

That meant the king had slept with the governess for the sake of procreation to please his queen, resulting in a decades-long affair. A twisted fairy tale that needed to be untangled. "You said 'until last year.' Does that mean Adan knows you were involved with his father?"

"Yes," she said quietly. "All the boys know. But they do not know I am Adan's true mother."

"It's not too late to rectify the deception, Elena, especially now that Adan has a son. A grandson whom you can acknowledge if you'll just tell Adan the whole story."

Elena's eyes began to mist with unshed tears. "I could not bear to tell him the rest for fear he'll hate me."

Piper leaned forward and clasped Elena's hands. "You're the only mother Adan has ever known, and it's obvious he loves you very much. He might need time to adjust, but I'm sure he'll eventually forgive you."

"It is because of my love for him that I want to protect him from more pain. And you must promise me, Piper, that you will say nothing to him."

The woman drove a hard bargain that could force a wedge between Piper and Adan should he ever learn she'd continued the ruse. "I'll allow you to tell Adan, but—"

"Tell me what?"

Startled by Adan's sudden appearance, Piper quickly shot to her feet. "We were just discussing…actually…"

"We were discussing Samuel's care," Elena said as she gave Piper a cautioning look.

"Am I doing something wrong?" Adan asked, sounding somewhat frustrated.

The lies would surely taste as bitter as brine going down. But it honestly wasn't Piper's place to enlighten him. "You're doing a great job. I basically asked Elena to keep encouraging you when I'm no longer here."

His expression turned somber. "We will discuss that following your departure. At the moment, I need to say goodbye to my son."

Piper remained rooted to her spot as Adan walked to the crib and laid a gentle hand on Sam's forehead. He looked so handsome in his navy flight suit, sunglasses perched atop his head and heavy boots on his feet. He also looked like the consummate father. And when he turned and came to her side, she desperately wanted to blurt out the truth.

Instead, she maintained an overly pleasant demeanor that inaccurately reflected her mood. "I guess we'll see you tomorrow evening, right?"

"Yes, and hopefully not too late." Then he brushed a kiss across her lips, as if this make-believe marriage had somehow become real. She knew better.

"Keep her company, Elena," he said as he kissed her cheek, unaware he was showing affection to his mother. "And do not reveal to her all my bad habits."

Elena reached up and patted his face. "Godspeed, *cara mia*."

After Adan left the room in a rush, Piper regarded Elena again. "I'll give you my word not to say anything to him, as long as you promise you'll tell him the truth. If you don't, I will."

Elena oddly didn't seem at all upset by the threat. "I will tell him before you depart. And I sincerely hope you will tell him what you have been concealing from him, as well."

That threw Piper for a mental loop. "I'm not hiding anything from Adan."

"Yes, my dear, you are." She started for the door but turned and paused before she exited. "You love him, Piper. Tell him soon."

Long after Elena left the nursery, Piper stood there aimlessly staring at the sleeping baby as she pondered the former governess's words. Did she love Adan? Did she even dare admit it to herself, much less to him?

Yet in her heart of hearts she knew that she did love him, and she loved his son as she would have her own child. Regardless, nothing would come of it unless Adan felt the same way about her. Only time would tell, and time was slowly slipping away.

At half past midnight, Adan arrived at the palace initially exhausted from performing his duties. Yet the moment he entered the corridor leading to the living quarters, his fatigue began to dissipate as he started toward his first stop—the nursery to see his son. After that, he would retire to his bedroom in hopes of finding Piper waiting up for him. He certainly wouldn't blame her if she wasn't, considering the lateness of the hour. And if that happened to be the case, he would use creative kisses in strategic places to wake her.

He found the nursery door open and the room entirely vacant. An empty bottle on the table next to the rocker indicated someone had recently been there to tend to Samuel, and he suspected who that someone might be.

On that thought, he traveled down the hall at a quick

clip, and pulled up short at the partially ajar door when he heard the soft, melodic sounds of a French lullaby.

"Dodo, l'enfant do, l'enfant dormira bien vite. Dodo, l'enfant do. L'enfant dormira bientôt."

The lyrics alone indicated Piper could be having difficulty putting Samuel to sleep, but Adan imagined her sweet voice would eventually do the trick. He stayed in the hallway, immersed in faint memories of Elena singing him to sleep. Sadly he'd never had the pleasure of recalling his own mother doing the same.

He wondered if Samuel would eventually resent him for taking him away from Talia. Provided Talia actually agreed to signing over her rights, and he didn't change his mind about asking her to do that very thing.

The sudden silence thrust the concerns away and sent Adan into the bedroom. He discovered Piper propped up against the headboard, eyes closed, her dark hair fanning out on the stack of white satin pillows beneath her head, and his son, deep in slumber, cradled against her breasts. Had she not been gently patting the baby's back, he might have believed she'd fallen asleep, as well.

He remained in place, recognizing at that moment how greatly he appreciated this woman who had stepped in to care for his child without hesitation. He'd begun to care for her deeply, more than he had any woman. But to expect her to continue in this role much longer would be completely unfair to both her and his child. She had another life in another country, and she would soon return to resume that life.

When Piper opened her eyes and caught his glance, she smiled before holding a finger against her lips to ensure his silence. He waited at the door as she worked her way slowly off the bed and approached him at the door. "I'll be right back," she whispered. "Unless he wakes again."

Unable to resist, he softly kissed the top of Samuel's head, remarkably without disturbing him, then leaned and kissed Piper's cheek, earning him another smile before she left the room.

In order to be waiting in bed for her return, Adan launched into action. He stripped out of his clothes on his way into the bathroom, turned on the water in the shower, then stepped beneath the spray and began to wash. He'd barely finished rinsing when the glass door opened—and one beautiful, naked woman with her hair piled atop her head boldly joined him.

Using his shoulders for support, she stood on tiptoe and brought her lips to his ear. "I missed you."

He framed her face in his palms. "I missed you, too."

All conversation ceased as they explored each other's bodies with eager hands as the water rained down over them. They kissed with shared passion, touched without restraint. Adan purposely kept Piper on the brink of orgasm with light pressure before he quickened the pace. She released a small moan, then raked her nails down his back with the force of her release. He soon discovered she was bent on reciprocating when she nudged him against the shower wall, lowered to her knees and took him into her mouth. He tipped his head back and gritted his teeth as she took him to the breaking point. Refusing to allow that to happen, he clasped her wrists and pulled her to her feet.

"Not here," he grated out, then swept her into his arms, carried her into the bedroom and brought her down on the sheets despite the fact they were soaking wet.

He slowed the tempo then, using his mouth to bring her more pleasure as she had done with him, until his own body demanded he hurry. In a matter of moments, he had the condom in place, and seated himself soundly inside her. She sighed when he held her closer, yet he couldn't seem to get close enough, even when she wrapped her legs around his waist.

All the unfamiliar emotions, the desperate desire, culminated in a climax that rocked him to the core. He had difficulty catching his breath as his heart beat a thunderous tempo against his chest. Piper began to stroke his back in a soothing rhythm, bringing him slowly back into reality. And that reality included an emotion he'd always rejected in the past. An expression he had never uttered to any lover. A word he dared not acknowledge now, for in doing so he would be completely vulnerable to a woman who was bound to leave.

He preferred to remain as he'd always been, immune to romantic love. Yet as Piper whispered soft words of praise, he wondered where he would find the strength to let her go. He would find it. He had no choice.

But not now. Not tonight.

Three weeks gone, one more to go.

As the first morning light filtered in from the part in the heavy gold curtains, Piper couldn't stop thinking about how little time she had left before she went home. And as she lay curled up in the empty bed, hugging a pillow, she also couldn't stop pondering Adan's abrupt change in mood.

For the past several days, he'd begun to spend more time with the baby when he wasn't at the base and a lot less time with her. She felt somewhat guilty for even questioning his paternal role, but she didn't quite understand why he'd started coming to bed in the middle of the night. Nor could she fathom why they hadn't made love in over a week when they hadn't missed a day since their first time together.

She questioned whether Elena had told him her secret, but she felt certain Adan would have told her if that had been the case. Blamed her for meddling, for that matter. Maybe the prince was simply preparing for their parting. Maybe the pretend princess would be wise to do the same. But lately she'd learned to lead with her heart, not her head. Her head told her to accept the certain end to their relationship. Her heart told her not to go down without a fight.

At the moment, her heart made more sense. For that reason, she climbed from beneath the covers to confront the missing sheikh, who she presumed was still in the nursery, tending to his son. After donning her robe, she padded down the hall to confirm her conjecture. And she did when she walked into the nursery and found Adan in the rocker, Sam cradled against his shoulder, both fast asleep.

All her previous concerns disappeared as she took in the precious sight. A scene worthy of being commemorated on canvas. Regrettably she didn't have one readily available, but she did have a sketch pad.

With that in mind, she hurried back to the bedroom she hadn't occupied in weeks, retrieved paper and pencil and then returned to the nursery. She moved closer to achieve a prime vantage point of father and son in the throes of blissful sleep. A souvenir to take with her that would enhance the wonderful memories…unless…

As she sketched the details with second-nature

strokes, a plan began brewing in her mind. A good plan. She quietly backed out the door and returned to Adan's quarters, closed the door, hid the pad in her lingerie drawer beneath her panties and picked up the palace phone. She expected Elena to answer, but instead heard an unfamiliar female voice ask, "May I help you?"

"Yes. This is…" The sheikh's fake spouse? The prince's bed buddy? She couldn't stomach lying again, even to a stranger. "With whom am I speaking?"

"My name is Kira," she said, her pleasant voice not even hinting at a Middle Eastern accent. "And you are the newest princess."

Apparently the woman thought Piper had forgotten her title. Bogus title. "Right. Is there someone available who could run an errand for me?"

"I will be up immediately."

Before she could offer to come downstairs, the line went dead, allowing her only enough time to brush her teeth and hair before she heard the knock.

After tightening the robe's sash, Piper opened the door to find a woman with golden-brown shoulder-length hair and striking cobalt eyes. She wore a navy blazer covering a white blouse and matching knee-length skirt, sensible pumps and a sunny smile. "Good morning, Princess Mehdi."

Piper would like to return the sentiment, but so far the morning hadn't started off well when she'd woken up alone. "Thank you for answering the summons so quickly, Kira, but this errand isn't really that pressing. I'm not even sure it's possible."

Kira straightened her shoulders and slightly lifted

her chin. "This is only my second day as a palace employee, and it is my duty to make this task possible."

Talk about pressure. "Okay, then. Is there a store that sells art supplies in the village?"

Kira seemed to relax from relief. "Thankfully, yes there is."

Things could be looking up after all. "Great. I need a canvas, the largest one available, and a basic set of oil paints today, if at all possible."

"I will gladly see to the purchase myself."

"Wonderful." Piper hooked a thumb over her shoulder. "I'll just grab my credit card and—"

"That is not necessary," Kira said. "The household budget covers all your expenses."

She didn't have the energy or desire to argue. "I truly appreciate that. And out of curiosity, are you from Bajul? I ask because you don't really have an accent."

"I was born and grew up here but I've been living in Montreal for the past few years. My mother was Canadian, and while she was working in Dubai, she traveled to the queen's mountain resort here one weekend, met my papa, fell madly in love and never left."

At least someone's whirlwind affair had turned out well. "That's a wonderful story. Now, if you don't mind, I have one more favor to ask."

"Whatever you wish, Princess Mehdi."

She really wished she would stop calling her that. "Please, call me Piper."

Kira looked just this side of mortified over the suggestion. "That would not be proper. I am a member of the staff and you are a member of the royal family."

Little did the woman know, nothing could be further from the truth. "How old are you, Kira, if you don't mind me asking?"

She looked a little confused by the question. "Twenty-seven."

"And I'll turn twenty-seven in three months. Since we're basically contemporaries, I'd prefer you address me by my given name while we're in private. If we're in a public forum, we'll adhere to all that ridiculous formality since it's expected. And in all honesty, I could use a friend in the palace. A female friend close to my age."

That brought the return of Kira's grin. "I suppose we could do that. A woman can never have an overabundance of friends."

Piper returned her smile. "Great. Now about that other favor." She gestured Kira inside the suite and closed the door. "Please don't say anything to anyone about the art supplies. I want to surprise Adan."

She raised her hand as if taking an oath. "I promise I will not say a word to the prince, even if it means residing in the dungeon while being subjected to torture."

"There's a dungeon?"

Kira chuckled. "Not that I have seen. And I apologize. At times I let my questionable sense of humor overtake my sound judgment."

"Well, Kira, since I'm prone to do the same, I believe that will make us fast friends. We can meet weekly and exchange smart remarks to enable us to maintain a certain amount of decorum."

They both shared in a laugh then, but all humor ceased when Adan came through the door without warning. He gave Piper a confused look before his gaze settled on Kira—and he grinned. "Are my eyes deceiving me, or has the caretaker's daughter come home?"

"No, Your Highness, your eyes are not deceiving you. I have returned, and I am now working in the palace with the sole intent to serve you."

He frowned. "Serve me grief no doubt, and what is with the 'Your Highness'? If I recall, I was the first boy to kiss you."

"And if I recall, I slugged you before you could."

This time Adan and Kira laughed, before he grabbed her up and spun her around, indicating to Piper this pair knew each other well. Possibly very well. She couldn't quell the bite of jealousy, even though she sensed nothing aside from camaraderie between the two. Or maybe she was just playing the ostrich hiding its head in the desert sand.

After Adan let Kira go, he kept his attention on her. "I thought you were engaged to be married."

"That didn't work out," she replied. "It's a long, sad story that is not worth telling. Luckily Mama and Papa mentioned my return to Elena, and here I am."

Adan finally regarded Piper. "Kira's parents were members of the household staff for many years."

"My father tended the palace grounds," Kira added. "My mother was the head chef at the palace."

Adan pointed at her. "And she was the resident holy terror in her youth."

Kira frowned. "If I were not your subordinate, I would possibly slug you again. But since I am, I will leave you both to your privacy as I have an important task to oversee. Princess Mehdi, it was a pleasure to meet you." She then did an about-face and left, closing the door behind her.

"She certainly left in a hurry," Piper said. "Evidently she had a very bad breakup."

Adan's good spirits seemed to dissolve right before Piper's eyes. "More often than not, relationships run their course and usually come to a less than favorable conclusion."

Piper's hope that he might have feelings for her beyond gratitude evaporated like early-morning fog. "I had no idea you were that cynical, Your Highness."

He disappeared into the closet and returned with khaki cargo pants, a navy T-shirt, socks and a pair of heavy boots. "I am a realist."

She leaned a shoulder against the bedpost as he shrugged out of his robe, finding it difficult to ignore his board-flat abdomen and the slight stream of hair disappearing beneath the waistband of his boxer briefs. "It seems to me both your brothers are happily married."

He tugged the shirt over his head, ruffling his dark hair in the process. "Perhaps, but they are the exception to the rule."

"Your relationship rules?"

He put on his pants one leg at a time and zipped them closed. "I didn't make the rules, Piper. I'm only acknowledging that failed relationships seem to be my forte."

"Are you referring to Talia?"

After rounding the bed, he perched on the mattress's edge to put on his boots. "Yes, among a few other non-intimate relationships, including my father."

Now they were getting somewhere. "You didn't fail him, Adan. He failed you."

"I suppose you're right. Apparently I never accomplished anything to suit him, no matter how hard I tried."

"Even learning to pilot jets wasn't good enough?"

He came to his feet and faced her. "I have no idea since he rarely mentioned my skills, even when he convinced the counsel to appoint me as the armed forces commander."

"Well, at least he had enough faith in you to believe you could handle the responsibility."

"Or he was possibly setting me up to fail. Fortunately I proved him wrong."

She smiled. "Yes, you did, at that. And if it's any consolation, I'm proud of your accomplishments, both military and paternal."

Discomfort called out from his eyes. "You never did say why Kira was here."

Time to lighten the mood. Or die trying. "She was seeking donations for the poor. I told her to take five or so of the watches in your extensive collection since I'm sure they'll go for a hefty price, and you probably wouldn't miss them."

From the sour look on his face, her efforts at levity had fallen flat. "Try again, Piper."

She folded her arms beneath her breasts and sighed. "If you must know, I sent her into the village for a few feminine unmentionables. But I'll be glad to show you the list if you're worried we were somehow plotting against you."

He held up both hands, palms forward. "That will not be necessary. I presently need to prepare for the day."

"Are you going to the base?"

"Not today. Following breakfast, I thought I would

take Samuel for a stroll around the grounds as soon as he wakes from his morning nap."

"Do you mind if I join you?"

"That is entirely up to you."

The lack of enthusiasm in his response told Piper all she needed to know—she wasn't welcome, and that stung like a bumblebee. "I'll let you and Sam have some father-and-son alone time. Besides, I have something I need to do anyway." Namely begin painting a portrait that would serve as a gift for the prince. A parting gift.

"That is your prerogative," he said in a noncommittal tone as he started to the door. "I'll tell the cook to keep your breakfast warm while you dress."

She wasn't hungry for food, but she was definitely starved for answers. "Before you leave, I have something I need to tell you."

Adan paused with his hand on the doorknob and turned to face her. "I'm listening."

She drew in a deep breath and prepared for the possibility of having her heart completely torn in two. "I'm in love with you."

He looked as if she'd slapped him. "What did you say?"

"Don't be obtuse, Adan. I love you. I didn't plan it. I really didn't want it. But it happened in spite of my resistance. My question is, how do you feel about me?"

He lowered his eyes to the floor. "I cannot be the man you need, Piper."

"That's my decision to make, not an answer."

His gaze snapped to hers. "You deserve someone who can give you the emotional support you require."

Meaning he didn't return her feelings. Or maybe he

refused to admit it. Only one way to find out. "What are you afraid of, Adan?"

"I'm not afraid, Piper. As I've said, I'm pragmatic."

"No, you're not," she said. "You're a risk taker, but you're scared to take a chance on us."

"I am only considering your well-being. I do care about you, Piper. Perhaps more than I've cared for any woman in my past. But I'll be damned if I break your heart because I cannot succeed at being faithful to one woman."

The surprising revelations took Piper aback. "Did you cheat on Talia during the six years you were together?"

"No."

"Have you cheated on any woman you've been with?"

"No, but—"

"Then why would you believe you would be unfaithful to me?"

"Because I could be genetically predisposed to adultery, compliments of my mother."

She could no longer allow him to think that his mother had taken a lover who resulted in his birth, in spite of her promise to Elena. Not when their future together could depend on the truth. "Adan, your mother was—"

The sharp rap suspended Piper's confession midsentence and caused Adan to mutter a string of Arabic words as he opened the door.

Piper expected a member of the staff. What she got was Adan's erstwhile lover, her platinum hair slicked back in a low chignon, her lithe body tightly encased in

a blue silk jumpsuit, her makeup applied to perfection
and her red painted lips curled into a snarl-like smile.

"Surprise, you bleedin' bastard. I'm back!"

Nine

The woman in the catsuit looked ready for a catfight, but Piper wasn't about to bite. "I'll leave you two with your privacy," she said as she targeted the door as her means to escape.

Talia stormed into the room, blocking her escape. "Oh, do stay, chicky. The party is only getting started."

Adan stepped to Piper's side and moved slightly in front of her. "Calm down, Talia. If anyone has cause to be irritated, it should be me. You might have had the courtesy of notifying me of your impending arrival."

"And you might have told me you married—" she pointed a finger at Piper "—this wench."

"Piper is not a wench," Adan stated with a touch of venom in his tone. "And your argument is with me, not her. If you will join me in my study, we will discuss our son."

Talia smirked. "Here seems fine. After all, you've obviously been taking care of the bonking business in the bedroom with her for quite some time, according to the press."

And Piper had only thought they'd covered all their media bases. "You can't believe everything you hear or read, Talia. Adan has done whatever it takes to protect Sam."

The woman nailed her with a seething glare. "Our son is not your concern."

"But he is my concern," Adan said. "And I am prepared to offer you a sizable settlement in exchange for retaining full custody of Samuel."

Talia flipped a hand in dismissal. "Your attorneys have already worked that out with my attorneys."

Adan's expression was a mixture of confusion and anger. "How is that possible when I have not consulted the palace barrister?"

"Maybe you should talk to your brother about that," Talia replied.

"The king knew you were coming?" Piper chimed in, earning a quelling look from Adan.

"Yes, he did," she said. "I had Bridgette call when I arrived back in Paris. Rafiq wouldn't let me speak to you, the duffer, so I hopped on a plane and came here. He practically met me at the door with the papers. I signed them and then I had to evade the houseboy on my way up here."

Piper knew very little British slang, but it didn't take much to interpret Talia's words. "Then I assume you're okay with giving Adan full custody," she said, sticking her nose in where it obviously didn't belong.

Talia screwed up her face in a frown. It wasn't pretty.

"No. I'm giving him to Adan. What would I need with a kid?"

A litany of indictments shot into Piper's brain, threatening to spill out her mouth. Luckily Sam's cry filtered through the monitor at that exact moment, supplying an excuse to bail before she blew up. "I'll take care of him." She brushed past Talia, resisting the urge to rip the expensive designer bag from her shoulder and stomp on it for good measure.

She took a few calming breaths as she quickly made her way to the nursery to see about the baby. The minute she walked into the room, Sam's cries turned into wails, as if he somehow sensed the stressful situation brewing down the hall.

"What's wrong, sweetie?" she said as she picked him up from the crib. "Did you have a bad dream or just need some company?"

His sobs turned to sniffles as she cradled him in her arms, and then she realized he was in dire need of a diaper change. After she saw to that task, she considered instituting Adan's plan to take the baby for a stroll around the grounds. She discarded that idea when she remembered she was still wearing her robe. Nothing like giving tabloid reporters more fuel for gossip should she get caught on camera. Of course, if any of the bottom-feeders had been hanging around in the past hour, which they had been periodically known to do since she'd arrived in Bajul, they would have a field day with Toxic Talia.

Her anger came back full throttle when she considered how the woman had agreed to relinquish her child without a second thought. Couldn't she see what a precious gift she'd been given? Of course she couldn't. She wasn't concerned about anything that didn't promote her personal gain…just like her own mother.

Piper refused to make this decision easy on the selfish supermodel, and with that goal in mind, she strode back down the hall with Sam in tow. She arrived at the open door to the suite in time to hear Talia say, "Now that everything's settled, I'll be on my way."

"You're not going anywhere yet," Piper said through gritted teeth. "Not until you take a good long look at what you're giving away."

Talia spun around and rolled her eyes. "For the last time, this is none of your business, ducky."

Undeterred, Piper walked right up to her and turned the baby around in her arms. "Look at him, Talia, and think about what you're doing. It's still not too late to change your mind."

Adan took a few steps forward. "It's no use, Piper. She's made her choice, and she chooses her career. She wants no part in raising him."

Ignoring Adan, Piper kept her gaze trained on Talia. "This is a life-altering decision. There's no turning back if you walk away now. Is that what you really want?"

A spark of indecision showed in Talia's eyes. "I can't raise him," she said, an almost mournful quality to her voice.

Piper's disdain lessened as she witnessed the woman's defenses began to crumble, one fissure at a time. "Are you absolutely sure?"

"If I were a different person, perhaps I could. But I'm never going to be good at it, and it would be unfair to him if I tried." Then she surprisingly reached out and touched Sam's fisted hand. "So long, little fellow. Be good for your daddy and your new mum."

Talia hurried out the door, but not before Piper caught a glimpse of tears in her eyes. "Maybe I misjudged her," she said as she placed Sam against her shoulder. "Maybe for the first time in her life, she's doing something unselfish."

Adan shoved a hand in his pocket, rubbed his neck with the other and began to pace. "Do you find it odd that all three of us have been betrayed by our mothers?"

In a way, he was right, but not completely. Piper had intended to tell him the truth before Talia's interruption. She now recognized she walked a fine line between breaking a promise and bringing him peace. Perhaps she could avoid crossing that line by handing him only a partial truth. "There are some things you don't know about your mother, and it's high time you do."

He faced her and frowned. "What are you talking about?"

"You need to ask Elena," she said. "She holds the answers, and she's prepared to tell you."

At least that was what she hoped.

A few moments later, Adan found himself standing outside Elena's private office, his mind caught in a maze of confusion. He had no idea what Piper had been talking about, yet he suspected he would soon find out, even if he wasn't certain he wanted to know.

When he rapped on the frame surrounding the open door, Elena looked up from her position behind the desk, obviously startled before surprise melted into a smile. "Come in, *cara*."

He entered, pulled back the chair opposite her and sat. "Am I interrupting anything?"

"Of course not. You are always welcome here."

He stretched out his legs in an attempt to affect a casual demeanor, when in truth his nerves were on edge. "Talia stopped by to sign over custody of Samuel."

"I heard," she said. "And I am very sorry that your son will not have the opportunity to know his mother. On the other hand, since I do know his mother's shortcomings, the decision she made was the best course of action in this case."

"Piper suggested it was an uncharacteristically unselfish act on Talia's part."

"Piper is correct, but then she has wisdom beyond her years."

The moment had arrived to transition into his real reason for being there. "And continuing on with the subject of motherhood, Piper also informed me you had information about my mother that she's convinced I should know."

Unmistakable panic showed in Elena's eyes. "I told her I would tell you in due time."

"Perhaps that time is now."

Elena hesitated for several moments, leading him to believe she might thwart his attempts at garnering information. "I suppose you are right."

"Then proceed," he said as he braced for the possibilities and prepared for the worst.

She picked up a stack of papers and moved them aside before folding her hands atop the desk. "First of all, I must clarify an incorrect assumption you have long held regarding your parents. Your mother always remained true to her husband during their marriage, and they both grew to love each other. Most important, Aahil Mehdi was your biological father, not some unknown man."

He had waited all his life for confirmation or a denial of his theory, yet something didn't quite ring true. "If that is a fact, then why was I the only son not raised and schooled here at the palace? Why was I the only brother sent away during my formative years?"

"To protect you, Adan."

"From what?"

"The chance someone could learn your true parentage, and you would suffer the consequences from being labeled the child of a concubine."

Anger began brewing immediately beneath the surface of his feigned calm. "Then you are saying my father was the adulterer and I am the product of his affair with a servant?"

"No. Your father was a good man, but you were the reminder of his failure to make his queen happy by giving her the baby she was not able to conceive." She sent him a wistful smile. "Yet you were the greatest joy in my life from the moment you came into this world."

Awareness barreled down on him with the force of a hundred wild horses. "*You* gave birth to me?"

"Yes, *cara,* as a favor to the king, and during the process of conception, your father and I fell in love. And as you already know, that love continued until his death, but I assure you we did not act on it until the queen's demise."

Questions continued to bombard his brain. He chose the one that took precedence over all. "Why did you wait to tell me this?"

"I promised your father I would never reveal the truth to anyone, even you."

Once the initial shock subsided, ire took its place.

"He had no right to ask that of you, and you had no right to keep this from me all these years."

"I realize that now," she said. "And had Piper not come to me and then pressed me to reveal the truth to you, I might have carried the secret to my grave."

Adan was torn between gratitude and resentment aimed toward both Elena and Piper. "How long has she known about this secret?"

"For a while."

One more betrayal in a long line of many. "She should have told me immediately."

"Do not blame Piper for not saying anything, Adan. I begged her to allow me to tell you."

"She should not have come to you in the first place."

"She did so because she loves you, Adan. She only wants what is best for you, and she believes with this information you'll find some peace."

Piper's declaration of love intruded into his thoughts, but he pushed it aside. "If that is so, then why would she subject me to this confession knowing it would cause such turmoil?"

"I suspect she recognizes that lies have the capacity to destroy relationships."

And so could the truth. His relationship with Piper had been fraught with lies from the beginning, and he wasn't certain he could trust her now.

Bent on a confrontation, he shoved the chair back and stood. "We will discuss this further after I have had time to digest this information."

Tears filled Elena's eyes. "Please tell me you do not hate me, Adan."

How could he hate the woman who had been the only

mother he had ever known? In reality, his real mother. "I could never hate you, Elena."

"But you might never forgive me," she said, resignation in her tone.

"I will try, and that is all I can promise at this moment," he said before he turned to leave.

"Where are you going, Adan?" Elena called after him.

"To have a serious conversation with my alleged wife."

"What possessed you to interfere in my life?"

Piper put down the art book she'd attempted to read in the common sitting area, moved to the edge of the uncomfortable chair and faced Adan's wrath head-on. "I assume Elena told you everything."

He released a caustic laugh. "You would be correct in that assumption, and you have yet to answer my question."

"Okay. You see it as interference, and I see it as making an effort to find the answers you've always longed for."

"I never sought those answers for a reason."

"And that reason is?"

"I knew nothing good would come of them, and nothing has."

She couldn't believe his attitude or his misdirected anger. "What's not good about finally knowing the identity of your real mother? Believe me, Sunny and I unsuccessfully tried to find our father, but we could only narrow it down to three prospects. One was in prison for insider trading, one was a money-hungry gigolo and the last was married with four children. With that field of prospects, we decided it wasn't worth pursuing. At least you now know you have a wonderful mother."

He ran a fast hand over his jaw. "I am not you, Piper. I had no desire to learn the truth. And now that I do know, I have been shown that even the most trustworthy person is capable of the ultimate betrayal."

She felt as if he'd placed her in that category, along with his biological mother. "Look, Adan, I don't agree with Elena concealing the truth for such a lengthy period of time, but on some level I did understand why she was afraid to reveal it. Seeing your reaction only validated her fears."

He paced back and forth like a caged animal before pausing before her. "How would you wish me to react, Piper? Should I be celebrating the lies I've been told my entire life? Or the fact that you knew the truth and concealed it?"

"Believe me, keeping it from you wasn't easy." A colossal understatement. "But it wasn't my place to tell you, although I would have before I left if Elena hadn't."

He narrowed his eyes into a hard glare. "It wasn't your place to go on a bloody fact-finding mission, either."

No matter how hard she tried to see it from his point of view, his condemnation hurt like the devil. Time to fight fire with fire. "Sometimes it's necessary to set a lie into motion to protect those you love, just like you're protecting Samuel by lying about our marriage."

"You are absolutely correct," he said, taking her by surprise. "And I plan to put an end to that fabrication immediately. Now that Talia has relinquished her rights, you have no cause to remain here any longer. I will make the arrangements for you to fly home as soon as possible."

As she came to her feet, she seriously wanted to cry, maybe even beg, but instead called on fury to give her strength. "So that's it, huh? I've served my purpose and now you're going to toss me out into the street like refuse?"

"I am not tossing you out," he said. "I am giving you back your freedom."

And he was going to hold her emotionally captive for a very long time. But deep down, hadn't she known all along this would happen? And she'd been an unequivocal fool to believe otherwise. "Shame on me for believing I meant more to you than just a quick fix to save your sterling reputation. And shame on you for leading me to believe you were honorable."

She could tell by the harsh look on his face she'd delivered a knockout blow. "I would be less than honorable if I kept you here any longer when we both know that I will never be able to give you what you need."

Battling the threatening tears, Piper snatched up the book and clutched it to her heart. "You're right, Your Highness. I need a man who can let down his guard and take a chance on love, even though I've recently discovered love is a risky business. But just remember, there's a little boy who's going to need all the love you can give him, since, like his father, he's never going to know his mother. Don't fail him because you're too afraid to feel."

Without giving him a chance to respond, Piper stormed down the hall to the make-believe lovers' hideaway, slammed the door behind her and started the process of packing. Only then did she let the tears fall at will and continued to cry until she was all cried out, though she inherently knew she was only temporarily done with the blubbering.

Not long after Piper finished filling the last of the suitcases, a series of knocks signaled a guest had come calling, the last thing she needed. Unless… On the way to answer the summons, she couldn't help hoping Adan had somehow come to his senses and decided to ask for a second chance. That he would appear on the threshold on bended knee with his heart in his hands and a declaration of love flowing from his gorgeous mouth. As if that fairy-tale scenario was going to happen. Most likely she'd find Abdul standing in the hall with his head slightly bowed, a live-to-serve look on his face while he declared his unwavering need to carry her luggage.

She discovered she'd been wrong on both counts when she opened the door to the ever-smiling Kira. "I'm so sorry to bother you, Your—" She sent a quick glance over her shoulder. "…Piper, but the art shop didn't have any canvases available and they only had colored chalk. They did offer to order the supplies for you."

She'd forgotten all about the painting she'd planned to give Adan. "That's okay. I won't be needing those supplies now." Or ever.

Kira appeared sorely disappointed. "But you seemed so excited over surprising your husband."

He's not my husband, she wanted to say, but opted for a partial truth. "I probably shouldn't mention this, but you'll know soon enough. The marriage isn't working out, so I'm returning home this afternoon."

Kira hid a gasp behind her hand. "I am so sorry, Piper. I was so certain seeing you and Adan together today that you were completely in love."

"Love isn't always enough, Kira," she said without thought.

"I know that all too well, Piper."

She sensed her newfound friend did, at that. "Oh, well. Nothing ventured, nothing gained, as they say. And I'm going to miss having the opportunity to get to know you."

"Surely I'll see you when you bring the baby to visit his father."

If only that were the case. Leaving Sam would be equally as difficult as leaving his father behind, never knowing what might have been. "Adan is going to have full custody. I travel a lot with my job and we both think it's important Sam grows up in his homeland with his people."

"But you'll be coming here to see him often, right?"

And now for the final, and most painful, lie. "Of course."

That prompted the return of Kira's smile. "That's wonderful. We can still have those smart-remark sessions when you're here."

"I'd offer to have one now, but I want to give Sam one last bottle before I go."

As Piper stepped into the hall to do that very thing, Kira drew her into a hug. "Goodbye for now, Piper. I wish you the best of luck."

"Same to you," she replied as she started toward the nursery, before she gave in to the temptation to tell Kira the truth.

As much as she wanted to see the cherished baby boy, Piper dreaded telling him goodbye. That didn't prevent her from lifting the sleeping Sam from his crib and holding him for the very last time. He opened his eyes slowly and didn't make a sound, as if he understood the importance of the moment. She walked around the room as one more time she sang the lullaby she'd used to put him to sleep. If only she could be his mother. If only his father had loved her back. If only...

"The car is waiting, Your Highness."

Piper wanted to tell Abdul it would just have to wait, but she saw no use in prolonging the inevitable farewell to the second love of her life. She kissed Sam's forehead, laid him back in the crib and managed a smile. "I love you, sweetie. I know you'll forget me once I'm gone, but I will never forget you."

Or the man who had given him life.

After one last look at Sam, Piper turned to go, only to discover Adan standing in the open door looking somewhat remorseful. "I did not want you to leave before I expressed my gratitude for all that you've done for myself and Samuel."

She truly wanted to tell him what he should do with that gratitude, but she couldn't. She honestly wanted to hate him, and she couldn't do that, either. "You're welcome, Your Highness. It's been quite the adventure."

He attempted a smile that didn't quite reach his eyes. "Yes, it has. And I also want to assure you that I will treat my son as he should be treated. I will make certain he has all that he desires."

Too bad he couldn't promise her the same. "Within reason, I hope. I'd hate to think you'd buy him his first plane on his first birthday."

He favored her with a dimpled grin. The same grin she'd noticed the first time she'd laid eyes on him. "Rest assured I will withhold that gesture until his second birthday."

"Good idea. We wouldn't want him to be too spoiled."

A lengthy span of silence passed as they remained quiet, as if neither knew what to say next. Piper had already said what she'd needed to say when she'd told him she loved him, even if he hadn't done the same. Now all that remained was the final goodbye. "Well, I guess I need to get my things and take to the friendly skies. I'd like to say give me a call if you're ever in need of ending your celibacy, but that wouldn't be wise."

He streaked a palm over the nape of his neck. "I suppose it wouldn't be, at that."

"And just so you know, I don't regret the time we've spent together. I only regret this little fake fairy tale didn't have a happy ending. But that's life. Goodbye, Adan."

When she tried to make a hasty exit, Adan caught her arm and pulled her into an embrace that didn't last nearly long enough. "You are a remarkable woman, Piper McAdams. I wish for you only the brightest future with a deserving man."

She was convinced he could be that man, if only he believed it, which he didn't.

Piper began backing away, determined to leave him with a smile. "I'm going to forgo the whole man-hunting thing for a while, but I've decided I am going to further pursue a career in art."

"I am pleased to hear that," he said sincerely. "Perhaps you can send me some of your work in the future. I will pay top price."

How badly she wanted to run back into his arms, but her pride had already suffered too many hits as it was. "I'll certainly give that some serious consideration. In the meantime, take care, Adan."

"I wish the same to you, Piper."

She chose not to afford Adan another look for fear she might do something foolish, like give him another kiss. But after she climbed into the black limousine a half hour later, she glanced back at the red-stone castle and caught a glimpse of someone standing at the second-floor-terrace railing—the someone who had changed her life.

The sheikh of her dreams. A prince of a guy. The one who got away…with her heart.

Ten

"This arrived for you a little while ago."

Adan turned from the nursery window to find Elena holding a large rectangular box. "More gifts from some sultan attempting to insert themselves in the government with bribes for the baby?"

She crossed the room and handed him the brown-paper-wrapped package. "This one is from the United States. South Carolina, to be exact."

He immediately knew what it contained, though he never believed she would actually honor his request. Not after the way he had regretfully treated her.

While Elena looked on, Adan tore through the wrapping and opened the box to find what appeared to be a painting, exactly as he'd expected. Yet when he pulled it from the box, he didn't expect that the painting would depict a slumbering father holding his sleeping son in remarkable detail, right down to the cleft in his chin and Samuel's prominent left dimple.

"Oh, Adan," Elena began in a reverent voice, "this is such a *bella* gift."

He would wholeheartedly agree, if he could dislodge the annoying lump in his throat. The baby began kicking his legs in rapid-fire succession against the mattress as if he appreciated the gesture.

After resting the painting against the crib, Adan picked up Samuel and held him above his head. "You are quite the noisy character these days."

His son rewarded him with a toothless smile, something he'd begun doing the past month. A milestone that had given him great joy. Bittersweet joy, because Piper had not been around to share in it.

"You should call her and thank her, Adan."

He lowered Samuel to his chest and faced Elena with a frown. "I will send her a handwritten note."

She took the baby from his arms without invitation. "You will do no such thing. She deserves to hear from you personally. She also deserves to know that you have been mourning your loss of her since she departed."

"I have not been mourning," he said, sounding too defensive. "I have been busy raising my son and seeing to my royal duty."

Elena patted his cheek. "You can deceive yourself, but you cannot deceive me. You are so sick with love you could wilt every flower in the palace courtyard with your anxiety."

He avoided her scrutiny by picking up the painting and studying the empty wall above the crib. "I believe this is the perfect spot, right above Samuel's bed so he will go to sleep knowing I am watching over him throughout the night."

"Since it is obvious you are not getting any sleep, why not watch over him in person?"

He returned the painting to the floor at his feet. "I am sleeping fine."

"Ah, yes, and I am entering the marathon in Dubai two weeks from now."

That forced Adan around. "Would you please stop assuming you know everything about me?"

She kissed Samuel's cheek before placing him back in the crib, where he began kicking again at the sight of the colorful mobile above him. "I do know you, *cara,* better than most. When you were Samuel's age, I stayed up many nights while you were teething. When you were a toddler, I put you to bed every night with a book, the reason why you were always such a grand reader. When you were six, and you broke your right arm trying to jump the hedges, I was the one who fed you until you learned to eat with your left hand. And when you were twelve, I discovered those horrid magazines beneath your bed and did not tell your father."

He'd forgotten that incident, with good reason. "I realize you've been there for me through thick and thin, but that does not give you carte blanche to lord over me now that I am an adult."

"I agree, you are an adult."

"I am pleased to know you finally acknowledge that."

"An adult who has absolutely no common sense when it counts most."

He should have expected this as soon as he opened the box. "If you're going to say I made the wrong decision by allowing Piper to leave, I would have to disagree."

"And you would be wrong." Elena leaned back against the crib's railing and donned her stern face. "As I have told both your brothers, you all have a great capacity to love, but it would take a special woman to bring that out in you. Zain and Rafiq learned that lesson by finding that special woman, and so have you. Piper is your soul mate, *cara*. Do not destroy what you could have with her by being so stubborn you cannot see what was right in front of you and you foolishly let go for good."

He hated that she had begun to make sense. "I am not being stubborn. I am being sensible. If you know me as well as you say you do, then you realize I have never stayed involved with one woman longer than six years, and we know how well that turned out."

Elena glared at him much as she had when he'd been a badly behaved boy. "Comparing Talia to Piper is like comparing a cactus to a down comforter. It's true Talia gave you a precious son, but she also gave you continuous grief. Piper gave you not only this touching portrait but also the means to heal your wounds with the truth. And you repay her by not admitting how you feel about her."

"I'm presently not certain how I feel about anything." Other than he resented Elena for pointing out the error in his ways.

"And you, *cara mia,* are guilty of propagating the biggest lie of all if you do not stop denying your love for Piper."

"I have never said I love her." He was too afraid

to leave himself open to that emotion, more so now than ever.

She pointed a finger at his face and glowered at him. "Adan Mehdi, before your obstinate behavior destroys what could be the best thing that has happened to you, listen to me, and listen well. First of all, consider how Piper selflessly cared for your son. How she protected you and Samuel by putting her life on hold while pretending to be your wife, only to be dismissed by you as one would dismiss a servant."

"But I never—"

"Furthermore," she continued without regard for his attempts to halt the tirade, "should you finally regain some semblance of wisdom befitting of royalty and decide to contact her, you will beg her forgiveness for being such a rigid *cretino*."

The woman knew how to deliver a right hook to his ego. "I take offense to my own mother calling me an idiot."

Her expression brightened over the unexpected maternal reference. "It means everything to hear you finally acknowledging me as your mother."

He laid a palm on her cheek. "I suppose I have known that all along. Only a true mother would tolerate my antics."

"And only a true mother would agree to raise a child that is not her own, and love that child's father with all her being despite his shortcomings."

He recognized the reference to Piper, yet he couldn't quell his concerns. "What if I try to contact her and she rejects me? And what do I say to her?"

"You must speak from the heart."

"Something I have never truly mastered."

She sighed. "Adan, your father also viewed revealing emotions as a sign of weakness, and in many ways you have inherited that trait from him. But in reality, it's a brave man who shows vulnerability for the sake of love. I implore you to call on your courage and tell Piper your true feelings, before it is too late."

Admittedly, Elena—his mother—was right. He had never backed away from a battle, and he shouldn't avoid this war to win Piper back. Better still, he had the perfect weapons to convince her to surrender—his well-honed charm, and his remarkable son.

When she sensed movement in the corner of her eye, Piper tore her attention away from the painting of the red-stone palace and brought it to the window that provided natural light. And after she glimpsed the tall man pushing the stroller up the guesthouse walkway, she blinked twice to make sure her imagination hadn't commandeered her vision.

But there he was, the man who'd haunted her dreams for the past four weeks. He wore a crisp tailored black shirt and casual beige slacks, his perfect jaw covered by a shading of whiskers, his slightly ruffled thick dark hair as sexy as ever. And she looked like something the cat had dragged into the garage.

She barely had time to remove the paint-dotted apron and smooth the sides of her lopsided ponytail before the bell chimed. After drawing in a cleansing breath, she opened the door and concealed her shock with a smile. "To what do I owe this honor, Your Highness?"

Adan reached into the stroller and retrieved the baby who had stolen Piper's heart from the moment she'd first held him. "This future pilot insisted on paying a personal visit to the artist who presented us with such a fine painting."

She couldn't believe how cute Sam looked in the miniature flight suit and tiny beige boots. "He really said that, huh?"

"He did."

"Wow. I had no idea three-month-old babies could talk."

"He's an exceptional child."

Born to an exceptionally charming father. A charm he'd clearly passed on to his son, evident when Sam kicked his legs and smiled, revealing his inherited dimples. "Well, don't just stand there, boys. Come inside before you both melt from the heat."

Balancing Sam in one arm, Adan leaned over, retrieved the diaper bag from the basket behind the stroller and slipped the strap over his shoulder. "We are accustomed to the heat, but this humidity is excruciating, so I will gladly accept your offer."

Once he stepped into the foyer, Piper showed him into the small living area and gestured toward the floral sofa. "Have a seat, as soon as you give me the kid."

After he handed Samuel off to her, he claimed the end of the couch and set the bag at his feet. "This is a very comfortable yet quaint abode."

"A nice way of saying *small*," she said as she sat in the club chair across from him and gently bounced the baby in her lap. "But the rent is cheap. Actually, it's free. My grandparents live in the main house and this is the guest quarters."

"Yes, I know. Your grandfather greeted me as soon as we left the car."

Great. "Not with a shotgun, I hope."

He laughed. "Actually, he wasn't armed. In fact, he was quite cordial. He's still very pleased that he's been granted the water conservation project, and that's going quite well, by the way."

"So I've heard," she said. "I spoke with Rafiq a few days ago."

"He never mentioned that to me."

"He had no reason to mention it, Adan. He's well aware that once I met the terms of our arrangement I'd go back to business as usual."

"And I presume you've done that?"

"Actually, I'm giving a few private art lessons, and I'm looking for a place to open a small gallery. Interestingly enough, my grandfather is willing to invest in the venture."

"How did you convince him to let you leave the company?"

"I told him that it was high time I had a life of my own that included pursuing my personal aspirations. And then I bribed my grandmother into taking up the cause by helping her with a fund-raiser. Between the two of us, he finally caved."

"I'm glad you're happy, Piper," he said, a solemn note to his voice.

She could think of one other thing that would make her happy, but that was only a pipe dream. "I am, for the most part. Are you?"

He rubbed a palm over his jaw. "I'm happy that I have a son and a fulfilling career. Aside from that—"

When Sam began to fuss, Adan withdrew a bottle from the tote, uncapped it and handed to her. "It seems he's getting hungry more often these days. The books

I've read clearly state that an increase in appetite in an infant signals a growth spurt."

"Spoken like the consummate father," Piper said, bringing the return of Adan's smile.

"I am certainly trying my best."

"And you're succeeding," she said as she laid the baby in the crook of her arm and watched as he downed the formula with gusto. "He's definitely grown. Before you know it, he'll be riding a bike. I can't wait to see that." The statement left her mouth before she'd considered how unrealistic she sounded.

"Perhaps he should learn to walk first."

That drew her attention back to Adan. "Yes, you're right. Time is too short to wish it away." After a bout of awkward silence, she added, "How is Elena these days?"

He leaned back against the sofa and draped an arm over the back of the cushions. "She is doing well. We've had several discussions about my father. She insists he was proud of my accomplishments, and claims he had difficulty expressing his emotions. I'm going to endeavor not to do that with Samuel. He deserves to know that his father supports him at every turn."

"And I'm positive you'll manage that just fine."

"You always have had more faith in me than most." He studied her eyes for a long moment. "I didn't realize how much I would miss your company once you left. But I have missed you. Very much."

She had no idea what to say or how to react. She certainly knew better than to hope. "That reminds me. I never saw where you released the statement outlining the reasons behind my departure."

His gaze drifted away. "That is because I never issued that particular statement. We led the press to believe you were on a sabbatical in the States, visiting family."

That made no sense to her at all. "What was the point in delaying the truth? You're eventually going to have to explain why I left and never came back."

Finally, he brought his attention back to her, some unnamed emotion in his eyes. "Perhaps that will not be necessary."

She put the now-empty bottle on the side table and set Sam upright in her lap. "You're hoping that if you sweep it under the rug, everyone will forget I ever existed?"

"I am hoping after you hear what I have to say, you will realize my mission entails alleviating that necessity."

The man insisted on speaking in riddles. "By all means, continue. I'm waiting with bated breath for clarification."

He pushed off the sofa and stood before her. "And I pray I have not waited too long to do this."

As if she'd been thrust in the middle of some surreal dream, Piper watched in awe as Adan fished a black velvet box from his pants pocket and lowered to one knee. She couldn't catch her breath when he opened that box to reveal a massive princess-cut diamond ring. "Piper McAdams, I have never met a woman quite like you, and I have never been in love until you. I probably do not deserve your forgiveness for my careless disregard, but I sincerely believe we both deserve to be together." He tugged the ring from the holder and held it up. "Now, will you do me the honor of being my real wife, and a mother to my son?"

Heaven help her, the cat that had dragged her into

the garage now had hold of her tongue. She could only stare at the glistening diamond, awed by Adan's declaration of love and the knowledge the fairy tale could soon come true. But then came the questions. Should she take this leap of faith? Could she trust that he really wanted her as his wife, not only as a mother for his child? Or was she overanalyzing everything? Then suddenly the baby reached back, grabbed a wayward tendril of hair at her nape and tugged hard, eliciting her involuntary yelp and Adan's scowl.

"That was not the reply I had hoped for," he said gruffly.

She laughed as she extracted Sam's grasp and offered him her pointer finger. "Apparently he was tired of waiting for my answer."

"And I am also growing impatient."

She pulled Sam up from her lap and turned him to face her. "What do you think about this whole thing, little boy? Should I say yes?"

When the baby squealed in response, Adan said, "I do believe he agrees that you should."

She turned Sam around in her lap to face his father and held out her left hand. "I do believe you're right."

After Adan slid the ring into place, he stood and motioned for Piper to join him. Then with baby Sam nestled between them, he kissed her softly and smiled. "I do love you, Piper. More than my MiG-20 jet."

He could be such a cad. A very cute cad. "And I love you more than my purple fluffy slippers that you always found so comical."

His ensuing smile soon disappeared. "On a serious note, as soon as we are wed, I want you to legally become Samuel's mother."

"I would be honored," she said. And she would.

His expression remained overtly somber. "He has a right to know about Talia, although I am at a loss over what to tell him."

"That's simple. When he's old enough to understand, we'll say that his mother loved him enough to give him up because she felt it was the best thing for him. And if I've learned anything at all, I suppose in some way that's what my own mother did for me and Sunny. She wasn't equipped for parenthood."

"But you are," he said. "And I've come to realize that not knowing about Elena did not discount the fact she was always the best mother a man could ask for. She's also a very good grandmother, and she is dying to have you as her daughter-in-law."

Piper couldn't ask for more. "Any idea when we're going to take care of the wedding business?"

"As soon as possible. Perhaps before we return to Bajul."

"We could always hold the ceremony in the family backyard. I provide the groom, and my grandfather provides the shotgun."

Adan laughed as if he didn't have a care in the world. "No need for that. I am a willing participant in establishing a future with you."

And very soon she would no longer be his pretend wife. She would be the real deal.

Epilogue

If a woman wanted to live in a palace, the gorgeous guy standing a few feet away could be just the man to make that come true. And three months ago he had—in a civil ceremony surrounded by her grandparents' lush gardens, sans shotgun. Now Piper McAdams was more than ready to legitimately assume her role as his princess during the elaborate reception held in their honor.

For the past twenty minutes, she'd been schmoozing with wealthy strangers while shamelessly studying her husband's assets. He wore a navy suit adorned with military insignias, a pricey watch on his wrist and a wedding band on his left hand. His usually tousled dark brown hair had been neatly styled for the occasion, but it still complemented the slight shading of whiskers framing his mouth. And those dimples. She'd spotted them the first time she'd laid eyes on him six months ago in the Chicago hotel bar.

And as it had been that night, he was currently speaking to a lithe blonde wearing a chic red sparkling dress, only she didn't see this woman as a threat. In fact, she saw her as simply Madison Foster Mehdi, her sister-in-law and recent addition to Piper's ever-expanding gal-pal club.

Speaking of expanding, a woman dressed in flowing coral chiffon that didn't completely hide a baby bump stood at the ballroom's entrance. She'd come to call her Maysa while most called her queen, and aside from the duties that came along with the title, she served as Sam's stellar doctor and Piper's confidante. The man on her arm, also known as the king, hadn't been as easy to get to know, yet he'd been warming up to his youngest brother's wife, slowly but surely.

All in all, Piper couldn't be happier with her new family. And she couldn't be more pleased when her husband started toward her with that sexy, confident gait that threatened to bring her to her knees.

Once he reached her side, he leaned over and whispered, "I have another gift for you."

"Giving it to me now would be rather inappropriate, don't you think?" she whispered back.

He straightened and smiled. "I'll reserve that gift for later when we are safely ensconced in our room. But this particular present is totally appropriate for the occasion."

Piper took a quick glance at her left hand. "I really think the boulder on my finger is quite sufficient, and so was the wonderful honeymoon in Naples."

"Have you forgotten our time on the beach?"

She faked a frown. "All right, that thing you did to me on the beach was very unforgettable."

"I thought you enjoyed that thing."

She grinned. "I did!"

He pressed a palm against the small of her back and feathered a kiss across her cheek. "Remain here while I retrieve your surprise."

As he headed across the room, Madison came to Piper's side. "Where is he going in such a hurry?"

"He says he has a gift for me."

"Oh, that," Madison replied. "I was beginning to wonder when he was going to get to that."

Piper's eyes went wide. "You know what it is?"

"Yes, I do. In fact, I assisted in acquiring it. And don't look so worried. You'll love it."

Knowing Adan, she probably would. "I'm counting on it."

Madison momentarily scanned the crowd before bringing her attention back to Piper. "I haven't seen Elena yet. She promised she'd come down once she had the babies put to bed."

"She told me she wanted to read them all a book."

"Good luck with that," Madison said, followed by a laugh. "I'm not sure year-old twins and a six-month-old will fit in her lap."

"She enlisted Kira's help," Piper added. "And believe me, Kira is amazing. I'm not sure there's anything she can't do."

"Except hold on to a man," Madison said. "At least according to her."

"A worthless man, maybe. She told me all about her broken engagement. Too bad we snatched up all the Mehdi brothers. She'd make a great sister-in-law."

Madison grinned. "Maybe there's one hiding in

the closet somewhere. Of course, there is their cousin, Rayad, although he's all into the military thing."

Piper still had a lot to learn about the family. "You'd better hope there's not a secret Mehdi hiding out somewhere. That means you'd be in charge of handling that scandal."

"True." Madison pointed at the double doors to her left, where Adan now stood. "Your husband is about to reveal your surprise, so wait and watch and get ready to be wowed."

Piper kept her gaze trained on the doors, wondering what might actually come through them. A new sports car? A pet elephant? Maybe even a…sister?

The minute Sunny caught sight of Piper, she practically ran across the room and engaged her in a voracious hug. And as if they'd been propelled back into the days of their youth, they momentarily jumped up and down until Piper realized exactly where they were and who she now was.

She stopped the girlish celebration, but she couldn't stop her smile. "Sunny McAdams, what are you doing here?"

"Answering your new husband's invitation."

She noticed they'd gained the attention of a room full of dignitaries. "Thanks to our boisterous show of affection, these people are now convinced the new princess is nuttier than a squirrel's nest."

"If the glass slipper fits," Sunny said as she stepped back and surveyed Piper from head to high heels. "You clean up good, sugar plum. Aqua is definitely your color, but I'm clearly underdressed."

Piper smoothed a hand down the bling-embellished satin strapless gown and grinned. "If you'd walked in here wearing something other than black slacks and a white silk blouse, I'd be asking you to return to the mother ship and give me back the real Sunny McAdams."

They shared in a laugh until Adan interrupted the camaraderie. "Did I succeed in surprising you, fair lady?"

She gave him a grateful hug and an enthusiastic kiss. "An excellent surprise, good sir. I do believe you've thought of everything."

"He wanted to make up for me not being at the wedding," Sunny added.

"That's okay, dear sister. You can make it up to me by staying here a few days."

"Unfortunately, I'll be leaving tomorrow. I'm meeting up with Cameron in Africa to cover a few of the most recent uprisings."

Piper hated how her sibling insisted on putting herself in danger, but she was pleased that she seemed to have found her match. "So how's it going with Cameron the cameraman?"

Sunny shrugged. "We're hanging in there. He wants to settle down in suburbia and have a few kids, but I'm not ready for that."

"Take it from me," Madison began, "you can balance career and motherhood. I've managed it with twins."

"And a very accommodating husband." All eyes turned to Zain Mehdi as he slid an arm around his wife's waist. "It's good to see you again, Sunny."

Piper momentarily gaped. "You two have met?"

"Briefly in Nigeria," Sunny said. "But I didn't know who he was until much later, since he was traveling incognito at the time."

Must run in the family, Piper thought when she considered how Adan had concealed his identity. They'd come a long way in a very short time.

As casual conversation continued, Piper noticed a man standing alone a few feet away, his attention focused on the group. "Does anyone know who that man is to my left, holding up the wall?"

"What man?" Adan asked.

"The one who keeps staring."

Sunny glanced over her shoulder before focusing on Piper again. "That's Tarek Azzmar, a corporate investor who hails from Morocco and a billionaire probably ten times over. I met him in Mexico City a few years back when he was opening an orphanage. He's a man of few words and rather reclusive. An enigma wrapped in a mystery, as they say."

"And Rafiq invited him," Zain added. "Apparently he's building a mansion not far from the palace. We'll be able to see his estate when we're standing on the west-facing veranda."

"So much for privacy," Adan muttered. "And with that in mind, if you fine people will excuse us while I have a few moments alone with my wife?"

"By all means," Zain said. "The courtyard outside provides enough protection to begin your honeymoon, if you so choose. My wife will attest to that."

Piper caught a glimpse of Madison elbowing Zain in the side, earning quite a bit of laughter as her husband led her away.

Once in the corner of the deserted vestibule, Adan turned her into his arms. "How does it feel to be an honest-to-goodness princess?"

"Unreal. Surreal. Wonderful."

"I'm glad you are up to the task, and I'm hoping you are willing to take on another."

She suspected she knew where this could be heading. "Hold it right there, hotshot. We have plenty of time to make a sibling for Sam."

"I would like to get to that in the immediate future," he said, "but this task involves your painting skills."

"What would you like me to paint, Your Highness? And please don't tell me one of your planes."

He gave her that earth-shattering, heart-melting grin. "As tempting as that might be, I'm referring to capturing the entire family on canvas. Rafiq, with the council's support, wants to commission you as the official palace artist in order to preserve history."

Piper could think of nothing she would like better. Actually, she could, but she'd take care of that later in bed. "I'm absolutely honored, and I will do my best to prove I'm up to the challenge."

"It is going to be challenging, at that. You'll have to rely on photographs of my father to capture his likeness. And we'll hang that in the foyer."

"I can do that," she said, thankful Adan had thought of it first. "What about your mother?"

"Since she's here for the sitting, that should not be a problem."

Another feat accomplished—his acceptance of Elena. "We'll hang that one in the nursery, next to yours and Sam's."

"And will you be able to paint one of all three of us?"

"Certainly, and I'll make myself look much thinner."

He frowned. "No need for that. You are perfect in every way."

So was he. So was their life, and their love. "Now

that we've taken care of the details, why don't we go up and say good-night to your son?"

"*Our* son."

"You're right. As of this morning, he's legally mine."

He brushed her hair back from her shoulder and kissed her gently. "He has been yours from the beginning, and I will be yours for all time."

In that moment, Piper realized she'd been very lucky to find the sheikh of her dreams. A prince of a guy. The one who got away…and came back, this time to give her his heart.

* * * * *

A sneaky peek at next month...

Desire™

PASSIONATE AND DRAMATIC LOVE STORIES

My wish list for next month's titles...

In stores from 18th July 2014:

2 stories in each book - only £5.49!

❏ The Fiancée Caper – Maureen Child
& Matched to a Prince – Kat Cantrell

❏ Taming the Takeover Tycoon – Robyn Grady
& Redeeming the CEO Cowboy – Charlene Sands

❏ The Nanny Proposition – Rachel Bailey
& A Bride's Tangled Vows – Dani Wade

Available at WHSmith, Tesco, Asda, Eason, Amazon and Apple

Just can't wait?

Visit us Online

You can buy our books online a month before they hit the shops! **www.millsandboon.co.uk**

0714/51

Join our *EXCLUSIVE* eBook club

FROM JUST £1.99 A MONTH!

Never miss a book again with our hassle-free eBook subscription.

★ Pick how many titles you want from each series with our flexible subscription

★ Your titles are delivered to your device on the first of every month

★ Zero risk, zero obligation!

There really is nothing standing in the way of you and your favourite books!

Start your eBook subscription today at www.millsandboon.co.uk/subscribe

The World of Mills & Boon

There's a Mills & Boon® series that's perfect for you. There are ten different series to choose from and new titles every month, so whether you're looking for glamorous seduction, Regency rakes, homespun heroes or sizzling erotica, we'll give you plenty of inspiration for your next read.

By Request

Relive the romance with the best of the best
12 stories every month

Cherish™

Experience the ultimate rush of falling in love.
12 new stories every month

INTRIGUE...

A seductive combination of danger and desire...
7 new stories every month

Desire™

Passionate and dramatic love stories
6 new stories every month

nocturne™

An exhilarating underworld of dark desires
3 new stories every month

For exclusive member offers go to
millsandboon.co.uk/subscribe

Discover more romance at

www.millsandboon.co.uk

- ❤ WIN great prizes in our exclusive competitions
- ❤ BUY new titles before they hit the shops
- ❤ BROWSE new books and REVIEW your favourites
- ❤ SAVE on new books with the Mills & Boon® Bookclub™
- ❤ DISCOVER new authors

PLUS, to chat about your favourite reads, get the latest news and find special offers:

- 🗗 Find us on facebook.com/millsandboon
- 🐦 Follow us on twitter.com/millsandboonuk
- ❤ Sign up to our newsletter at millsandboon.co.uk